THE FINERY

RACHEL GROSVENOR

First published 25th of July 2023 by Fly on the Wall Press
Published in the UK by
Fly on the Wall Press
56 High Lea Rd
New Mills
Derbyshire
SK22 3DP

www.flyonthewallpress.co.uk
ISBN: 9781915789037
Copyright Rachel Grosvenor © 2023

A CIP Catalogue record for this book is available from the British Library.

For my mother, Hilary, with thanks for her infinite love and support.

Chapter One

There had been a murder. Wendowleen knew this as soon as she woke up. Apart from the knowing, the morning was much the same as usual. Her wolf lay sleeping at the bottom of her bed as she woke, and she gave him a small nudge with her large toe. Nothing stirred but the dust surrounding him, which billowed in tiny mushrooms from the duvet to his fur.

"Oi."

Nothing. She rolled her eyes and nudged him again. This time his nose wrinkled slightly, and she viewed it with satisfaction. He was awake.

"There's been a murder."

At this, the wolf knew better than to open his eyes. Many of his mornings had started this way in the past year, and he wasn't going to get involved. He rolled his head lazily from one side to the other and let out a large snort.

"Well, you might think that, but if you're not willing to help, what are you good for?"

Another snort. This wasn't a magic wolf; he couldn't speak English (or any other language for that matter). He was fluent in wolf. Wendowleen was not.

"Useless. Get a wolf, they said. It'll keep you company in your old age."

She pulled her dust-laden bed covers back and lifted her legs out of bed. They were heavy and weighted with swollen ankles, a sign that she had done too much the day before. This was the thing about getting older. The ankles that once carried you began to look like hams.

"Bloody hams."

The wolf opened one eye and stared at her. This was a word he did know. In fact, he was excellent with all food-related words in every language. Mention a kobasica, salsiccia, a korv or a selsig, and you could expect to look down to see a sizeable greying wolf waiting patiently by your side.

Wendowleen glanced over at him and reached out a hand to touch his fur. They had only lived together for a year. He had been a retirement gift from her university. And it was a shock, because she had not once mentioned that she fancied getting a wolf. Not once in the forty-five years that she had taught there. Many people did, of course, especially the elderly. And those who lived alone. She sighed at him. Perhaps she ticked both of those boxes now. But the wolves that were companions for the elderly were at least meant to do something. They opened doors, put the kettle on, that sort of thing. This wolf had none of the skills she had expected him to have. Early in their cohabitation, she had left him to sort the laundry and had come back half an hour later to find him asleep in a pile of her dirty knickers. And that had rather put her off trying to make him useful. He seemed to be a wolf in name only, so she didn't bother to name him at all, referring to him only as Wolf.

Wendowleen stood and shuffled her way to the landing, leaving Wolf to sleep among the dust. As she took the stairs carefully, one at a time, she stared at the photographs that adorned the walls. The ones at the top were expertly hung in her younger days, and by her young love, Arthur. There, at the highest point, their cohabitation day. A little below, her first graduation. Then, her second. Then, ornamented in a golden frame, her doctorate. Arthur smiling proudly beside her in each, as she stood awkwardly in a ridiculous hat, looking exhausted. Lower, there were the ones that she had tried to hang recently. Her retirement party, barely out of arms reach, because every time she got the ladder out to do it, Wolf had growled and pulled at it. Stupid animal. Her promotion to Professor, a little higher than that. A beautiful frame that she had always meant to fill above that one, holding nothing but a blank space.

At the bottom of the staircase was the kitchen. It was a small, but tall house. Each room was accessible by stairs only, with one room on each floor. There were five floors and five rooms. These days Wendowleen mainly spent time in the bottom two, her bedroom and the kitchen. Of course, she had to visit the third floor every now and then, for the monthly bath. She had a toilet outside in the garden though, so it wasn't as serious a situation as all that. The fourth floor was a guest room, and the fifth was...well, what was the fifth room? She paused in front of the kettle and closed her eyes tightly; it had been so long since she ventured up there. Ah. The library. That made sense. The house nestled in between two other houses of a very similar layout. In her youth, she and Arthur had discussed the possibility of buying one someday and knocking the walls through to create floors with at least two rooms. But even then, she knew that this would never be possible. It wasn't just the money, but the city would never allow it. There were rules, you know, and she was breaking them anyway by occupying a house with two bedrooms. That wasn't *how it was done* in Finer Bay (a name that brought to mind a coast much nicer than the one that actually gave the city its title). She had been warned by the Finery (law enforcement – aptly named) that they would indeed be fining her if she didn't move someone in or move out herself by the end of the year. They had given an exact date, but that date had sifted through her mind and disappeared within a week. Anyway, she knew the mayor of the city. She had taught him at the university when he was just a show-off without a golden medallion. If the Finery really did come round to bother her, she would just get him involved.

She filled the kettle with water and placed it on the stove, watching the flames rise around the metal. A chill on her skin caused her pores to push upwards, jostling for position. She stared at her arm and shook her head.

"A sure sign."

There had been a murder, after all.

Chapter Two

In every city there are problems. Homelessness, starvation, criminality... For the Finery, this was all the better: they wanted crime, murder, and anguish. After all, who makes money in a perfect city? Nobody. Who makes money in a city filled with crime? The Finery. Small children who wanted to make money in their future saw the Finery as the way forward. And, as the Finery only wanted a very specific sort of person involved in their society, you could only sign up to join them if you were under the age of fifteen. Once the contract was signed, you couldn't change your mind. You didn't actually get to officially work with them until you were twenty, of course, but by securing those born with ideals of an unfair society early, they succeeded in having troops that did not question their decisions. Ever. If you were unlucky enough to be robbed, you could rely on the Finery to arrest the robber. However, you should also expect to be fined and given a warning yourself for being an easy victim. The force were always there, on the streets and in your mind. They would pace the pavements, carefully looking for trouble. Giant posters covered billboards and walls, showing officers in uniform, with slogans like "Watch Your Step" and "We See You".

Versions of the Finery existed in other, smaller, cities and towns throughout Rytter, but they were not as feared as those in Finer Bay, and those in Finer Bay didn't like Wendowleen Cripcot. Oh, they knew there was a title in front of her name, be it Professor or Doctor, but they weren't going to use that.

She just wasn't right for Finer Bay or even Rytter as a whole. She must have been a hundred years old if she was a day, and her binder at the Finery headquarters was now more of a cabinet than a file. And the most infuriating thing about her was that she acted as though she wasn't scared of the Finery at all. If there was anything to make the institution crumble, it was a lack of fear. This was taught to you on your first day as a recruit. Even the officers were afraid of each other. You made friends in the Finery, that was a given, and some even found their spouses there, but you never for a moment turned your back on them. The tales of in-depth files being kept by a spouse on their partner were endless. It was expected, even. Jokes were made at cohabitation ceremonies about it – "I knew they were meant for each other when I saw the way he'd underlined Proud's name in silver in the daily threat report." Cue nervous laughter from Proud and hurried notes taken later that day. That sort of thing.

Two young recruits had been ordered to visit Wendowleen that morning. They hadn't met her before and had been told to remind her of her moving date and bring fear into her heart. This, in turn, inspired fear in them, as they hadn't done an official visit of this kind before, and neither of them could decide who was going to do the talking.

"Please – you do it. You're much scarier than I am. Look at me." The young woman stood back and held her arms out slightly. Their starched blazers were stiff in the wind, shoulder pads pointing out severely from their shoulders.

"You're terrifying. You do it." The man smirked in response, tufty hairs sprouting from around his upper lip. They marched onwards in silence, irritation stinging the air around them until they reached the street that Wendowleen lived on.

"Such a weird street. Look at the gaps between the houses. What a waste of space. Look at those front gardens." The woman sighed.

"Exactly. And to live here and have a bedroom spare? Who does she think she is?"

They stared hard at each other, puffing their chests out, pigeons ready to fight.

"I'll do it," the man said firmly.

"No, you won't."

They jostled up the front garden, treading the carefully planted golden flowers that followed the path into the dirt, and wrapped their knuckles on the oak door in unison.

Wendowleen answered sleepily, chestnut broth in hand. The pair stared at the tall, plump woman and flashed their Finery badges.

"Wendowleen Cripcot?" they spoke in unison.

"Dr Cripcot to you."

They glanced at each other. This is what their superior had meant. The young woman stepped forward slightly.

"Wendowleen Cripcot, we are from the Fi-"

"You bloody idiots! Look at my awatoprams!" Wendowleen pushed passed them to her golden flowers and knelt carefully beside them, gently pouring chestnut broth into the earth. "There, my dears, this may help a little."

"Miss Cripcot – do you know who we are?" The man took over, red rising from his neck to his face. Wendowleen stood and turned slowly, the inch difference in their height suddenly becoming a tower.

"Did you just call me Miss? What did I tell you my name was?"

He stared into her eyes, watching their colour darken dramatically. She was a citizen, how dare she make him feel afraid! She was nothing compared to him.

"We are from the Finery." He rose onto his tiptoes to try and gain a little height. "And we have come to talk to you about your *spare* bedroom."

Wolf wandered out of the house and sat squarely in front of the door, staring at the uniformed woman. She glanced at him briefly. Wolves could sometimes be something to be wary of, but old peoples' wolves were often nothing to worry about. This one looked tamer than a rabbit.

"Oh, get out of my way, you stupid boy." Wendowleen batted the man out of her stride and moved slowly toward the front door. The woman stepped forward in front of her path and held her hands up in front of her.

"If you do not cease all activity immediately, we will be forced to arrest you."

"Who is your superior?"

"That is none of your business!" The woman stamped her foot, much to Wendowleen's joy.

"Do you know, young lady...there's something so familiar about you."

"No, there isn't," she responded quickly.

"There is. I know your face. Is your mother Roma?"

The pause told Wendowleen everything she needed to know. "Oh goodness, what a crying shame. She was such a bright woman – I taught her philosophy at university. All those years ago. Who'd have thought she'd have a child in the Finery?"

"My mother supports all of my decisions," the woman sputtered, thrown by this turn in the conversation.

"No, dear, she doesn't. Oh, such a shame. She did so well too."

Wendowleen frowned gently at the woman and shrugged her shoulders. It was an entirely different life to be in the Finery. Once signed up, you didn't get the option to go to university. That wasn't a choice. Universities and education were too dangerous for the officers, they might be encouraged to think something themselves. As soon as that dotted line was signed with your name, you were whisked out of mainstream education to a Finery boarding school and encouraged to cut all ties with those who had not joined. It was often the case that parents never heard from their child again, unless, of course, they did something to put them in front of the Finery. No parent supported the decision to join unless they were a part of it too.

The male officer stepped forward, shining new boots crunching on the soil beneath his feet.

"You have one month to the day. If you have not moved out of this house by then or moved a lodger into your spare room, you will have broken law 532 and will be dealt with as the Finery sees fit. There will be no court case. There will be no opportunity for you to argue your side."

They turned on their heel in unison, something that had definitely been planned, and stalked down the pathway, this time avoiding the crushed golden petals of the awatoprams. When they reached the gate, the woman turned and fixed Wendowleen with a shaky smile.

"You should move to the country. There are no bedroom laws there."

Wendowleen rolled her eyes and walked back inside, beckoning at Wolf, who was watching the pair leave with interest.

"You weren't much help, were you?"

Wolf glanced at her momentarily and licked his lips. Wendowleen didn't know what he meant by that and so closed the door behind her, leaving him on the step.

Chapter Three

Wendowleen first saw Arthur at a protest. There he was, skinny arms holding a banner aloft, protesting against...now what was it again? Wendowleen closed her eyes and tried to focus her memory. Obviously, it was probably something to do with the Finery. She was wrong, however, because it wasn't. It was the university wanting to knock down the old library to make way for a new one. The plans for the new library were very fancy, futuristic, even. Glass walls, stairs that only had space for one foot. Daft things, meant to encourage those from not only Finer Bay but the whole of Rytter, to visit. The protests were not just against the idea of knocking down the old library but against the filtering of the books. There was also the suggestion of moving all of the graduate theses from the library to storage. This irritated Wendowleen, an absolute atrocity. Her great-grandmother's thesis was there, displayed for all to see, and she liked to visit it now and then while working on her own. It was like getting a handshake from a friend. What was to become of life if everything worthwhile was put into storage?

Eventually, the new library wasn't built. The fury was too much for the Vice Chancellor, who was furious in turn that his plans would never come to fruition because the public thought they knew better. Outrageous.

But this isn't just where Wendowleen and Arthur's story began, it was where Wendowleen's file began at the Finery headquarters. In short, she bit somebody. Of course, the Finery were there; where else would they be on the day of a protest? An officer put his hand on Wendowleen's shoulder, and she bit his finger. People have been thrown in jail for life for less. Luckily for Wendowleen, the mayor had just arrived and trudged his way over. This particular mayor only lasted two years in post, as he was forced out by those not as gentle as he. His calm manner got him voted in one moment but ousted the next.

"Excuse me, young man — what are you doing touching members of the public who are peacefully protesting?"

The officer glared at him in response; here was confusing ground to tread on. He was in the Finery; after all, his actions were the law. But on the other hand, the mayor was the man with the keys to the city. He held up his finger begrudgingly.

"She bit me."

The mayor laughed and shook his head, peering at the finger with feigned interest.

"Well, I would probably bite you too if you laid a finger on me, sir."

The 'sir' at the end of the sentence was low and long, drawn out and stretched. Wendowleen barely stayed to see the response to this and quickly stepped through the crowd until she reached Arthur, the man she had previously admired. He grinned at her.

"Did you just bite an officer of the Finery?"

Wendowleen laughed and shrugged her shoulders and then reconsidered this move, understanding that Arthur was seemingly interested in those who fought against the establishment. She stopped laughing and stared at him in a serious, but not unfriendly, way.

"That was nothing. I've done worse."

This was a lie, but it didn't matter. Arthur had already fallen in love with her. Unfortunately for Wendowleen, a different officer had been standing nearby, had heard this, and had written her name down in capital letters in his notebook. One officer returning from a protest with your name on their lips is not ideal, two officers returning with your name on their lips is worse. The number of officers that eventually wrote Wendowleen's name down for further investigation that day was actually five. One count of finger biting, one count of admission of crimes, one count of purposefully stepping on an officer's boot, one count of taking part in an illegal protest, and one count of indecent behaviour at said protest (kissing Arthur, it turns out).

Chapter Four

Wendowleen slammed her mug down on the kitchen counter, the force causing a tidal wave of chestnut broth to spill over its edge. She stared at it. Wolf growled outside the front door. She should have let him in, really, but she needed a moment, just a minute, to calm down. How dare the Finery come to her house that way to demand that she move a stranger in or leave. They had long done stupid things, but now she was getting fed up. She turned and marched to the front door, yanking it open to reveal Wolf glaring at her. He stood and purposefully padded into the house, tail straight to show his annoyance.

"That's it," she said to him, and he stared at her, eyebrows furrowing. He recognised her tone. She closed the door softly this time and leaned on the small three-legged table propped up against the wall. Wolf sat and watched her read a number carefully from a square of paper glued to the surface. She dialled it awkwardly, saying the numbers under her breath.

"The mayor."

A pause.

"It's Dr Cripcot."

Another.

"Just you put him on the phone – all right?"

Wolf moved closer and pricked up an ear, leaning in.

"Hello? Wendowleen, is it?"

"Yes, hello. I'm calling about the Finery."

"Of course you are. It might be better if you booked a phone call with my PA – he really knows his stuff."

"He doesn't have any power, though, does he?"

A stifled laugh from the other end.

"What is it that you need, Wendowleen?"

"Do you remember when you used to call me Dr Cripcot?"

"Yes. I stopped around the same time you started visiting me when I didn't answer the phone, I think. What is it that you *need*?"

"The Finery have given me a date to move a stranger into my house or move out. What do you have to say about that?"

"I'd say that it's their prerogative. They are here, as I have explained numerous times to you, to enforce the law. And this law makes sense."

The mayor had only been in his position for four months. He had already had multiple dealings with Wendowleen.

"You listen to me —"

"You really shouldn't call me so oft -"

"LISTEN. I am going to be one hundred and one years old in two months. Why in the world should I move? I've lived here for over sixty years!"

"If you want the finer details of the law, I'll have my PA send it over to you."

"Are you telling me that there is nothing you can do, at all?"

A pause.

"Yes. Take my advice. Think about the countryside. I've tried to help you before, Wendowleen, but really, enough is enough. Time to hang up the protest banner, I think."

Wendowleen slammed down the phone, hoping that the suddenness of this caused the mayor to jump. It certainly made Wolf flinch, who watched her with interest. He hadn't understood the conversation, but he knew that it wasn't the outcome Wendowleen had wanted. She drummed her fingers on the table, causing it to rock back and forth on its three legs. She glanced at him.

"Who on earth could I move in that I wouldn't mind living in close quarters with?"

Wolf cocked his head to one side.

"I could dress you up like a person."

He cocked his head to the other, trying to find the hidden snack within her speech.

"Arthur's sister moved to the country," she said to no one. With that, she rounded her shoulders and began to trudge up the stairs. Wolf waited a step behind, as always, but followed her. Once they arrived at the first landing he paused, waiting for her to enter the bedroom. She didn't. He let out a low murmur at this, was it bath time already? Had it been a month? She began to climb to the next story, each step more laboured than the last. He paused when they reached that landing, too, as Wendowleen made no move toward the tub. She stepped forward again and took a deep breath, hand poised over the bannister.

Onward and upward, the dust building beneath her feet the higher they went. The fourth floor, the spare room. Wendowleen stopped and stared at it. A single bed sat in the middle, still made from well…it must have been the last time she had guests. When on earth was that? She had no idea. It was wrinkled slightly from Wolf, who had decided that it may as well be his bed on occasion.

Wolf watched her. She turned and began to climb the final set of stairs. He let out a low howl. He wasn't very well trained, but he knew enough. He perceived that she was starting to struggle.

"Quiet you."

He howled again, louder this time. She stopped on the third step and turned awkwardly.

"If you howl one more time."

He put a paw on the first step and seemed to nod at her expectantly.

"I'll just be quite cross, that's all."

That was no threat, and he didn't understand it, anyway.

Wendowleen reached the top with a heavy breath and a heavier step. The tips of her ears were burning. It reminded her of what she had forgotten. The murder. She rested her hand on the wall and stood for a moment, surveying the room. Wolf rested his chin on her foot, and lay down, whining. She said nothing, rolling her watery eyes at him and wiggling her toes, causing her chin to ripple. Her ears throbbed again as though nudging her.

"The murder. I keep forgetting."

Wolf watched her cautiously. Wendowleen had had a sense like this before, many years previously. But where had she gotten to with that investigation? It was while she was still at the university, teaching the masses. Her ears burned every day for a month, and she knew, she just knew that something was very wrong. The mayor died a week before her ears finished burning. By that time, welts and marks had begun to show, and the alienist had discounted the issue as mental. She had thought seriously about investigating the mayor's death, she really had. But the turnover of mayors was so high in Finer Bay. One couldn't go around delving into every single death or abduction of a mayor – who would have the time? Especially when the likely culprit was obvious. The Finery would have nothing to do with a mayor who couldn't take instruction.

Of course, the answer to Wendowleen's rhetorical question is that the Finery had the time. They were rigid note-takers, every one of them. They took more notes than they had hot dinners, which was funny, because they also took notes about their hot dinners. It was, on the whole, a massive waste of resources. For each ten-hour shift, at least five hours were spent typing up notes such as "Saw a beetle – suspicious?" and then filing your notes under "B" for Beetle and "S" for suspicious, making sure that you cross-referenced them with the date.

Wendowleen touched the top of her right ear and felt a small bump form. She stared at the room before her. The study.

Her books. She viewed them as old friends. She made a step toward the large mahogany bookcase that swayed beneath the strain of her collection and reached a hand out toward them, misjudging the distance. She began to fall, and Wolf saw her, slow motion, sinking to the floor. He padded over to her and nudged her with his cold nose, pressing it against her cheek. He whined loudly and made a gruff little sound at the bottom of his throat. Wendowleen was okay, she had landed on her bum. A little awkwardly, yes, but she was fine on the whole. Her hand was still outstretched, the fall doing nothing to stop her from touching the leather that encased the largest book on the shelf – her PhD thesis. She grasped it and pulled it toward her, shifting until it was on her lap. She smiled at the lettering, golden, her name before it was special. Ironically, how that now made it more special, the name without the Dr marching before it. She opened the book to the first page and frowned at what was written inside.

"For my boys."

She paused, staring at the words and then at Wolf.

"Plural?"

Wolf stared back and sat down heavily. Wendowleen narrowed her eyes at him, confused.

"When did you move in? No, no, no. Don't be daft. It's not you."

She pulled her gaze back to the first page, thinking of the photograph of herself and Arthur at her graduation. Who would she have been referring to? Her PhD supervisor? Surely she would never have been so personal as to call him 'her boy', that wasn't her style at all. In fact, it wasn't really her style to call Arthur that, either. She closed the book and checked the name again. Yep. There it was.

"Wendowleen Cripcot," she said aloud.

The sound of a bell came pounding up the stairs and through the room. The clock was striking five. Wolf listened patiently and then put a paw onto Wendowleen's lap. His dinner was in half an hour.

"Bugger off a minute."

She put the book down in front of her and reached for another, smaller, leather-bound book. This one had a single silver heart on the front, and she touched it gently. She hadn't thought about this in years, but now that it was in front of her, she remembered every dimension and bump in the leather. She opened it with care. There were she and Arthur on their cohabitation day. She was in grey, he in fuchsia, traditional to the last. They held a bundle of twigs between them, meant to signify the many years of memory gathering ahead of them. Of course, the cohabitation traditions of Rytter were extensive and varied, and to recognise them all would be costly and even heavy. In some cases, as with the tradition of exchanging boulders (signifying a sharing of each other's burdens, but you could have worked that one out), they were almost impossible. Wendowleen grinned as she inspected their smiles, both gazing into the camera, staring into their future. She wasn't one to cry but felt, just for a small moment, that if pushed, a tear could fall. She missed him. That was all there was to it. Arthur's departure from this world had been so…she tried to remember, desperately. Unexpected? It must have been that. And how long had it been? She closed her eyes and took a deep breath in. He died of old age, isn't that righ –

"OoowwweeewwweeeeeooOOOOO," Wolf howled low and long into her ear and shook her from her thoughts.

"You bloody –"

"OOOOwwweeeeeeoooOOOOOOOOOOO," he said again, standing and glaring at her.

"Fine, but afterwards, we're coming back up here."

Wendowleen leaned on his shoulder and stood up doggedly, using him for guidance. They began to start the great trek to the kitchen, when suddenly, she noticed something. A piece of paper that had fallen from her the book she had been pouring over. She bent down to grasp it.

Chapter Five

The mayor shuffled the papers in front of him nervously. They didn't need shuffling, they never did, but he had seen it many times in movies growing up, and it now brought him comfort to shuffle his way through difficult decisions and moments.

"Sir, what do you think?"

"Yes, yes, just give me a second."

The decision he had to make was not a difficult one. It was simple, really. Did he want tuna or ham for dinner? The answer was that he wanted neither. He scratched the ever-growing bald spot on top of his head.

"You decide."

The assistant nodded briefly and stalked out of the room, leaving the mayor staring at his papers once again. The nerves were about the top paper in the pile, awaiting his signature. It was from the head of the Finery, the Director. The clock struck five behind him with short, sharp dings. He sucked in a deep breath of stale air and stared at the dotted line. If he signed this paper, the only people allowed in any restricted access area of a university library would be the Finery. They had a lot of power now, but the need for them to control education in Rytter made him very nervous. He thought back to his own research days, fondly letting himself drift away for a moment, remembering the scent of the old books, the tang of machine-made chestnut broth and the hours debating inside professors' offices. He shook his head. How would the signing of this have an impact on those days, though, really? After all, they were gone. Dead and buried, already happened. The current students, they shouldn't be going into the restricted areas of research without cause anyway, it wasn't as though they could just wander in willy-nilly. He reread the paper before him, his eyes pausing upon the following:

No member of the public (including University staff and students) shall be allowed access under any circumstances. Any files wished to be seen by the public may be requested. If the request is approved by the Finery, a summarisation and re-wording of the file will be provided on the basis of a one-time usage.

"Summarisation and re-wording," he said aloud.

"Sorry, sir?" The assistant walked back into the room with a plate in either hand, clearly deciding that the tuna or ham decision had been too significant a burden to bear.

"Did you go to university, Rowan?" the mayor asked.

"Yes, sir," Rowan answered, only mildly irritated that the mayor didn't already know this and that it seemingly had no impact on his ability to get a job next to the second most powerful man in Rytter.

"And did you ever use the restricted access area, in the library?"

"Yes," Rowan said, nervous that something was coming that he couldn't foresee.

"But, why did you? What did it offer you that you couldn't get elsewhere?"

Rowan stood awkwardly before the mayor's desk, plate still in either hand.

"Sit."

He sat, sandwiches poised before him.

"Well, to be honest, sir, I went because I wanted to see what all the fuss was about. Why was it restricted? That's what I wanted to know."

The mayor listened with interest, Rowan's accent had changed slightly, and he realised that he had possibly never heard him say a full sentence before.

"And so, what did you find out?"

"Not much, sir. There were a few research books about evil doings, you know, bad history. A few books about unusual animals. I can't think what else."

"Bad history?"

A knock came suddenly at the door, and the mayor turned to see it open slightly. The head of his receptionist popped through the gap.

"Are you busy, sir?"

The mayor stared at his receptionist in surprise; he had never seen him knock on his door previously. Not waiting for an answer, he spoke again.

"There's someone here from the Finery. It's the Director, sir."

The mayor felt for his pen, trying not to seem surprised or bothered by this unexpected visit. After all, he was the mayor. And that had to count for something, didn't it?

The door swung open, the receptionist cowering to one side. There stood the Director, smiling from ear to ear. As with all the leaders in history, he was dressed fairly casually in comparison to the Finery uniform. He wore a soft woollen suit, with a white shirt beneath it. His hair was combed expertly to one side. He stepped forward with bright, shining brogues and reached out a hand to the mayor, who stood with difficulty, still fiddling with his pen. After the handshake was over, the Director stared expectantly at the assistant.

"You can throw those in the bin. The mayor will be taking his dinner with me tonight."

The mayor stared at the sandwiches as they left the room, wishing desperately that they were to be his only company.

Chapter Six

The world watched from their windows, hiding behind curtains, afraid to join, afraid to speak, afraid to fight. It had been this way for as long as Wendowleen could realistically remember. She tried to remember her first experience of it, her first real taste of the way life was to be.

Just a child, or perhaps a little older than that. Still with the baby knuckles of youth, but wearing her mother's jewellery, straining to be older. It was a cinema trip, to see an old film her mother loved. Wendowleen remembered being excited to see what was so interesting about this film, that her mother might pay to see it again with her. They stood, tickets in hand, waiting in line. The air was chilled, almost winter, the promise of snow to come. The queue was not long, they wouldn't have to wait. They stood, shivering in unison. Then, a group of men (were they officers? Wendowleen wondered) marched up to the queue. They stood, in a group, laughing and muttering under their breaths. Wendowleen stared at their clothes with interest. The shiniest leather boots she had ever – "WOOF!"

She jumped back, shocked. One of the young men had barked in her face. He laughed at her response, holding his hands aloft in a mock "sorry" position. They were joined by another man from the front of the queue.

"Sold out. No bloody tickets left."

Grumbles. Murmurs of plots.

"All right." The man who had barked stared at Wendowleen and her mother, hard.

"We're going to need your tickets, ladies."

The group dispersed, seemingly to ask the other members of the group the same thing. Wendowleen held her ticket close to her chest.

"Did you hear me?"

Her mother stood up straight and growled in response: "You've no right."

The officer sneered, his long jaw reaching a smile. "Are you part of the government, madam?"

"Sorry?"

"I'll take that to be a no then. We are members of the Finery, madam, and as such, you are a second-class citizen in our company. If you do not hand over your tickets for tonight's performance, there may be trouble. Your husband runs the local barbers, doesn't he?"

Wendowleen stared at her mother, who went completely white. There seemed to be a moment of thought, and then she took Wendowleen's ticket and handed them both over, without a word.

"Much obliged, madam. There's always next time, isn't there?" He winked, and stalked off up the queue, his jeering team following in unison.

Wendowleen and her mother walked home in silence.

"Don't tell your father," her mother muttered as they reached the front door. Wendowleen didn't dare.

Chapter Seven

We went on holiday to the seaside, and on the way we stopped in TOWEN. We ate bean burgers and drank broth, and walked through the market SQUARE. On sale there were lots of nice things to EAT. We only ate some of THEM.

Wendowleen peered at the words, the handwriting, and squinted. Was that her writing? It was hard to say. It had changed so much as she had grown. The curve of the capital letters was familiar, as was the decision to make each last word capitalised. That was something she would have done, wasn't it?

"Think back, woman."

Wolf murmured softly. Wendowleen watched the letters squirm on the page. Yes. That must have been her. A vague memory pushed its way forward from the far depths of her mind. Not of her writing it, it couldn't be said to be as clear a memory as that.

Chapter Eight

"We'll have the lobster."

The mayor stared at the sharp smile of the Director, who took the menu from him before he had time to open it. The lobster. At least that decision was dealt with, the mayor thought, ticking an invisible item off his non-existent to-do list.

"Have you ever had lobster here?"

The mayor fidgeted in his seat and copied the Director's body language, leaning back slightly, hands clasped loosely in front of him. He listened to the question with interest, noticing that it was the first time since he became mayor that a sentence hadn't ended in 'Sir'.

"No…no, I've never been here before."

That was true, he hadn't. It was expensive, you could tell by the clean sign outside the door, the fact that the menu had no prices whatsoever on it. That had always made him avoid the place, the fear of having to ask for the bill. Who knows how expensive a meal could really be? It could be humiliating.

"Well, the lobster is really very good. Of course, they know me here. I've become rather a fixture."

A waiter brought over two glasses of something dark and placed them in front of the men. The Director nodded at him, no eye contact. "I've become a piece of the furniture," he murmured, to no one, grasping the glass.

The mayor followed suit and lifted the glass to his lips, tasting the liquid. He tried not to pull a face. On closer inspection, it was like tar, not treacle, and tasted like soil, and, unusually, the scent of leather. The Director glanced at him.

"An acquired taste, perhaps."

The mayor straightened up, time to take back some power. "Oh, I drink it all the time."

The Director smirked. "I voted for you, you know."

"You did?"

"Yes. So did the establishment, of course. I knew you would win. Always best to vote for someone you have *faith* in."

The mayor nodded enthusiastically, smiling.

"Of course," he continued, "the role of Director isn't one that you vote someone in for. Rather you fight your way to the top." He laughed the laugh of a man who had never found anything truly funny.

"Well, I had to do a fair amount of fighting to get the mayor's role, let me tell you!" the mayor began, jovially. The Director's eyes narrowed.

"Did you *really?*"

"Well, not physically, you understand."

"Hmmm."

A waiter came toward the table with the lobsters, one each. They looked giant, and the mayor stared at the protruding black eyes and wished that he could change places with them.

"Dig in, Mr Mayor."

The mayor reached a shaky hand toward a claw, and pulled firmly. He was nervous. He wished that he had been given some prior warning about this whole situation. The Director was, technically, at the same level as him in terms of job role, but really he knew that this counted for nothing. The Director was a job that only one person had until they died. After that eventuality, the next Director would have to battle their way to the top, stopping at nothing. Mayors could come and go, could be ousted. He glanced at the Director as he sucked lobster meat from within the claw, and wondered how many people he had killed. You could be certain that it wasn't a case of whether he had killed anyone, because that was a definite. The Director caught his gaze and smiled.

"So, why did I invite you here?"

The mayor shook his head. "I'm afraid I'm not sure."

"Yes, you are. Come on chap, give it some thought."

The mayor placed the claw down uncomfortably. He could tell that he wasn't really going to get a chance to eat anything properly during this meal. That was always the way with working mealtimes.

"The Library Law?"

The Director nodded, grinning broadly. "That's the one. See? I knew you knew!"

The mayor tried a smile in return and felt the broad hand of the Director slap him on the back.

"Now then, let's get down to business. You haven't signed the paper yet, have you?"

"No, well, it's at the top of a very large pile, Director, that's the prob-"

"That shouldn't be a problem."

"Right." The mayor didn't know what to say, so closed his mouth, and watched as the Director pulled a folded paper from his soft woollen blazer pocket, and straightened it out on the table before him, and the barely started lobsters.

"It's always tricky when you have just started a role, Mr Mayor, to find the priorities of your particular job."

"Yes, I agree, but it's also my job to consider what I am signing, to really understand the laws that are passed and make sure that they are for the greater good of the...city."

The Director stared at him for a moment, and then smiled broadly again, clapping his hands together loudly. "Wonderful, Mr Mayor, wonderful. I couldn't have said it better myself. It's that sort of thing that leads to you gaining this prestigious position, isn't it?"

The mayor nodded silently.

"And how we, at the Finery, respect you for it. But, here's the awkward conversation that I always have to have with a new appointee...your priority is signing the Finery laws. We take a lot of weight off your shoulders when it comes to keeping the peace, we make it easy for you to do your job so, Mr Mayor, you really must do us the same kindness, don't you think? Now, this may be on your to-do list, but you have had this paper for almost a month. That's too long."

The mayor stared at the paper again and sighed. He took a deep breath, and pushed it away from him.

"Director, may I be frank with you for a moment?"

The Director stared at the paper and then back to the mayor, his face unmoving. The mayor took this as an encouragement to go ahead.

"There are some laws that are easy to sign...the onion law, for example, I'm happy with that one, it made sense. But this law is...Director, if it's not too bold to ask – did you go to university?"

The Director leant back in his chair. "Of course, you know that members of the Finery are trained from an early age, thus meaning that attendance at university is not necessary, or, rather – allowed. I myself was enrolled, in fact, a rare occurrence, but I saw the light before I actually attended."

The mayor stared at him. He had asked the question already knowing the answer, of course, the Director had not attended university. It wasn't just non-compulsory not to attend as a member of the Finery, it was more or less illegal. "You enrolled?"

The Director nodded. "Yes. It was a curiosity, above everything. What are they teaching members of the public?"

"But you didn't go?"

"No, I didn't. Because I saw an opportunity. An opportunity for a position that could really make a difference."

"So...this law...this is because you want to control what members of the public are learning, isn't it?"

The Director laughed and shook his head. "Goodness me, no. Do you see me going into the University of Rytter, taking over lecture theatres and vetting free speech? Of course you don't." He pulled the paper closer to the mayor, and jabbed a slender finger at it. "This is about the *restricted* information. Do you know who gets to decide who has access to the *restricted* information, Mr Mayor?"

The mayor thought back to his university days. "Well, you make an application to the Restricted Admissions Office, and they decide whether your case is approved."

"Yes. And who works in that office, who makes those all-important decisions about access?"

"Um…an admin team?"

The Director nodded and raised his eyebrows. "Exactly. A team of administrators. A team of people I wouldn't even have as my PAs."

"Well, with all due respect Director, they are trained."

"Trained? To do what?"

The mayor watched the Director carefully, sensing danger. "To do their job."

"Are they trained to understand exactly what they are letting members of the public, unwitting students and senile professors, have access to? Are they trained to understand the deeper parts of the human psyche, Mr Mayor? Are they trained to deal with the result of letting potentially dangerous and unstable individuals get their hands on extreme and loathsome information?"

The mayor tried to think of something to say, anything. He could feel the Director's breath on his skin. "Director, while I understand your point – I don't believe that anything has ever happened as a result of allowing access to the restricted part of the library. The University of Rytter stands for the expansion of knowledge, for the development of enquiring minds…"

The Director suddenly sat back and clapped his hands together again, laughing loudly. "Well, Mr Mayor, you cannot say that I didn't try! Here, finish your drink." He handed him his glass, and together they downed the rest of the thick, blackening liquid. "I hope you won't think me rude, but I must dash off." He raised a hand and called the waiter with a click of his fingers. The waiter scurried over. "Put it on my tab."

The mayor looked hungrily at the lobsters, barely touched on his plate.

"Oh goodness me, Mr Mayor, you must stay and finish the food, of course." The Director smiled, the expression not reaching his eyes.

The waiter scuttled back to where he had come from as the Director stood, and pulled his coat on.

"Thank you, Director, it's very generous of you." He smiled, a genuine smile, pleased to have won the discussion. He was proud.

The Director buttoned up his coat and leaned forward, over the lobster, casting a shadow on the paper, nose to nose with the mayor. "Parenthetically, if anything ever does happen, and I view it to be as a direct result of this paper not being signed, I will hold you personally responsible. You, your family, and those you hold dear. On that matter, you have my word."

With this, the Director stood up straight and stalked out of the restaurant, leaving the mayor's appetite waning. The mayor called the waiter over with a shaking hand, and asked for another drink, and a pen, if he would be so kind. Upon his return, he downed the drink, signed the paper, and devoured both lobsters.

Chapter Nine

Wendowleen had wound her way down the stairs by now, one step at a time, slowly taking each step with a wobble as Wolf carefully padded along beside her. They reached the kitchen, to his relief, and he let out a low whine. It was time for food. If he didn't remind her, she might not remember.

"Yes, yes. I know. Impatient beast."

As Wendowleen reached for a cupboard door, the telephone began to ring in the hallway. Wolf let out a single bark as he saw her hand drop back down by her side, and received a sharp tap on the nose for it. House wolves were not supposed to put their own hunger issues ahead of their owner's business. No one had ever told Wolf this. Wendowleen curled her way past him to the phone.

"Hello?"

A pause. Wolf stood next to her, ears pricked forward. He heard a muffled voice on the other end of the phone. Wendowleen smiled.

"Oh, hello. Are you well?"

More muffling.

"Well, yes, it has been too long. Absolutely. It would be lovely to see you, Sylvia, of course, but all the way to Snorington? It would take around eight hours. With Wolf too. Between you and I," she glanced down at Wolf and cupped a hand around the receiver, "he is becoming a right grump in his old age."

Wolf glared at her.

"Why don't you come here?... Hmmm...Yes. The city is that, especially at the moment...All right. Yes, yes, fine.

When?...I'll book a train...oh don't be daft Sylvia, I'm not going to hire a horse to travel all that way...Do they?... Well, that's the countryside, isn't it?"

Wolf listened to this discussion with bored attention, his only interest being in when it had actually finished. Wendowleen put the phone down and turned to look at him.

"Now then. Your dinner, and then we better pack our bags."

Wolf understood only dinner, his tail wagging wildly behind him.

Chapter Ten

By the time Wendowleen and Wolf were on the train, the sun had set firmly in the sky, and they stared out of the window at their reflections. You should know that the train you are thinking of is perhaps not the type of train that Wendowleen and Wolf sat in. Trains in Rytter are horse-drawn, by six, or eight, horses. They have a series of short carriages, as you should expect, and follow tracks made specifically for the train service. They stop at stations, of course.

Wendowleen had packed as quickly as possible, and that had made for some odd choices in clothing that she wouldn't realise until they had arrived. It had been a few years since she had last seen Sylvia, her sister-in-law. She made the visits less frequent as travel became harder, or at least, that was the line that she told Sylvia. In all honesty though, it was the constant reminiscing that kept Wendowleen away. She loved and missed her Arthur dearly, but talking about every single thing he had ever done did grow tiring. They hadn't had conversations like that when he was alive, why have them now he was gone?

Wendowleen leant her head back and closed her eyes, resting them. How long had it been since she had left Finer Bay, really? She couldn't decide. Certainly, before Wolf had come to live with her. She opened her right eye slightly and peered at him. He was yawning widely, his full belly making gurgling sounds that ricocheted off the tinny walls of the old train carriage. There was no one else in the carriage to mind. Wendowleen closed her eye again and sighed. Only eight hours left to go.

"SNOOORINGTON…ARRIVING IN SNOORINGTON!"

Wolf barked suddenly and the clash of noises woke Wendowleen with a shudder. She glanced around and saw the soft light of the morning sun penetrating the windows. Wolf barked again, a single, shrill noise and Wendowleen rapped the table in front of her crossly.

"Enough!"

They weaved out of the carriage and onto the platform, Wolf carrying the luggage in his mouth while Wendowleen organised herself. She patted down the pockets of her long cardigan, making sure that she had collected everything she owned, despite not having removed anything in the first place.

"Wendy, darling!"

Wendowleen paused. No one called her that. She looked up to see Sylvia standing before her, and immediately remembered what she had completely forgotten. Sylvia shared Arthur's eyes, albeit, under heavy make-up. It made her stare.

"Are you quite all right?" Sylvia stepped forward and took her hand gently, patting it, pulling her from her daze.

"Yes, Sylvia. Gosh, I haven't been called Wendy in…" Ever, Wendowleen thought. "Years."

Sylvia grinned, her bright pink lipstick spreading from her lips to the creases around her mouth. "My darling, it has been years. Come, come, there is a cake to be eaten, and it won't eat itself…at least, I hope it won't."

Wendowleen glanced at Wolf to roll her eyes, but Wolf understood the word 'cake' better than the eye roll and ignored her.

Chapter Eleven

The mayor was standing in front of his kitchen sink when he heard the letterbox go. He paused, hand hovering over the hot tap. What time was it? The kitchen clock, a gift from his mother, ticked loudly above the cooker and signified to him that it was early. Far too early for the postman. He sighed. Since becoming mayor these things would happen, the local community thought that he was constantly on call. He must have received fifteen letters a day from his neighbours, all to do with daft things he cared nothing about. The Saturday market started too early, the local butcher had stopped selling bacon and fig muffins on a Sunday, the drainage in someone's garden had stopped working entirely. He thought about that last one. That was probably one he should do something about.

Slowly, he made his way to his front door and predictably saw a letter sticking out of it. He grabbed it and felt his stomach clench as he recognised the signature on the front. A note was scrawled across the grey envelope:

I admire a man who can make up his mind in a hurry. Here is another, personal, favour. Yours in Admiration,

The Director

He groaned audibly, noticing with anguish that there was no address written on the front. They knew where he lived. The Director won't have posted it himself, he thought, but it still meant bad news. He turned the envelope and slit it open with his fingernail. Inside there was a sheet, another law to be signed into existence. No accompanying note. The mayor stood in his hallway, the draft of the cold dark air outside creeping beneath the door and up the legs of his pyjama trousers, and scanned the page. It was to do with search warrants, or rather, the abolishment of having to have proof for gaining them. It was the idea that you could forcibly enter one's house on suspicion of something, without proof. That part was suitably vague, and the mayor wondered what suspicion you may need for this to be put into action. As he was staring at it, a knock suddenly shook him back into consciousness. He saw a shadow behind the door and reached a hand awkwardly to the handle, pulling it open. It was a member of the Finery, one he hadn't seen before.

"Mr Mayor." The young officer bowed his head respectfully and smiled.

"Oh. Hello." The mayor stared at the uniformed boy standing before him, from the shoulder pads to the shining boots on his doorstep.

"I take it you have read the —"

"Do you know how early it is?" the mayor boomed. He was fed up. This wasn't the Director, this was some child training to be a pawn.

The boy glared at him and bowed his head once more. "Yes, sir. I respect that you must be busy. However, I am under strict instructions to —"

"Bother me when I'm not at work?"

The boy had murder in his eyes at this second interruption and forced a smile. "Apologies, sir. If you could just sign the paper, I will be on my way."

The mayor noticed him glance down at his socks, and felt momentarily self-conscious.

"I will sign this to get rid of you, but you tell your boss that if one of you flunkies ever come to my front door again, there will be a price to pay."

The boy grinned and held out a silver pen for the mayor, who took it furiously. He scribbled his name on the paper and thrust it into the boy's hands.

"Thank you, sir, and I'll be sure to pass your message on to the Director." His eyes gleamed with something that the mayor couldn't quite place. Arrogance, pride... he reached out in a rage, grabbing the boy round the collar.

"Don't you ever threaten me, child. I'm the mayor of this town."

The boy, much to the mayor's surprise, didn't even seem to react. His lips remained in a smile, his eyes seemingly brimming with joy. The mayor suddenly saw the Director's face in his mind, and hesitated, letting the boy down gently. He coughed uncomfortably.

"My apologies, young man. I don't believe I meant to do that."

The boy nodded, still grinning a sickly smirk. "No problem, Mr Mayor. I didn't think you did."

Chapter Twelve

Wendowleen was exhausted. The journey had taken it out of her, and she just wanted to go and have a nap, but Sylvia had not stopped talking all morning. She was jabbering constantly in an almost nervous attack, and Wendowleen was struggling to fit a word in between her breaths. Wolf had sloped off long ago to discover an unused (at that time anyway) bed, and had curled up beneath the quilt, happily snoring away the cake he had managed to steal.

"Anyway, that was years ago. Can I get you more cake?"

Wendowleen held up her hand and shook her head. "No, I've had enough."

"It is so lovely to see you though, Wendy, it truly is."

"Yes. You too. What made you think to call?"

Sylvia began to laugh, and then, much to Wendowleen's concern, didn't stop. Wendowleen stared at her nervously, as she rocked back and forth in her chair, hooting and whooping into the air.

"Sylvia? Are you all right?"

Sylvia swept tears from beneath her eyes and gasped for air. "Oh, of course! What an amusing idea that I *shouldn't* think of calling you. You are, after all, my sister."

Wendowleen nodded, silently entering the 'in-law' bit to the end of her sentence. "Yes, but it has been a long time, I mean, when Arthur died, I didn't really hear from you at all."

The sentence passed through the air quickly, leaving a gaping hole behind it. A pause. Sylvia seemed to be thinking of something complicated, her brow furrowed in concentration.

"Well, it was a difficult time. It was unexpected losing my brother. I suppose I wanted to distance myself."

Wendowleen stared at her, interested. This was possibly the first time she hadn't called her 'darling' in a sentence since she arrived. "And so what changed, Sylvia? I don't want to force the point…"

She began to laugh again. "I think you do, Wendy. Come now, I'll show you to your room. You must be wanting a nap."

Wendowleen heard the word with relief, and stood, following Sylvia into a room painted brown. Upon closer inspection, Wendowleen noticed that the brown shapes on the walls were pictures of chestnuts. It was an odd choice, she thought, as Sylvia left her alone. She stared at the bed, noting the shape beneath the covers. Wolf had already made himself at home then.

Chapter Thirteen

The lock was easy to break. A single blow with a hammer was all it took. There had been murmurs about whether to knock first, but they had been quashed quickly by the man in charge. The Director's head of staff was the man to give the order, but never the man to make the blow. He stood squarely in the garden, staring at the front door through the fading light as it was shifted open. His shining toe caps kneaded the already bent golden awatoprams into the dirt.

"We're in, sir." One of the lower members of the Finery nodded to the man in charge.

"Good."

He stalked forward, shifting the officers out of the way. As he stepped through the door his nose wrinkled automatically. The smell. It was oily fur and…chestnut broth. He surveyed the scene. A small home, very slim. Smaller than it appeared from the outside, certainly. It looked as though it hadn't been cleaned for a long time. He ran a finger along the telephone that sat to his right and peered at the dust that lay heavy on his glove. Something caught his eye directly above his finger, a note pinned to the table. He leaned in and read it under his breath.

"The mayor's number," he said quietly, "the irony."

He turned on the threshold of the kitchen, rolled his shoulders back and clicked his heels together sharply. The group of officers standing at the door followed suite, waiting for their order.

"The study will be on the top floor. Clear it out." He glanced at the staircase, noticing the photographs that adorned the wall behind it, blinking twice at the empty frame in the centre. "Including those, take them." He glanced around at the kitchen and shrugged. "The rest is trash. Burn it."

The officers didn't falter.

Around an hour later, thick blackening smoke filled the air of Finer Bay. The city watched with limited concern. There was no need to worry. Mothers pulled their children back from the window and kissed them lightly on the forehead.

"Come now, if anything were truly wrong, the Finery would raise the alarm."

Far away, in a very quiet room adorned with chestnut wallpaper, Wolf stirred.

Chapter Fourteen

Wendowleen woke to find Wolf standing over her, breathing sour dog breath into her face. She pushed his snout away firmly and coughed.

"That's new. I hope that doesn't become a habit. Now, where...?" She stared at the wallpaper, and let all of her thoughts slot into place. "Oh. Yes."

Wolf let out a low whine, and Wendowleen glanced back at him, sighing. "I know."

She stood awkwardly and pulled an old cardigan over her nightgown, shuffling her way from the chestnut bedroom to Sylvia's kitchen. Wolf followed impatiently, whining the entire time. Sylvia stood over the stove, a battered copper kettle heating in front of her. She made no move when Wendowleen entered, and didn't even seem to register the noises from Wolf.

"Hello Sylvia," tried Wendowleen. Nothing. Sylvia stood firmly, staring at the kettle. Wendowleen moved forward and placed her hand on Sylvia's shoulder, causing her to screech suddenly and reel around. Wolf began to bark loudly at both women, ears pricked to attention.

"Oh, you surprised me, Wendy."

Wendowleen tapped Wolf on the snout and demanded quiet. He took up his growling again, much to Sylvia's dislike. She eyed him nervously, one hand poised over the kettle as though it might turn into a weapon at any moment.

"Oh ignore him, Sylvia, you probably burst his eardrums."

"Well, I'm not used to having guests, that's what it is. Did you want some broth?"

Wendowleen nodded, "Yes, we'll both have a little. He's not used to having guests either, you know."

Sylvia rolled her eyes at Wolf and poured some of the treacle-like broth out of the kettle into three mugs. Wendowleen took hers and took a seat at the kitchen table, pausing momentarily at a photograph of her late husband, which was nailed to the wall.

"It's a good photograph."

Sylvia nodded and sat opposite, her own cup held tightly. Wendowleen noticed the whites of her sister-in-law's knuckles.

"Yes. I miss him every day."

Wendowleen nodded and took a sip of her broth. It was stronger than she would usually make it, the taste of the chestnut sweetened with sugar. It wasn't really to her taste, but she tried not to pull a face.

"It was hard to find a way...through," Wendowleen said.

"Pardon, my dear?"

"I mean, past the sad times. The grieving."

Sylvia raised her eyebrows and sighed a long, stilted sigh. "I don't like to think about him."

Wendowleen cocked her head to one side, interested. She had certainly mentioned him enough previously. "Then why the photograph on display?"

"Well, he was my brother."

"Yes."

Silence filled the kitchen, the low growl of Wolf creating a backdrop of white noise. Wendowleen coughed, which caused Sylvia to stare at her expectantly.

"Well..." she began, "what are we to do today?"

"I suppose it depends, really, Wendy. How much time do we have? How long do you suppose you might stay for?"

"Not more than a few days."

Sylvia smiled a hard, and yet kind smile, as though she were lecturing a student.

"I have errands to run, that's the only thing. It's a quiet sort of town this, not what you'll have been used to." There was an edge to this, as though it were an insult.

"Arthur and I liked the city, it's true, but we had our trips to the country. One to stay with you, as I recall. It was the hot season, wasn't it? We had pie made by your mother."

Sylvia went silent for a moment, staring into the space beside Wendowleen's right shoulder, eyes glazed. She nodded gently. "Yes. I'd forgotten all about that."

"Yes and," Wendowleen's memory began to pick up speed, "you all drank the homemade quanberry juice, and it made you all quite funny in the head! Arthur fell asleep on the lawn after singing about bringing down the government, do you remember?"

The ladies began to laugh, recalling Arthur taking turns dancing with the women of his life, twisting about the garden.

"Oh, that was rotten stuff! Mother only ever made that one batch. Lethal."

"But do you know Sylvia," Wendowleen closed her eyes momentarily, "I cannot remember why I didn't drink any myself."

Sylvia stopped laughing suddenly and frowned at Wendowleen, shaking her head. "I don't know what you are talking about."

The low growl of Wolf continued.

Chapter Fifteen

The Finery head of staff stood with the spoils of his task in front of him. He was waiting for his boss patiently, ignoring the murmuring of nerves inside his stomach. He held his breath as the door handle turned behind him.

"Ah, Mr Snid. I was informed that you were waiting for —" the Director paused as he saw the stolen framed photographs laid out before his head of staff. He stared at the faces.

"These were taken from the witch's—"

"Professor," the Director interrupted. In a world where a witch was a profession, it made no sense to get Wendowleen's employment history wrong.

"They're from her house, anyway."

"And the rest of the house?"

"Burnt."

The Director nodded, satisfied with this result. His hand hovered above his subordinate's shoulder, the promise of approval. Mr Snid (Bob, to his friends), felt its presence.

"Anything else?"

"Yes." Bob pulled the new law, freshly signed by the mayor, from his pocket, and passed it to the Director.

"Excellent work. Now get out."

Left alone in the room, The Director leaned over the photographs, the frames, the faces. He picked one up of the happy couple on the day of their cohabitation ceremony and stared at it. Wendowleen was much younger, obviously, and he peered at her creaseless face. Then Arthur's, in his strange too short suit, gleeful to be beside his new cohabitee.

"The Cripcots," the Director read aloud. He placed the photograph down carefully and selected another. It was of Wendowleen on the day of her graduation. "Dr Cripcot," he said, blowing dust from the frame. "Well, Dr Cripcot. Professor. It is a shame that your house burnt down. I suppose you had it coming really, ignoring the laws of the land. We'll have to build another house right on top of it."

He placed this down carefully and picked up the empty frame, inspecting it for damage. He nodded to himself, his face flushing with pleasure. "Funny, isn't it, Professor Cripcot, what an unscholarly little boy can do."

Chapter Sixteen

The mayor had heard, of course, what had happened at Wendowleen's home. He was also aware that she was out of town currently, or at least had guessed this, because she would have been banging on his door and ringing his phone from sunrise to sundown if not. And with fair reason, too. He sat at his desk and closed his eyes. Surely, that paper he signed wasn't anything to do with what had happened to Wendowleen's house. And even if it was, that didn't hold him to blame, did it? You didn't blame the person who invented the ink for a bad novel, of course, you didn't. You didn't even blame the bookseller, and that was far closer to it. You blamed the writer. The mayor tried to blame himself in many ways for this unfortunate eventuality, but it was clear to him that he was not the writer of this particular novel. He was just a man, separately doing a job.

So why did he feel so sick?

The mayor's stomach rumbled beneath him. He had noticed that this was becoming common in his day, even when he wasn't hungry, his stomach would murmur and growl. He patted it uncomfortably and pressed the buzzer for his assistant.

The young man marched in almost immediately, clicking his heels to attention before him.

"Yes, sir?"

"You don't have to stand to attention like that."

"Yes, sir." The young man purposefully slouched his shoulders, giving the impression of an uncomfortable captain of a ship.

"Have you read the papers today?"

"No, sir."

"Right, well, get me them, would you? Isn't that supposed to be part of your job?"

The assistant practically ran out of the room while still walking, and the mayor watched him, twinges of guilt sparking in his brain. Why had he just spoken to him like that? He glanced at a framed photograph on his desk, the face of his late mother.

"Remember, just because you have an important job, it doesn't mean that you are important," he said aloud to nobody. This was perhaps the problem, he concluded. He thought he had always been important up until the last week or so. Suddenly he felt like a puppet. Well, enough was enough! He grabbed the phone and dialled a number quickly. As the line rang he hesitated. There was the familiar sound of a *click* as it was answered. He hurriedly placed the phone back in its cradle. Puppet or not, there was no need to be stupid.

Chapter Seventeen

Sylvia and Wendowleen had decided to take a walk down the garden path, and Sylvia was showing off her various plants with pride. Wendowleen looked at them half-heartedly, knowing that her own garden was in fact, much more beautiful. She nodded and smiled at the right times, and kept an ear open for Wolf, who was napping indoors, and not his usual self today.

"Of course, you can only plant these in the Shallow Spring, otherwise, they will never come up in time for the Mighty Freeze."

Wendowleen followed the long finger of Sylvia's hand as she pointed to, well, nothing. Simply earth.

"Do you have a garden, Wendy?"

"Yes, I do."

"Oh good. It is important I think, to work on one's garden."

"Indeed. Although it was Arthur that inspired me to garden really, taught me a lot about it. Before him, it must be said, I didn't know a whole lot about it."

Sylvia paused and sighed, turning to face Wendowleen.

"I did tell you that I didn't like to talk about Arthur much, didn't I?"

"You did, but it confused me a little because you seemed to love to chat about him the last few times I saw you. Besides, you must be the only person in this whole land that actually knew him. Don't you find it a pleasure to reminisce anymore?"

Sylvia scowled and folded her arms. "I am *not* the only person that you can reminisce with."

54

"All right, Sylvia!" Wendowleen raised her hands in protest, "I didn't mean to offend you in any way at all. Honestly."

Sylvia didn't seem to want to back down however, she stood squarely and frowned at Wendowleen. "I am just saying, that this is my house."

"That you *invited* me to stay in!"

"Yes, well. The less said about that, the better!"

Suddenly she paused, and thought for a moment, and then her whole stance changed. She slouched once more, awkwardly gazing at her garden, and then her feet.

"Gosh, I am sorry Wendy. You must think me an awful brute. Just ignore me, won't you? I just need a lie-down."

Wendowleen nodded, shocked at the sudden change in her behaviour. Although, she thought, as she watched Sylvia wander back down the garden path, she always was a funny one. That was the whole reason that Arthur and herself kept a little distance, only seeing her on very special occasions. And her reluctance to talk about Arthur these days was different. Wendowleen had been sort of dreading the amount they used to chat about him, but now she was here, had started to find it enjoyable. Wendowleen glanced around the garden. She had only been there one night, was it too soon to leave already? Pah. She was over one hundred years old. She could do whatever the hell she wanted.

The nap was agreed on by the both of them, each needing a break from the other. Sisters-in-law by name, and certainly not by blood. They both struggled with the other in close proximity, irritated by their presence. Wendowleen sighed and pulled the strange-smelling duvet around her face, closing her eyes slowly. She was tired. It wasn't like her to nap during the day, she believed that sort of thing was for the elderly, and she did not consider herself to be that. Wolf was curled up at the end of the bed, still growling softly beneath his breath. He didn't like being here either, Wendowleen thought, as she drifted into sleep.

The smell took over all of her senses, touching her nose at the tip and reaching the back of her throat. It was blood, she recognised it as that, but it was not so repulsive as she had imagined. There was something softer as well, like sour milk, curdling in her thoughts. She reached out her arms to him and brought him close to her chest, skin on skin, sight on sight. He gazed at her with such need that she felt overwhelmed. And then, the voice. Arthur. The laughter that followed. The murmurs that she couldn't quite make out. She knew though, that it was joy. Arthur's joy, and by extension, her own. She clasped him to her and laughed along, not trying to make sense of it, not attempting to break the spell. Arthur and she, and now the three of them, all together. She brought her blanket up to cover his naked body, and kissed his cheeks. His gaze continued, driving into her, focusing on her eyes, her mind. She felt the tears begin to drop, and waited for them to land on his cheeks. He blinked slowly, beginning to close his eyes.

"I don't want him to sleep," Wendowleen said aloud, "I want him to stay awake, with us."

More laughter from Arthur followed, the murmurs continuing, the blanket being wrapped around the both of them. She kissed his forehead, waiting for the eyes to spring back open. They did not. She watched his tiny chest rise and fall and began to cry real tears, that splashed and gathered on the blanket, on her skin, on his skin. Still, he did not wake. The laughter quietened, as though disappearing down a corridor.

"I don't want him to sleep, Arthur." But there was no response. She was quite alone, the babe sleeping in her arms was not really with her. She stared at his face. What about those lips, did she recognise those? Were they her own, or Arthurs? But they weren't either. And neither was the nose. Those cheeks that were kissable, were unlike anything she had ever seen before. He opened his eyes again, staring at her own, and her heart leapt with joy.

"Wendowleen."

His mouth formed words neatly, quickly. She stared.

"Wendowleen."

He didn't move this time.

"Wendy."

Wendowleen's ears began to burn.

Chapter Eighteen

Wendowleen's neighbours stood in front of the pile of rubble and ashes, and shook their heads sadly. What a shame it was, they muttered to each other, what an absolute disaster.

"Has anyone tried calling her, or writing to her, at her... sister's, is it?" one neighbour said to another.

"Well, I'm not sure if it's a sister or a friend, but thank goodness she wasn't inside."

"Yes, but has anyone tried to contact her?"

"No no, I don't have any telephone numbers at all."

No, none of them did, they all agreed.

"Still," the one who asked the first question spoke up again, "I am certain that *someone* will have contacted her to inform her of this. After all, the Finery, the mayor, someone will have that responsibility."

Murmurs of agreement came from all.

"There is nothing that we can do, not us."

"No, I was saying that only earlier today. It is absolutely not our responsibility."

And then they left, treading awkwardly over the shattered glass from her windows, comfortable in the knowledge that it was nothing at all to do with them.

Wendowleen opened her eyes to see Sylvia standing by her bed. She pulled herself up, as quickly as her age would allow.

"Did you have a good nap?" Sylvia asked.

Wendowleen nodded in response and clicked her fingers to Wolf, who was baring his teeth behind her sister-in-law.

"I'm sorry if I was short with you outside. I'm really not used to having guests and it has been a long time since we last spoke. I wondered, is there a time that might be suitable to book you a train home?"

"Oh, well, yes I suppose..."

"Not that I want you to *leave* per se, Wendy, it's just that space is a vital ingredient to the happiness and harmony of this home."

Wolf bared his teeth again, silently, behind Sylvia. Wendowleen watched him with interest. Was he actually going to bite her?

"It's the shame of losing touch I'm afraid, one loses one's ability to converse with estranged relatives," Sylvia continued.

"Sylvia..." Wendowleen reached out a hand as Wolf began to rise slowly, leaning forward. His gaze seemed intent on Sylvia's head.

"Oh, I know, it's the comings and goings of life..." and then, he sprang. Wendowleen shoved Sylvia out of the way, pushing her to the floor with one hand, and grasping Wolf by the scruff of his neck with the other. The room was silent for seconds. Wendowleen stared at Wolf in surprise. This was the first time he had ever done anything like this.

"What in Rytter are you doing Wendowleen?!" Sylvia screeched as she pushed herself up from the floor, brushing dust off her skirts.

Wendowleen kept a firm hold of Wolf's scruff, keeping him heeled at her side. "I'm sorry Sylvia..."

"Well, you really must leave now. I don't know, I didn't think you would take having your holiday cut short well, but that was really too much." With that, she stalked out of the room, muttering about rudeness and inability to visit relatives.

Wendowleen pushed the door closed and finally let go of Wolf. She stared at him hard, and he sat patiently and stared back, a couple of occasional glances to the floor, to show that she was still in charge.

"You listen to me." She leaned in closer. "You absolutely cannot eat people. Is that understood? If you do anything like that again, that'll be it for you. I mean it. I have enough problems with everything else."

Wolf glanced down at the floor again, seeming to understand that an act of contrition was needed now although he didn't understand exactly what he had done wrong, because he was simply trying to protect his pack leader, which was what he had been taught to do. Still, humans were odd and unusual creatures, with whims and fancies that made little sense to a wolf, and there was no sense in trying to understand the incomprehensible, he decided.

Wendowleen straightened up and sat down on the bed, and sighed deeply. It wasn't that she was upset about being asked to leave, after all, it was hardly a holiday. Sylvia was awkward and difficult, and Wendowleen found life without her much easier. It was something else, an uneasy feeling that sat awkwardly somewhere beneath her intestines. Wolf shifted toward her and placed his chin on her knee, closing his eyes for a little snooze. She stroked the soft wiry fur on the tip of his head and smiled.

"Good pup," she said, and he understood, in some way, that he had done the right thing.

Chapter Nineteen

The neighbours didn't have to worry for too long, because work began fast on Wendowleen's patch of land. They just assumed that she was involved, and it was easier to think that than find out.

They watched from their windows as a low-ranking member of the Finery marched around, pointing out areas that needed digging and clearing, building and shining. The officer stared at the blueprints in her smart uniform, demandingly clicking her fingers at a man in a purple hard hat.

"You! Come here and look at this, do you think that this step here looks anything like that one there?"

The man stalked over, grumbling, irritated that she was there at all. Why was she there? None of the builders knew. This was not usual.

"Mam, sometimes small things change on a build and…"

"You listen to me - things do not change on *this* build, no matter how insignificant you may consider them to be, without my approval first. Do you understand?"

The builder took off his hard hat and scratched his head for a moment before responding.

"Not entirely, mam, no. That step on the blueprint there is far too high for a domesticated house. The woman that lives here is over one hundred years old apparently, and my construction degree from Finer Bay University tells me that…"

The woman from the Finery snatched his purple hat from his hand and slammed it into the ground, the sane reaction of many a member of the Finery to the mention of a degree. "We have our reasons for everything, and everything we do is to ensure the safety of this Rytter. Every step, every brick, every mound in the garden of this house has to be exactly as specified in these blueprints. Do you know why?"

The builder stared at her, bewildered by this sudden change of atmosphere. He shook his head.

"Because that is what the Director wishes. He drew these up himself, with an architect."

"An actual architect or a Finery architect?" The builder said the words before he could stop himself, and visibly flinched as the question fell from his mouth. The words sat between them, waiting to be picked up. Eventually, the member of the Finery moved, pulling a notepad and pen from her pocket. She reached for the hat and plucked it from the ground, staring inside the rim. Eventually, she found his name and wrote it down, scribbling for a full minute. She handed it back to him with a smile, and a nod, and he took it awkwardly. Walking away, he stared at the name inside the hat. It was the name of his best friend, the wrong hat he had selected that morning. He said nothing, and kept on moving.

Later that evening, the notes were typed up, copied and filed away. The knock at the hat owner's door came around two in the morning. No claims of confusion could stop the strike of the ever-growing law.

Chapter Twenty

Wendowleen had packed her bag quickly after Sylvia had asked her to leave. What was the point in trying to force a relationship with this woman anyway? She had never been quite right. Even when Arthur was alive, she had some sort of issue with the union. Wendowleen stood and stared at the handle of her canvas bag for a moment, and then rolled back her shoulders. Why on earth was she invited here? What sense did this make? The woman changed her mind on a dime, as ever.

"That's it, Wolf, heel."

Wolf, not having been trained to heel or to understand what that word meant, stared at her with a wrinkled brow. Wendowleen shrugged at him and turned to stalk out of the door, into the kitchen, where she found Sylvia, speaking into the telephone with limp murmurs.

"Yes, I understand. Thank you."

She placed the received down and sighed a sigh that sounded like relief.

"Who was that?"

Sylvia jolted in surprise and turned slowly to face her sister-in-law.

"Oh, no one."

"Right...well I'm all packed up." Wendowleen folded her arms and waited for a response. An apology, or some kind of recognition of insult, would be ideal. Sylvia simply nodded.

"I did want to ask you something, though, Sylvia."

"Yes?"

"Why did you invite me here?"

"I thought that —" The telephone began to ring, mid-sentence. Sylvia's face froze, and she smiled rigidly, answering with an intake of breath.

"Yes? Hello. Yes. Okay. Goodbye."

She placed the receiver on the kitchen counter and stepped toward Wendowleen, who in turn, stepped backwards.

"I would like to apologise if I have come across as rude in any way, Wendy. Won't you stay for another night?"

Wendowleen shook her head firmly. Was she unwell? The way she leapt between decisions was alarming. "Absolutely not, Sylvia. I've got my bags packed, and I'm going home on the next train."

Sylvia launched forward and grasped her by the arm, tightly. Wendowleen stared at the hand that puckered her already puckering skin for a moment and laughed gently.

"There's a phrase in Finer Bay, which I used to utter to students who had no idea of the hierarchy of academia."

The grip tightened. "You mustn't leave tonight."

Wendowleen stood still and stared at her sister-in-law, "Learn a lion's temper before you pull its mane."

Sylvia loosened her grip and moved her hand down until it was holding Wendowleen's own.

"I am begging you, Wendy. I'm not quite right. Haven't you noticed? I know that, I know that. You must stay one more night. You are the only family I have now, aren't you?"

Wendowleen squeezed Sylvia's hand and shook her head. What to do? She wanted desperately to be back in her own narrow kitchen, climbing the staircase to her own bed. But Sylvia was right, she was the only family she had. And clearly, she wasn't well.

"Oh, I don't know Sylvia. I don't know what to say. Okay, what about a compromise? Is there a hotel nearby that I could stay in for the night? And that way, at least Wolf will be less cooped up. I'll come back for dinner."

Sylvia stooped and sighed, nodding slowly. "You'll have to let me have some time to call them...arrange your stay. It would be much simpler for you to stay here, you know."

"For whom?"

"Well, for both of us."

"Hmmm. Make your call."

Wendowleen stepped out of the kitchen into the living room and flicked on the lamp that stood awkwardly by the door. Nothing happened. She leant forward slightly to check it, all the while trying to listen in to Sylvia's telephone conversation with the hotel.

"Yes, she wants to leave...the local hotel...The Squid's Inn, that's right." Wendowleen paused. Who was she talking to now? There was no one apart from Sylvia who might care about herself and Wolf's whereabouts, surely.

Wendowleen glanced at Wolf, shivering as a memory dragged itself to the front of her mind. Sharp words delivered by pretend soldiers in shining boots, "You should move to the country. There are no bedroom laws there." They were the only people who might care that she was in the country, Wendowleen mused. But the Finery had other things to be dealing with and talking to Sylvia of Snorington would be a strange priority. She nodded, as though putting the thought to bed, and stopped listening. Why wasn't that lamp working? Wendowleen pulled the lampshade from the base, tapping the lightbulb a couple of times. There wasn't the ting of glass that she expected, but rather the thump of...what was that, rubber? She flicked it again, and the same dull thud repeated itself. Sylvia's voice floated through the wall.

"How long do you need? Yes. I can do that."

Wendowleen twisted the strange glass looking lightbulb from the lamp and held it up to her face. It hummed in her hand. She squinted at it, weighing it between her fingers. What was it?

"Thank you, yes. I will deliver her to you in around an hour."

The phone clicked in the kitchen. Something told Wendowleen that Sylvia wouldn't like her messing with the lamp, so she hastily pulled the lampshade back on and stuffed the strange rubber bulb under a cushion on the couch.

Sylvia moved into the living room slowly, "Oh! You're right there. Well, it is organised. You'll be staying at The Squid's Inn tonight. They are quite friendly there."

Wendowleen nodded, smiling. That was welcome news, getting out of here was the first step home.

Chapter Twenty-One

The Squid's Inn was an oval shape, the rooms being rounded and curved, with furniture to match, that followed the edges of each wall carefully. The name had been carefully picked, Wendowleen mused, to match the immense array of decorations that covered the walls surrounding the staircase. Which came first? The squids, or the name?

Wendowleen sighed and sat down on the cream curved bed in her new room, and watched Wolf explore his new surroundings. It was clean, quiet, and the giant squid sculpture stuck to the ceiling did not bother her one bit. It was better than chestnuts, anyway. Wolf eyed it with mistrust and groaned quietly.

Wendowleen lay back and closed her eyes. The staff *had* been very friendly, just as Sylvia had said they would be, and Sylvia had been clearly pleased to pass the responsibility of a guest on to somebody else. In fact, she couldn't leave quickly enough, nodding at everything as though the furniture was asking a series of questions, and hurrying the staff along. Wendowleen had watched her in amusement, seeing nothing of Arthur in her at all.

It had been a little strange when she arrived, that was true. There were three staff waiting behind the very small squid shaped desk, and if Wendowleen hadn't known better, she would have thought they were waiting specifically for her. They practically pounced on top of her as she entered the foyer, pulling her bags from her hands, patting Wolf nervously on the head, and shooting glances at Sylvia that were bordering on desperate.

"Do you get many guests?" Wendowleen had asked them as she was signing in.

"Oh, once in a while, madam, once in a while," one of them answered, quickly.

"And are there any other guests staying tonight?"

The staff glanced at each other and shook their heads.

"Well then, does that mean I get an upgrade?" Wendowleen grinned and thought she may as well ask.

Nervous laughter from the three staff. "Yes, madam. We have already given you the best room."

The best room in The Squid's Inn. Wendowleen opened her eyes and sat up slowly, looking around. Well, the best room didn't account for too much. For a start, she could now see that there were clear dust marks between each tentacle of the squid-shaped bedside lamp.

"What do you think, Wolf?"

Wolf glanced at her at the sound of his name and let out a snort, before lying down carefully on the wooden floor. She nodded in response.

"You're right. It's a better alternative."

The night was not without its disturbances. Wendowleen, once washed and ready for bed, slipped into an easy rest, with Wolf curled at her feet. It was a relief to be in her own space again, though she dreamt unevenly of her home, with its own scent and corners that she knew well. She missed her bed, the curve of the mattress as it held her familiar shape, and even longed for the faucets of the bathroom sink, the accustomed stopcocks, nozzles and valves.

The first disturbance was subtle but irritating. It woke Wolf first. The slow but soft noise of electricity in the air. A dull but existent buzzing, almost invisible to sound. Wolf whined as it reached him, grating on his senses. The whine, in turn, woke

Wendowleen, and she murmured a request for quiet. And then, as she was slipping back into an unconscious state, it reached her. That soft, lead, electrical hum. Her eyes flicked open, and she listened. How irritating. She rolled over so that she was facing the ceiling and stared at the second interruption. A tiny red light, holding its beam in the darkness, on the ceiling above the bed. Was that to blame for the noise? She peered at it, frowning. Indeed, it was. Right, this would take some manoeuvring. Her hand reached for the squid lamp beside the bed and flicked it on. Wolf raised his head at this, staring at Wendowleen with annoyance. He knew it was not the morning yet, and he certainly could have slept through that noise and the tiny light. He watched as Wendowleen shakily clambered to her feet on top of the mattress and obediently woke fully and stood beside her for support. She reached toward the light. What was that? Whatever it belonged to seemed to be embedded in the ceiling. She tapped it a couple of times. The ceiling was sticky, almost wet. A leak? Perhaps.

"Best room in the house? I think not," she said aloud.

At that, a knock on the door suddenly distracted her from the light. She glanced at Wolf in surprise and then at the model of a squid eating a clock that hung on the wall. It was two in the morning. Who on earth could be knocking? And there it was again, a more insistent, slow knock.

"What?" she yelled, as loud as she could, from the bed.

"Madam, would you please come and open the door?"

"Oh, how annoying!" she murmured, clambering slowly to her knees, and then her bum, and shifting herself off the bed. As she reached the door, she rounded her shoulders and pulled at it with a grimace.

"What do you want?" she demanded, staring at the young man in a crumpled uniform before her. His blazer had a squid emblazoned on the right lapel, causing Wendowleen to roll her eyes.

"We heard some commotion coming from your room, Madam, are you in distress?"

Wendowleen stared at him for a moment.

"What? You heard commotion?"

"Yes, madam, strange noises."

"Right, I do understand the definition of commotion. My query is rather that there was no noise coming from my bedroom."

The young man nodded in a very understanding, albeit condescending, way. "Well, I just thought I would check on you, madam, to see if there was anything you needed."

Wendowleen rolled her eyes again, this time at the way the boy said 'madam' repeatedly, in his northern drawl.

"Best room in the house, is it?" she said, widening her eyes expectantly.

"Yes, madam, oh certainly."

"Is it really...and if I wanted to move rooms?"

The young man shook his head quickly. "No, well, it wouldn't be possible. Fully booked."

Wendowleen paused, a smirk spreading across her lips. "Did you just say fully booked?"

The young man nodded, awkwardly waiting for whatever the punchline was.

"Well, I do find that *interesting*. Only a few hours ago there was nobody else staying but me. After all, it can't be a very busy time for you, not really. It's not a holiday season, is it?"

There was a definite pause as the young man stretched his brain as far as it would go, and coughed slightly. "It is almost the Artomia festival, though, madam, and people are getting prepared."

"Are they *really*." It wasn't a question. Wendowleen knew the festival wasn't for another couple of days, at least. After a pause, in which she stared at the young man until he was confident that it was probably, definitely, a bad idea to knock on this door and that the next time his boss told him to do something, he would go and hide in a cupboard, Wendowleen stepped aside and motioned that he should come in. He shifted from one foot to the other, his brow beginning to dampen beneath Wendowleen's stare. For what reason could they be lying to her? She wondered. Laziness, most likely. Too lazy to make another bed up, perhaps. There was something else there, though, in the gaze of the young man. Wendowleen recognised it as fear, the whites of his eyes more visible than before, his gaze flitting from her to the room beyond.

"There's a leak in my room, an irritating red light, and the blasted buzz of some kind of electrical equipment that I can't locate."

The man paused and hesitated, then shook his head, remaining on the threshold of the room. "Yes, that's the fire alarm. We can't turn that off, madam, otherwise, you would be in danger. We recommend just leaving it and going back to bed."

Wendowleen nodded carefully, watching as the youth straightened his small tie, clutching at his neck as though being strangled. The boy was terrified.

"Come now, I'm not scary, am I? Come on in, please, and take a look at the leak."

"It isn't a leak."

"I haven't even told you where it is yet."

A pause in which the young man scanned his mind again for possible responses.

"The Squid's Inn," he began, voice shaking with effort, "is well known for its realistic portrayal of how it might be to live among...squids. I'm sure if you require anything else, I can fetch the night manager. Goodnight."

Wendowleen watched him stalk away quickly, almost running down the hallway. Despite having had nothing resolved, she grinned. It took her straight back to the good old days when failing students would visit her office, begging for their final papers to be re-marked. Now that was fear. The thought of having to tell their parents that their studying years had been spent in the bars of Finer Bay was a deterrent indeed. But the fear in that boy's eyes was slightly different. Less of shame and more of desperation. The smile fell from Wendowleen's face, and she closed the door in front of her and sighed. There was an uneasiness in her stomach, the taste of worry in the air. The conflicting answers of the staff here, Sylvia's strange behaviour... it was beginning to feel purposeful, planned. Oh, to be at home, without all this absolute nonsense. She patted Wolf on the head, and he closed his eyes, tired from the early visit.

"Wouldn't it be something to be at home, Wolf?"

He murmured, understanding the need for a response, noticing the inflexion at the end of the sentence.

Together, they got back onto the bed and tried to ignore the light, the buzzing, and the confusing dampness in the ceiling. Eventually, this must have worked, as they slept soundly enough to forgive each other's snoring.

Chapter Twenty-Two

With the evening's disturbances, Wendowleen and Wolf explored their unconscious minds until the sun had settled firmly in the sky, and breakfast for one had been served in the dining room, and then cleared away.

Then, there was another precise knocking on the door, causing Wendowleen to stir. She got up, stomping her way through the room. The door opened to reveal Sylvia, who smiled and offered a mug of warm chestnut broth, which Wendowleen accepted gratefully.

The two women moved back into Wendowleen's room, where they perched next to each other on the bed.

"How was your evening sleep, Wendy?"

Wendowleen took a sip of her drink and sighed sleepily. "It was a shambles. I'll head home today."

"Oh, not at all. Why don't you stay here until Artomia? It's always a great celebration here." Sylvia nodded hurriedly as she spoke.

"Well, I should think it's probably better in the capital Sylvia, don't you?"

There was a pause as Wendowleen stared into her mug at something that had bumped her top lip as she took a sip. It was half a chestnut. She grimaced slightly. That would never have happened in her own chestnut broth. It was uncouth. She glanced at Sylvia, who was nervously knotting and unknotting her fingers beside her, knitting skin upon skin.

"Oh, what is wrong with you now, Sylvia?"

Sylvia shrugged. "Nothing! Nothing at all. I'll go and tell the staff you plan on leaving then, shall I?"

"Well, yes, that would actually be very helpful."

Sylvia stood and left, closing the door gently behind her. Alone with her thoughts (apart from Wolf, of course), Wendowleen closed her eyes and breathed in deeply. The sweet scent of the poorly made broth filled her nostrils, and the sound of…hang on…"That bloody buzzing again!"

Wendowleen slammed her mug down next to the squid-shaped bedside lamp and climbed to her feet on the bed once more. She pressed the red light that still shone above the mattress, feeling that the ceiling around it was still damp. Her fingers dug into the plaster slightly, and she pushed harder, eventually pulling some off. It fell onto the bed, and Wolf whined loudly at her. She pulled a little more from the ceiling, and the buzzing grew louder. And there it was. A strange black box, hidden in the ceiling. She grabbed it, pulling it hard until it came away in her hands.

"What the hell is this?"

At that exact moment, the door burst open, and Wendowleen looked up to see the young man from the previous evening standing side by side with Sylvia. Suddenly, it all made sense. She held up the black box and grinned.

"Well, isn't that perfect timing?"

Chapter Twenty-Three

The Artomia festivities were held every two years when the seasons went from chilly to colder and hot again. The switch was quite sudden, the weather in Rytter being cold most of the time. The heat was celebrated for as long as it lasted, and many residents still remembered that sweet time sixty years ago when the sunshine had stayed high in the sky for over three weeks. Now *that* had been worth celebrating. At the time, Wendowleen had been at the height of her career and took the students outside to learn in the sunshine. They had read in the quickly growing grass and slept at lunchtimes with their heads on their books, and she hadn't minded at all. The sunshine was brief and for enjoying.

The Director of the Finery had known the deadline for completing Wendowleen's house as soon as he had sat down with the architect. It was to be a week before the celebrations of Artomia began. The reason was simple – no Finer Bay resident would miss the festivities in their own hometown. To do so would be unthinkable. He also knew that Wendowleen decorated her house in the season, so she would be back to organise herself with time to spare. He had made this clear to Sylvia, who had managed to make a complete mess of what was a straightforward job. Why could she not just invite Wendowleen to stay for a week without any nonsense? She was unhinged, the stupid woman, incapable of organising anything. In retrospect, it would have made more sense to have sent Wendowleen away on holiday, and it could have been done with a competition or...

well, nevertheless. The Director leaned back in his chair and let his eyelids fall until darkness sat before him.

"Is she on her way back?"

"Yes, sir. Sylvia saw her onto the train, and the staff that accompanied her said that her reaction was very strong. He had no backup, sir, he was only a member of staff at the Squid's Inn. Didn't expect to get a phone call, he said. There was only one option, he said, to send her back here. Her assistance wolf was turning aggressive, and she's only an old –"

The Director's eyes opened slowly, and the action put the assistant on pause. He was using the phrase 'he said' like a shield, distancing himself from the actions of his country colleague.

"She's inept."

"It's the only family I could find, sir."

"And she doesn't have any friends?"

The assistant shook his head quickly. The Director nodded and thought about steepling his fingers before him, but it was such a cliché that he couldn't bring himself to do it. Cripcot was on her way back, which was fine, the housing project had been completed that morning. And yet, it was not to the letter of his order, and therein lay the problem.

"You must be able to tell that I am not pleased. Send a letter to The Squid's Inn. I want a list of the people on duty over Cripcot's stay."

Chapter Twenty-Four

Ah, to be back on the train, moving away from her only remaining family member. Wendowleen allowed Wolf to sit beside her on the seat, which was usually strictly off-limits. This confused him, and he flexed his paws repeatedly, trying to ready himself for jumping down. Well, she mused, it was certain. Sylvia was not the scatty and irritating sister-in-law she believed her to be. She was much worse than that, an easy to manipulate, untrustworthy coward. Wendowleen stared out of her window into the ever-darkening landscape, clutching the purse on her lap as though it was Sylvia's throat. She thought of Arthur and blinked hard. She would never cry; that wasn't Wendowleen's way. In fact, she hadn't cried since she was in school, not even when Arthur had died. Her grip tightened as her mind jumped to her escape from The Squid's Inn. To be back in her house, with her own things, far from any illegalities. The realisation of what the black box was had filled her chest with a tightness that she had never experienced before. They were watching her.

Sylvia sat in the waiting room shaking. She was terrified, that was a given, but she was even more scared by the fact that they hadn't offered her a drink. I mean, that was just inhumane. She folded her hands under and over each other, again and again, the clamminess spreading. The high-speed train (smaller carriages, ten horses, higher galloping to time ratio) had been exciting, that was true. She had never been on one before. She could have done without the hustling, and shoving, and the general rudeness. That was uncalled for. After all, she had done her best, hadn't she? She wasn't made for this sort of thing. She didn't even like her sister-in-law, so to have her in her own home had been a favour in itself, let alone all the nonsense that surrounded her stay. They were making her wait to build tension — she was sure of that. How rude! The young boy from The Squid's Inn coughed quietly beside her, and she glanced at him quickly. Sweat was weaving its way down his forehead and settling onto his eyebrow. Should she say something?

"It'll be okay, you know."

He shyed at her voice, and shook his head, not taking his eyes from the sign on the door before them. He was too afraid to respond to her.

"You will be —" But, he would never find out what he would be, according to Sylvia, because the Director's door swung open.

Chapter Twenty-Five

Well, the word 'escape' might be a bit extreme for the reality of Wendowleen's leaving of the inn. The young man had stood at the door, Sylvia in tow, staring uncomfortably at her as she grasped the black box.

"Well, isn't that perfect timing?"

And Sylvia began to laugh, a strange, deep-throated reach for mirth, that took the young man by surprise. He stared at the two old women, undoubtedly wondering what his place was in all of this, and how an evening position at The Squid's Inn to save up for university had led him to this moment. He tried to assert his authority.

"Please, madam, get down from the bed."

Wendowleen stared at him and placed her hand on the ceiling, pushing at it, until it crumbled into damp dust on her head.

"This is wet plaster. Who put this above the bed?"

The fact was, it wasn't anyone who worked at the inn, although he certainly wasn't brave enough to say that. After all, he had opened the door for its installation.

"I couldn't say. I don't know." He paused thoughtfully. "I don't know what it is."

And with that, Sylvia fell silent. Wendowleen turned the black box in her hands, still keeping her balance on the lumpy mattress. The fact was that she wasn't the best at dealing with electronics. She had watched her classroom change from hastily written pages to perfectly spelt essays, and that wasn't a good thing. You could tell a lot from handwriting, from the letters' curves to the uncrossed T's. You could tell who you were dealing with. An illegible scrawl could tell Wendowleen more about the ego of one of her students than the content of an essay. When screens had begun to fill the classroom, she had put up a fight and had even given evidence to the vice-chancellor on the unrealistic improvement of work. She had always said the same thing at the start of her course, "If you're going to be late don't come at all, and if you can't spell 'chiaroscurist' you are not welcome in my classroom." Sometimes she actually had students stand up and spell words like 'gneissoid' and 'pfeffernuss' just to see if they could. Of course, the name of a biscuit was not something they would ever need to learn to spell in her classroom, but it gave them the right impression. Firstly, there were no easy classes. Secondly, she was in charge of the curriculum. Ironically, the students who had the ability to spell those words usually went on to be her least favourite. They were usually know-it-all's, show-offs, too clever for their own good. They said things like, "When I was growing up, we had more books than floor space," and expected her to be impressed. She wasn't impressed. Any parent who brought their child up walking over books instead of carpet was bound to be incompetent.

And then, the screens came, and suddenly every single student could not only spell every word correctly, but they could give the definition immediately. But it wasn't genuine knowledge. It wouldn't be like the time she bumped into an old student in the supermarket, who told her that he had never forgotten the word 'staphylococci'. Instead, they could barely remember what she had said the previous week, and she watched them hastily check their previous typed documents when she asked them a question and swore against electronics for the rest of her life.

The red light still shone on the box, and she stared at it, then flipped it over in her hand. A lens the size of her fingernail stared back at her. She glanced up at the boy again.

"Is it customary to spy on guests?"

He understood the word 'spy' perfectly well, but, unfortunately, struggled with the word 'customary'. Sylvia stared at him, her mouth flung open, and then spoke up.

"Yes, is it?"

He stared from Wendowleen to Sylvia and raised his eyebrows.

"Come on," he hissed at her, and she mocked effrontery, stalking over to Wendowleen's bed. Wolf watched her with yellow eyes, his growl becoming louder by the second.

"Oh, call off your wolf, Wendy, I'm just going to help you down from the bed."

Wendowleen said nothing but shook her head. She trusted Wolf's judgement of personality. Instead, she climbed down carefully herself, using a post from the bed for assistance.

"Who is watching?"

Sylvia shook her head and turned back to the boy, "Go on, answer her!"

His shoes shifted beneath him, puckering the worn carpet. "I don't know."

Wolf's growl grew deeper.

"I think you do know. Have you met Wolf?"

Wolf's right ear flicked backwards at the sound of his master saying his name, but his attention remained on the two.

"Wolf is an assistance wolf. But really, I don't need one. And that's good because he's a lot wilder than they are supposed to be. He's not the meek, gentle, beast they usually send out to retired folk. But then, I'm not the usual retiree, so we are well matched." She took a step forward, and Sylvia glanced at Wolf and determinedly moved back toward the doorway beside the boy. "The Finery trained him. Renowned for bloodthirst, after his sixth killing they thought it was best to get rid of him –" she cupped her hand around her mouth, faux whispering "– as in, put him down. But the serum made him stronger, and worse, he was angrier than ever. And then, he came to me. So, when I ask you a question, I expect an answer, because it would take only one word for Wolf to level up his number of killings to seven." Wendowleen smiled sweetly from the boy to Sylvia. "Or eight."

The boy nodded hastily and opened his mouth to answer her, but not before Sylvia jumped in and took his words. "We had no choice. They think you know something...they want us to keep you here."

Wolf leaned forward, his behind in the air, shoulders moving visibly beneath his fur. The boy stared at him and back to Wendowleen, panicking. "Please – call him off."

Wendowleen shook her head slowly, "I can't."

And with that, Wolf understood the need for them to leave and sprang forward. The boy and Sylvia scattered as quickly as he moved. Wendowleen collected her things and left The Squid's Inn with Wolf. On the train, she smiled at him and rubbed the tip of his left ear.

"You're a good boy," she said, musing momentarily on the elaborate story she had told. "But you're not a killer."

Chapter Twenty-Six

The Director wasn't standing at the door himself, oh no. That would have been a mistake. His head of staff was standing instead, acting as a bodyguard, glaring out at Sylvia and the boy. He could be as stern, if not sterner, than the Director himself. After all, you don't get to open the Director's door by being weak. You get there because the Director has seen you act the way he saw himself act as a young man. Ruthlessness, discretion, and little hesitation in breaking the law were the critical components of the role. He was not the same person who hesitated with the Director's lunch or answered the phone for him. In fact, that was so far below him that it had never been his position. It was no secret that he was planning on being the Director at some stage in his career. There was never any question about his ambitions, and though others may have kept him at a distance, the Director liked to keep him at his side. After all, he was an enemy of sorts, and the more the Director could see, the less chance he would have to plan something. And it was exciting, in a strange, adrenalin-spiking sort of way, having a man who may kill you for your position be your assistant. It was perhaps the most passionate relationship either man had ever had in their lives.

Bob was tall, as could be expected, and naturally stocky. Perhaps he would have felt the need to work out in another life, but in this one, his job involved plenty of heavy lifting, squatting, cutting...although that last one couldn't really be said to improve his physique. The result of this was a thickness that many found menacing to behold, not least the boy from The Squid's Inn. He stared at him with wide eyes. Sylvia, on the other hand, was getting fed up. Who was this chap, standing and staring at them like this? What was she, a fish in a bowl?

"Are you the Director then?" she asked, still seated, her eyes twinkling. She knew, in fact, that he was not.

The assistant grinned, genuinely touched at the thought, and shook his head. "Would you like to come in?" He stepped aside.

Sylvia considered this and shook her head. "No, I wouldn't. If someone has got something so important to say that they hustled me onto a train, well, I think that they should come and say it to me." She leaned forward, eyes narrowing. "I've travelled the majority of the way, after all."

The assistant laughed, but his eyes stayed frozen. "You have changed your tune, haven't you? What could have transpired in the last hour or so that's given you a sudden shot of bravery?"

Sylvia shrugged, "I realised that I've got nothing to lose."

"No? Not your house? Not your...family?"

Sylvia glared. "I don't call it family."

"Well, maybe it doesn't call you family, either. Anyway, we can see the boy first if you're having trouble standing."

The boy stood to attention immediately, hastily glancing at Sylvia. Was she insane?

Chapter Twenty-Seven

It was late in the evening when the train slowly fidgeted its way into the station. Wendowleen had snoozed on and off, and felt a strange feeling as she stepped onto the platform with Wolf. It was a feeling of peace, a pleasure to be home, but there was also a deeper murmuring inside her stomach. She stood for a moment, watching as the station staff carefully decorated for Artomia. The familiar sight of the paper fawns being hung from benches, the lights shaped like chestnuts dripping their way across signs. She thought of Arthur then, as she always did at this time, the memories that were synonymous with Artomia. The scent of leaves falling from the trees in their garden, the grass beginning to grow. Arthur, decorating the lawnmower with green string, a celebration of its use. Ice-cold drinks on the front doorstep, and the whisper of warmth in the air. Arthur trying to find the decorations in the cellar. Giving up and buying new ones. Being able to stay awake until the official midnight start, something she had left to her youth. She smiled to herself, wrapped in the memories of her formative years. All the Artomias that merged into one confused her. Cooking for more than both of them, especially. Laying the table for three. She had no memory of Sylvia staying, or her students…who could have been – Wolf licked her hand, bringing her back to the station. She glanced down at him and nodded, and together they weaved their way to the street, beginning the short walk home.

The curves of the road were familiar beneath Wendowleen's shoes. She knew the dips of the cobbles, and as she stepped, she mused over how easy it was to get home with only the moon for light. She believed that she might even be able to get home by the sense of touch alone. And then, as she reached her house, her senses completely deceived her. Where her tall house once stood, prime of place at the end of her beautiful garden, was a brand new building. For the first time in her life, Wendowleen doubted her feet. She stared at the house next door and squinted in the darkness. That looked the same as her neighbour's, didn't it? Did it? She turned and walked back up the road to stare at the street name. It was the right sign, but that couldn't be correct. Perhaps some youths had swapped it with another as a prank. Wolf whined softly at her.

"Wolf – take me home." This was something that Wolf could actually understand. His training was such that he was bred for this very reason, helping lost older folks find their way back to safety. But he, too, was confused. Wendowleen nodded at him.

"Take me home."

He stepped awkwardly back down the street, over the familiar cobbles, and to the new building. Sitting before it, he barked loudly, distressed at being unable to complete the task. Wendowleen nodded again, understanding beginning to dawn on her. She stared at the ground where her garden used to be and blinked hard. Then, the door opened.

"Can I help you?" A young woman stood, silhouetted by cold white light, in the doorway. She smiled kindly and then noticed Wolf, a look of recognition spreading over her face.

"Ah, you must be Wendowleen." She stepped out, jerking slightly at the height of the front doorstep, and held out her hand, the nails of which were painted pink.

Wendowleen shook her head. "Who are you?"

"I'm one of the new lodgers."

"One of...?"

"Yes, there are three of us, in all. Including you."

Wolf barked again, causing the young woman to flinch.

"I don't have lodgers."

"Well, with all due respect..." A swallow, a lowering of the offered hand. "It is all of our homes. Though, I appreciate you have been here the longest."

Wendowleen breathed in deeply. "Been here the longest? Where exactly, where is my home?"

The woman lingered slightly and frowned. "I don't really know what to say. I think maybe you should come in? I mean, there has been some post left for you. I don't think that whatever this," she gestured at the empty space in front of her, "is, is my responsibility."

Wendowleen glowered. Her responsibility? The indication was clearly that Wendowleen's age had something to do with her confusion, as though her house hadn't disappeared entirely. She sighed, pretending to give in. "Show me inside."

They ambled toward the step, and the woman held out her arm. "This step is pretty big; you can hold on if you like."

Instead, Wolf was leaned on for support as Wendowleen climbed toward the front door. She stepped inside the hallway and blinked slowly. The small corridor that once led to the kitchen and staircase was gone, and in its place, there was a large white square room with three front doors, each with its own set of numbers. The woman grinned.

"I'm 32A, and you're 32C, remember? I've been putting your post beneath your front door. You left your keys in the lock, but I wouldn't worry; it's a pretty safe neighbourhood."

Wendowleen felt a shiver shift down her spine, her century old response to condescension. She felt the desire to shout and scream at this woman, this stranger, telling her that she was the original owner of this land, that she had been decorating the walls since before this young woman was born, let alone laid her head here. And yet, there was a threat in the air. What would happen if she did?

While Wendowleen considered her options, the woman wrinkled her nose with faux concern. A patronising tap on the arm offered, she left Wendowleen standing in the brightly lit square, staring at her new front door, its shiny illuminated numbers brazenly staring back at her. She pictured the last time she was home, receiving Sylvia's phone call, and shook her head. Sylvia. A distracting rouse to enforce the bedroom laws. How elaborate! Surely, that wasn't usual practice? Wolf stood next to her, vaguely understanding that something was really very wrong and squirming from paw to paw. He dreamed momentarily of his warm, soft space at the end of Wendowleen's bed, and sighed. Why on earth couldn't they just go home now?

Wendowleen turned the keys that she didn't leave in the front door that was not her own. A click, a turn of the handle, and she and Wolf were in. The lights turned on automatically, and Wendowleen sighed, irritated by the fact that she enjoyed not having to grope for switches and at the same time feeling furious by the change. The woman in the hallway seemed to think that she had been there before, which, in a way, she supposed she had if you were talking about the actual space where the house was. The flat that she was now standing in was entirely different to her tall house.

For a start, everything seemed to be beige. The carpet, the walls, the furniture. Behind the front door was a whole room, including a kitchen, sofa, table and chairs, and a staircase at the end. Wendowleen moved forwards to frown at the kitchen. Her own belongings had been mixed with brand new ones; spatulas with familiar dips were side by side with long silver forks that she couldn't see a use for, an odd beige mug with a giant chestnut on it that she rather liked but…had never seen before. She picked it up and looked inside, seeing the familiar brown marks of a

Chapter Twenty-Eight

After around half an hour, the Director's door reopened. By this time, Sylvia was absolutely livid. She was angry that she wasn't at home, she was furious that she had been bundled on a train and sent to the capital city, and if anyone had bothered to ask, which they hadn't, she had missed her dinner. Which, she remembered with even more irritation, was waiting on the side in the kitchen and would be ruined by the time she got back to her house.

Sylvia stared at the head of staff with a rage that didn't surprise even him. Nothing surprised him. He grinned. Work was always more fun when someone had a bit of fight.

"Sylvia, are you ready to see the Director?"

She stood without saying a word, and marched toward the door in a fury. The Director sat behind his desk, eyes twinkling.

"Sylvie! Come on in, and sit down, won't you?"

"I prefer to stand," Sylvia said, raising her chin. The Director grinned.

"Don't be daft. Sit down."

Sylvia sat but pointed her finger firmly in the face of the Director. "I am sitting, but only because I choose to sit. It has nothing to do with you, young man."

The Director laughed gleefully, his eyes not showing any signs of mirth. "Oh, it's just like my youth."

"Not exactly," Sylvia retorted, and the two sat and stared at each other for a few beats. The Director's head of staff looked between them, frowning, and then awkwardly sat at the side of the room.

"So," Sylvia began, still clutching her handbag on her lap like an otter grasping a clam, "where did the boy go?"

"Back to The Squid's Inn, I should think." The Director shrugged gently. "Anyway, we are here to discuss you, are we not?"

"And what in particular?"

"In particular? A job badly done."

Sylvia rolled her eyes and tutted loudly – the cliché of an irritated aunt. The Director watched her, his eyes darkening.

"I loathe the tut, Sylvia. Say something, or say nothing. There is no in-between."

"Well – I didn't ask for the job, did I? And," she leaned forward, "I was lead to believe that there was really no choice in the matter. You should have heard the threats."

Silence took over, and the Director leant back in his chair and waited. He was a man who understood the power of silence. Sylvia watched him carefully, unafraid to speak.

"You know, I really haven't thought about the Finery in years. At first, I wasn't even sure who you were."

"But now you know."

"Yes…"

More silence.

Sylvia sighed softly. "I know what you're afraid of."

"That's an exciting statement – do-"

"She doesn't remember anything."

The Director was not used to being cut off mid-sentence. His head of staff glanced at him, afraid to give his full attention but aware that the situation may blow up any moment. Who on earth did this woman think she was?! He stood up, and the Director stared at him suddenly, as though surprised that he was there at all.

"Out."

Bob hesitated. Surely he wasn't serious. "Sir?"

No verbal response was necessary. The Director gave him a look that pricked his stomach with doubt. In recent years he had been privy to everything that happened in the Director's professional life. He glanced at Sylvia again and simply nodded. There was absolutely no chance that he could do anything else.

Bob walked out of the office into the hallway, and closed the door quietly behind him. He stood for a moment, alone, wondering what to do next. He could go home, have dinner, shine his shoes for the following day. But, not before he had checked on the boy.

Beneath them all, four floors down, the boy from The Squid's Inn stood. His feet were square on a round platform, suspended half a meter from ice-cold water. The walls of the cell around him were steep and smooth, the only rough surface was chipping paint. The air, thick with murmurs, whispers, threats, told him not to twitch, not to fall. There would be little recovery from that. The boy thought of Sylvia and wondered how she was fairing above him. Surely Sylvia, the poor old woman, would be in a much worse position than he, who was young and strong? In reality, though, Sylvia had finally been offered a hot drink, and a little supper wouldn't go amiss either.

Chapter Twenty-Nine

Wendowleen awoke to the noise of chatter in the hallway outside her front door. She couldn't hear the words exactly, they were muffled, but the occasional burst of laughter irritated her greatly. She was used to waking up to the sound of the birds at the window, of Wolf whimpering in his sleep, and other such things that conveyed homeliness and comfort. As it turns out, Wolf was not murmuring in his sleep at this point but was sleeping with his eyes open. He did this occasionally, and Wendowleen liked to think it was when he knew they had to be alert. It was actually when Wolf was too tired to even close his eyes, and his last bit of energy had gone on climbing into a comfortable position, but neither of the two needed to know that.

Wendowleen pulled herself into a sitting position and nudged Wolf with her foot, who blinked rapidly for a moment. She looked around the room, at the accuracies and the inaccuracies, at the bits she recognised and those she didn't. So who could she go to? She stared at Wolf and then decided. The mayor. The covers flew back, and she shuffled down the short staircase to the phone. It was, she was relieved to see, her old phone, but the piece of paper that she kept pinned beside it was now gone. The piece of paper that had the mayor's number on it. She grumbled. It would have to be the operator – they would put her through. She lifted the receiver, surprised for a second at its weight, and dialled 0.

"Hello?"

"Operator, where can I direct you."

"The mayor's office."

A pause, a beep. "Putting you through now."

The phone on the other end began to ring, much to Wendowleen's approval. At least some things remained the same.

"Hello, mayor's office. How can I help?" A woman's voice reached Wendowleen's ear.

Wendowleen tutted. "Hello, I would like to speak to the mayor."

"And what would that be regarding?"

"Well…do I have to tell you?"

"If you do tell me, madam, I can ensure that you get put through to the correct person."

"The correct person is the mayor."

"With all due respect…"

"I did have the mayor's direct number, and I call him all the time."

"It appears that you have come through from an operating service…"

"Yes, yes." Wendowleen took a deep breath, reminding herself that the friendliest people got the most help from strangers. "I just need some help. I've been away for a few days, and I have come home again, and well…my home is where I left it, but it isn't the home I left – if you see my meaning. As an example, I did have the mayor's number pinned to the table, and now that's gone."

There was a pause on the end of the receiver, and then the woman spoke again in a very gentle, faux soothing voice. "Is there anyone there with you, madam, that I might be able to speak to?"

"Well, no."

"It sounds to me like you may need a little help –"

"That's what I just said."

"Yes, madam, I can put you through to the Caring Carers Society, if you would like?"

Wendowleen took another deep breath. "Why? Is the mayor with them? We don't seem to be getting anywhere here. Would you do me a kindness, please and just pop upstairs to tell him that Professor Cripcot is on the phone."

"I'm afraid that I cannot just interrupt the mayor because you would like to talk to him, Miss Cripcot."

"Firstly, I just told you that I was Professor Cripcot, so you can banish the Miss to wherever your last brain cell has set up camp, and secondly – it is the job that is important, not the man. He can be interrupted at any time of the day – just as I can."

"I'll put you through to someone who can help."

Wendowleen rolled her eyes, knowing that it was unlikely to be the mayor's office – she just wanted her off the phone. Still, she waited. Perhaps they could help.

"Hello, you're through to the CCS. How can we help?"

Wendowleen replaced the receiver which as much force as she could muster. She wasn't for the glue factory just yet. Wolf padded over to her slowly, recognising the uncomfortable atmosphere, and watched as she pulled an old coat from the coat stand – the coat he knew, it was the coat stand he had never seen before – and pushed her bare feet into boots. He grumbled, but only quietly, as heading outside before breakfast was not his idea of a good time. And yet, despite his meagre protest, out they went.

Wendowleen slammed the door behind her and Wolf and stood in the still too bright hallway. She strode purposefully toward the front door, and dropped awkwardly down the large step, with Wolf's help. Once outside, in the bright light of the early morning, she turned and marched toward her neighbour's house. The air tickled her skin as she walked down their garden path, and she paused for a moment to smell the sweet, almondy scent of awatoprams in full bloom. She missed her garden, with its tendrils and tricks, the way the sun would bounce from the cordelias as they pushed up the paving. Another deep breath. Wendowleen stepped forward and knocked firmly on the door.

The door opened almost instantly, and the middle-aged man that had bought the house five seasons previous answered in a short nightgown.

"Ah – Cripcot! You caught me on my way for my morning piddle. Enjoying the new house?"

Wendowleen frowned, trying not to glance down at his knees. "Keuy! So you know about it then?"

"Well, you didn't hire silent builders."

"I didn't hire anyone at all. I didn't know this was happening."

"Heh heh. Well, nice to see you again."

"Wait, Keuy – I'm serious. I went to my sister-in-law's, and I came back, and the whole house has been ripped down. Other people are living there!"

Keuy stared at Wendowleen and fidgeted slightly. The cold air was blowing into his house, and the goosebumps on his legs were not making his need to wee any easier.

"The truth is, Cripcot, I'm not sure what to say at this point."

Wendowleen rolled her eyes. "Well, did you see the people who did it?"

A nod, a glance around. "Yes, builders, like I said, and a couple of Finery folk. Nothing unusual there."

"Right. And you didn't say anything to them?"

Keuy let out a short burst of air from in front of his teeth. "Far be it for me to interrupt! For all I knew, you were sitting up high telling them to cause a racket – in actual fact, I felt quite cross with you."

Wendowleen's eyes narrowed, and she curled her lip in irritation. She turned swiftly, almost tripping over Wolf.

"You're bloody welcome!" Keuy shouted after her as she stalked down the garden path.

Wolf stayed behind, just for a moment, staring at the wooden door that had just slammed in his face. He thought about growling, barking, and making a fuss, but he wasn't confident he could get the bit of wood to open again. Plus, it would mean staring at those knees for a little longer, and he could do without the pleasure.

Chapter Thirty

Wendowleen found herself back in her hallway, behind the bright square of front doors. So, what next? She could visit the mayor in person, perhaps...but that was a risk in itself. If the Finery had knocked her house down, maybe she should start with them. She stared at a new piece of furniture that had been leaned against the wall. It was a small table and appeared to have been bashed with a hammer to create artificial ageing. Wendowleen imagined going to the mayor, to the Finery, telling her tale of confusion. What would they say? She suspected the worst. They would tell her that she was getting old, her memory was failing. They would point to the items in her house as evidence of longevity...or, perhaps they would even have some forged proof that she had commissioned the build. She couldn't put anything past them now. On top of the new old table lay a small pile of post, just as the neighbour had told her. She picked it up, hastily looking over the writing on the front of the envelopes. Bills, nothing out of the ordinary, except...Wendowleen frowned and stared at a browning packet on top of the pile, childish handwriting scrawled over the front. A strange scent of earth seemed to be emanating from it. She opened the packet quickly and looked inside. Dirt. It was a package of soil. Not caring at all for her new house, she tipped the large envelope up, watching the dirt cascade over the floorboards. It touched her shoes and sank between the cracks in the floor. And there, within the pile, Wendowleen saw a small off-white square of paper. She bent forward as best she could, momentarily cursing the decision to empty the pile in such a way, and grasped the paper. In the same, strangely juvenile scrawl, was the following message:

You didn't choose this. Neither did we. Meet our carrier in The Malted Mash. They will be waiting for you.

Wendowleen read and re-read the message, only vaguely becoming aware that Wolf had re-entered the house and arrived behind her, and was now moving the dirt around with his long snout, sniffing for clues (he wasn't actually looking for clues, but was instead enjoying a chance to get appropriately dirty – a treat for any pup).

"The Malted Mash," she said aloud, trying to place the name. She hadn't heard of it. Re-reading the note, she noticed that there was no time or date on it either. "How bloody annoying," she said to Wolf, who growled in agreement with her tone. She would get a taxi, perhaps...if it wasn't a downright bizarre idea to go at all. She considered her options, staring at Wolf and his now filthy snout. Mayor, Finery, stranger...to stay and do nothing was not an option. Besides, the day still held promise. It was only just breakfast. What danger was there that lay in sunlight?

Horse-drawn taxis were easy to find in Finer Bay, despite the general population choosing to take more modern engine driven vehicles. The carriages had remained due to the ease with which they bumped and glided over cobbled streets, the low cost of hiring one for a trip (horses did not have to pay taxes, of course, and they were often, if not always, named as the rightful owner of the cart), and the fact that the older population insisted on hiring them relentlessly. The mayor had tried his best, encouraging the Caring Carers Society to promote the use of engines, putting up posters on the difficulty of cleaning horse poo from between cobbles – but, it was for nothing. Wendowleen, aged one hundred, was a horse and cart hirer without exception, and she stood in front of one now, Wolf beside her.

"Good day – could you take me to The Malted Mash?"

The taxi driver looked down from his wooden seat and grinned at her, shifting his large stomach from one side to the other. "Bit early to start, isn't it?"

"Sir, I did not ask for your opinion on my destination, rather that you might take me to the destination itself."

One of those types, the driver thought, before nodding and beckoning that she should climb in. He waited until Wendowleen has successfully placed herself on the wooden seat behind him and then clucked at his horse, driving him forward. "You'd be lucky for a laugh from this one," he murmured to the horse more than himself. The horse did not respond but flicked one ear back, to acknowledge the comment.

Wendowleen watched the streets of Finer Bay from her uncomfortable seat, distracted only by the occasional bump which caused Wolf to lose his balance. She closed her eyes, listening to the horse's hooves on the cobbled streets, the chatter of people as she moved slowly past, and let her thoughts dissipate. They stretched far beyond her problem to the soft crunch of a hoof on gravel outside her and Arthur's front door. A taxi hired for a day, packing up the cart for a picnic for three. Small sandwiches with the crusts cut off, biscuits and juice, chestnut broth in takeaway mugs. The patchwork quilt for the damp ground, stained after –

"The Malted Mash."

Wendowleen came to, finding herself sat once again in the cart, now parked outside a small door with the words 'The Malted Mash' written above it. A wonky wooden sign read *Open, if you can pay* above the handle. Wendowleen didn't much like the look of the place, but she resolved herself to step inside. With the help of Wolf, she gingerly climbed down from the cart and waited until the taxi had moved on. Once alone, she pushed the heavy door and entered.

The stench of malt hit Wendowleen's nose instantly, and she stepped back into the already closed door and sniffed. Wolf had a similar reaction, wrinkling his nose and widening his mouth at the combination of strong senses — the aroma seemed to be dripping from his nose into his throat. He shivered slightly. Wendowleen widened her eyes in an attempt to see the room clearly, the darkness surprising for this time of day. Her sight began to adjust, and she saw some obscure figures hunched over a bar in the corner, a candle lit beside each. No one looked up toward her or seemed to acknowledge her presence at all. She stepped forward into the gloom, one hand on Wolf's back for courage. The bartender glanced up as she made her way through the room and lit a new candle, placing it by an empty stool at the bar. He smiled in the darkness.

"Welcome. What can I get you?"

Wendowleen stared at the bottles that lay in the shadows behind him and breathed in the scent once more. It wasn't unpleasant. She had no idea what to order.

"I'll have a…glass of your finest, thank you."

The barman nodded and stretched up toward a bottle high on the shelf. He uncorked it with ease, and Wendowleen accepted a glass gratefully, pleased that her order had worked at all. The barman glugged a treacle-like liquid into the glass, and stepped back.

"Most kind," Wendowleen murmured as she lifted the receptacle to her lips. The warm thick liquid filled her mouth, and she closed her eyes for just a moment. Down her throat the honeyed corn lit on fire, leaving a residue of bitter plum, coaxing out taste buds that had not risen their heads in years. She opened her eyes. The bartender grinned at her, his front four teeth missing, and nodded.

"That's the stuff."

Wendowleen smiled in response, but inwardly agreed, that it was indeed the stuff she was hoping for — despite never having had it previously. She placed the glass rectangularly on the bar in front of her and glanced at the other guests as subtly as she could.

There were three figures hunched in the candlelight. The furthest away seemed to be drinking something similar to Wendowleen and talking under their breath. A hood crowded their face, and Wendowleen couldn't see anything but shadow and rapidly murmuring lips. Beside them sat a young woman, dark hair cropped to her head, stirring a cup with a spoon silently and seemingly intent on the action. Wendowleen glanced at the figure closest to her, who was, in turn, nervously watching Wolf from their stool.

"Oh, he doesn't bite – I wouldn't worry."

The figure's attention snapped to Wendowleen, and she noticed that she couldn't get a grip on what they looked like at all. One eye seemed to glint in the darkness. They sat back on their stool, their face hidden by gloom.

"My mother always told me not to trust a person who doesn't order malt at a malt bar," the woman with the spoon spoke clearly across the bar to Wendowleen and placed her spoon beside her cup, smiling. Wendowleen nodded in response, unsure whether to speak. The woman glanced down at Wolf in the darkness and smiled.

"This must be Wolf." And with that, Wolf moved toward her, and gently started nuzzling her leg.

"Tsk – Wolf, you pest. I am sorry, he has absolutely no manners." Wendowleen noticed her eyes getting used to the darkness and saw the woman glance back at her. She laughed, the sound tinkling across the glasses on the bar.

"Ah, he must be smelling the poncetiyus biscuits I have in my pocket." With this, her long fingers reached inside her cloak and deftly produced a treat for Wolf. He sat patiently, pleased finally to have something akin to breakfast. The woman snapped her attention back to Wendowleen and leaned forward slightly,

"Professor."

Wendowleen nodded, nervously turning the glass before her.

"We'll take a seat by the back window, Seneca."

The barman lifted the candles from in front of the two women and led the way to a small darkened table at the back of the room. The young woman followed him holding her cup, her dark robe sweeping across the floor. Wendowleen stood, in turn, and motioned to Wolf that he should join them. Mouth still full, he trotted obediently along.

The stools by the table were not as comfortable as the ones at the bar, but a crack of light streamed through the boarded up window in front of them, and with the candles, it improved visibility, which was much to Wendowleen's preference. Once seated, the young woman unbuttoned her cloak, revealing a short, curved knife holstered to a leather belt. Wendowleen glanced at it briefly, uncertain whether the showing of it was by design.

"You are the carrier mentioned in the note?" Wendowleen began.

"I am, though were I not, you would have given rather a large amount of the situation away in that one sentence. But yes, it is not a name I give myself – but rather the title I have been given. I am Auri."

"I feel that I must have kept you waiting here rather a long time – I only just received the note, I'm afraid."

Auri shook her head warmly. "To sit in the warm with a mug of broth and a good book is no trial. Besides, I had a feeling that you would come in the morning – and as such, I've only been waiting until lunch each day. So, you have a new house."

Auri sipped from her mug and waited for Wendowleen to speak.

"You certainly know a lot for one so young. Yes. But it wasn't my choice."

"No, I'm aware of that – unfortunately, you appear to be very visible to the Finery. Of course, it'll be to do with your obvious connection, but –"

"I have no connection to those purloiners."

Auri paused and nodded slowly at Wendowleen. "I should tell you that anything said between us will go no further, Professor. And that this is a safe place. The Finery will not come into this establishment."

"If I could find it, they can."

Auri grinned. "They can't, actually. A simple trick I performed a couple of years ago after the last raid. An officer left his coat on the back of a chair while he used the toilet – the Finery emblems help them get into their buildings – I removed the chip from the officer's emblem and placed it into the door sign. Obviously, it wasn't as easy as all that, but the result is this: when a Finery member arrives at the door, the sign doesn't show what you saw. It reads *Abandoned and Dangerous Building*. Seneca keeps the blinds drawn, we use candles instead of electric light – but I think it just adds to the atmosphere."

Wendowleen noticed a shimmer across Auri's eye in the candlelight, the very faint reminder of a scar.

"How old are you, Auri?"

"I'm young enough to be drinking broth, old enough to be doing it in a malt bar. And you, Wendowleen, are pushing one hundred and one. And you're still upsetting the Finery by your presence – I admire that. We want to help you."

With that, Wolf began to nuzzle Auri's side again, hoping that the presence of his damp jowls would encourage this kind stranger to bestow another of her delicious biscuits. Unfortunately, Wendowleen snapped her fingers in front of his snout. He lay down begrudgingly.

"When you say "we" – whom do you mean?" Wendowleen asked carefully.

"You won't be aware of us."

"Try me."

Auri laughed gently, and Wendowleen noticed that tinkling again. "This isn't a trick – I am one of the only people above ground who knows."

Wendowleen glanced at the bar, at the two figures hunched aside their candles and drinks. She leaned forward and whispered, "what about them?"

Auri turned and followed Wendowleen's gaze. "Oh, they're akin to holograms. They're not really here – this is their resting station. They can be here or from underground – but we're getting far too ahead of ourselves. We must begin at the beginning."

Wendowleen reached out and touched Auri's shoulder, hesitating slightly when she felt resistance. "Sorry, I wasn't sure…"

"I am here, Professor. Let me buy you another drink." She called for Seneca over her shoulder, who came with a couple of bottles. Wendowleen watched him pour, fascinated. As he walked away, Auri reassured her, "he's really here too."

Chapter Thirty-One

"Well, it took a while for you to get in touch with me, director," Sylvia said, crossing her legs.

The Director rolled his eyes. "It's Director. Capitalise the D."

"What have you done to the boy from The Squid's Inn?"

The Director shrugged. "It's sort of beneath me, to be honest, Sylvia. My head of staff would have dealt with that."

Sylvia leaned forward and straightened the golden name plaque on the desk in front of the Director. "Why now? That's my question. I thought the Finery were finished with me years ago."

The Director smiled sharply, shark-like. "Because I'm concerned, Sylvia. There are certain remedies to particular problems," his eyes darkened, "that do not last forever. And we might have assumed that this would not be an issue-"

"Yes," Sylvia responded, "but age is perhaps more of a fluid concept than it once was."

"Exactly."

The two sat before each other, nodding in silent agreement.

"So, am I free to go home?" Sylvia asked, her eyes purposefully stern.

The Director took a moment to think, staring into the distance at some inanimate object that hadn't focused in his vision. Slowly, he shook his head.

"I'm not sure, Sylvia. After all, I sort of feel that you owe us after the failure of your set task. Perhaps you could do something helpful like move in with her? We can arrange that."

Sylvia shook her head firmly. "She doesn't like me, Ayin."

The Director's eyes sharpened, "Have you forgotten where you are?"

"Oh, for goodness sake. Director. Sir. Lord. You're not too old for a telling off."

Unfortunately for Sylvia, the Director was too old for a telling off. This is something that she realised as his fist slammed into the table. Sylvia twitched, watching the reverberations echo through the wood.

"Do you know what lies beneath us?"

Sylvia glanced at the floor warily, unsure whether she would be able to tell from the floorboards. She shook her head.

"Many padded rooms." The Director stared into the distance. "It was an interesting day, the day I realised that to really get to someone, to get inside their head and change their way of being, required almost no physical contact whatsoever." He grinned, leaning back in his chair. "And up here, isn't the air sweet? Isn't the silence glorious?"

Sylvia nodded, carefully choosing her words. "Yes. Apologies. Perhaps it's been a stressful sort of week."

"Perhaps it has." The Director agreed, his smile widening.

"I can visit her, ask her about moving in. I'm not sure what she'll say or how I will accomplish it, but I suppose it would be...helpful...just to try?"

The Director nodded.

Chapter Thirty-Two

As they settled into their chairs, Wendowleen began to feel very warm and calm. The drink was clearly having a positive impact on her stomach, and she smiled as the last week's issues dissolved quietly among her thoughts. Auri watched her amiably, occasionally sipping from her cup.

After a while, she began to speak.

"So, I'm going to make an assumption, and I want you to tell me if it's accurate."

Wendowleen nodded from within her cosy quilt of malt.

"You haven't heard of the partisans."

"No – well…I know the word."

"Of course, but the movement?"

Wendowleen shook her head. Auri grinned.

"That's great news. It's always a worrying moment for me. If you'd have said yes, it would have meant that the secret was out."

"So you're part of the partisans, Auri?"

Auri thought for a moment and then shook her head. "No, not exactly. The partisans have existed as a movement for hundreds of years, and of course, over that time, the face of Finer Bay and Rytter has changed, and so has their reason for existing. And now, as the Finery grow in power, they have begun to think of recruiting for the first time ever. And that is why," Auri leaned toward Wendowleen and smiled, "you and I are talking. My parents are in the movement. I chose a life above ground."

Wendowleen took another sip of her warming malt and felt tiredness sweep through her body. She blinked hard, forcing herself to stay awake. The darkness of the bar, the smoothness of her drink, the strange occurrences over the last few days – all of these moments were paving the way for an early night, despite it still being bright outside. She yawned and then shook her head as if to shake herself.

"You'll have to excuse me, Auri – I'm not usually so docile, if that's the word."

Auri nodded, "I know. It's part of our discussion, I'm afraid, Professor. There is, of course, the possibility that you could not want to join, and in that situation, you would wake up remembering none of this conversation. It won't harm you, and as soon as we have finished our talk and you are back outside, you'll feel much more yourself. More awake. It's the only way we can ensure that the partisans stay a secret, as I'm sure you understand."

Wendowleen would have felt at the very least indignant if she didn't feel so sleepy. She stared at Auri through hooded eyes. "Why recruit a one-hundred-year-old retired professor with an assistance wolf?"

"The partisans have, through many years of practice, become exceptional at precognition. They can make incredibly accurate, logical predictions of what is going to happen. And Professor, for you, it does not look good."

Wendowleen forced herself to sit up straight and frowned. "Go on."

"There is going to be a loose series of events that lead to the same thing – you being committed to a high-security care centre, or, death. Without Wolf. Without choice."

"What? I wouldn't allow it. Outrageous."

"But you won't have a choice. Have you ever tried to convince somebody that you're not losing your mind? They see you as a problem. You're not afraid of questioning them, you've previously had the mayor on side, and then there's the issue of *who* you are."

Despite her doubts about what her drink had in it, Wendowleen threw caution to the rain and took another sip. "All right. I'm not entirely sure what you mean, but I am listening. What if I choose to join this group then? How will I be any better off?"

Auri cocked her head to one side, her eyes drifting off for a moment, focusing on the candle in front of her. She blinked slowly and then brought her attention back to the conversation.

"You will be safe. Physically. We can create one of those," she gestured to the holograms sitting at the bar, "and put it in your house. You can check in through that when you feel like you need to. You'll go underground – quite literally – to join their world. They know what's happening up here, so you won't be missing out, and you can use your hologram to speak to those you love if required."

Wendowleen stared at her and shook her head. "I don't think that there is anyone I would miss in Finer Bay." The thought of it pricked her eyes with tears, and she paused for a moment. When had that happened? At what age had she stopped making an effort with people? Her mind wandered, as it so often did, to Arthur.

Auri spoke, shaking Wendowleen from her thoughts. "It's a closer community in the partisans. Everyone helps each other."

"I'm still unsure as to how you know about me, though?"

Auri grinned. "You taught both my mother and my father philosophy at university. Because of that, they have always remembered you fondly and have been checking in on you from time to time. They heard of your house being knocked down."

Wendowleen nodded sleepily. "I've taught thousands of students. Who are they?"

Auri shook her head in response. "I won't say. But if you decide to join, then you will meet them, I'm sure."

"I suppose there is only one thing that I need to know for certain." Wendowleen motioned to Wolf.

"Well, that's up to you, Professor. I'm not going to lie to you and tell you that there are plenty of animals there – because that wouldn't be true. You know Wolf, only you can decide whether he would fare better up here."

Wolf, as if understanding what was happening, nuzzled Wendowleen's leg, and she sighed loudly. "Can a hologram of me feed him and such?"

"No, Professor. They aren't solid to the touch, just figures, really. Seneca and I have the skill set required to shift their appearance. With an image of you, we can transmit a likeness that could confuse your own family. And that image will stick until we change it."

Wendowleen nodded and scratched Wolf on the head, "So, I'll take him. Decision made."

"You would like to join then? I might urge you to take a little more time, Professor. Once you go under, we cannot guarantee that you can decide to come back without your memory being altered."

Wendowleen downed her drink and nodded, "I understand, Auri. But it feels rather like the decision between the truth and a lie. If I say that I don't want to go, then I am deciding to forget an event in my life, and I am giving you – or potentially the barman –" Wendowleen glanced toward the bar, "permission to alter my mindset. In a way, the decision was made for me as soon as I was invited."

Auri nodded, smiling. "If it's worth anything at all, I think that you have made the right decision. You will have a happier life. The partisans have already worked out the likelihood of that."

Auri stood and swept her cloak from the back of the chair onto her shoulders, fastening it over her left shoulder with a strange pin. Wendowleen tried to focus on it in the darkness, frowning. It was some sort of flower, with red petals overlapping each other. Auri followed her gaze and glanced back.

"A rose. A flower invented by my great grandmother – but you won't find them in this world." She bent forward to stroke Wolf on his left ear and smiled up to Wendowleen, "You will be collected at midnight. Wear black, comfortable shoes. Leave no sign of your having left."

She left without any further words, the light from the front door illuminating the bar for a split second. Wendowleen watched her go and glanced at Wolf, "Well then. We have some preparing to do."

Wolf crunched his teeth together in a sign of comfort, something he had learned from Wendowleen (although she didn't know it).

Outside The Malted Mash Auri glanced down the street, blinking in the light. The day was wearing on, and she was relieved. Wendowleen had to be kept safe. She had seen the alternative in a flash of fire; the predictions were too terrifying.

Chapter Thirty-Three

Sylvia stood in front of Wendowleen's new house and squinted at the numbers on the door. It certainly had changed a lot since the last time she was here, in the Arthur days. She shook her head quickly as she realised why that was, accidentally getting confused over what she was, and wasn't, supposed to know. She knew the reason that Wendowleen had been visiting her, of course she did. Her brain had developed a clever trick since the Finery had been in touch – as though it was encouraging her to forget things that she wasn't sure she should have knowledge of. She took a deep breath and raised her hand to knock.

"Ahem."

Hand mid-air, she turned to see Wendowleen standing behind her, Wolf in attendance.

"I can't seem to shake you, can I, Sylvia?"

Wolf lowered his head and bared his teeth in a silent but present growl.

"Oh Wendy, I'm so pleased to see you." Sylvia stepped toward Wendowleen, who stepped back automatically.

"You've always had an air of insincerity about you, Sylvia, but recently it's become more of a stench."

Sylvia frowned, "Well, I only wanted to come and make sure you were okay. I could do without the dramatics." She folded her arms and sighed.

Wendowleen observed her. "What do you think of my new house then?" she asked, changing tack.

Sylvia smiled politely, turning briefly to glance at the door as though that could give her a complete impression of the building. "Flats, isn't it? Very economical. Much better for the community as a whole. Good for you, Wendy."

A silence descended over the two women, and they stared at each other in irritation. Wendowleen wondered how she might get rid of the sister-in-law without raising suspicion, and Sylvia how she might get inside the house and make herself at home. The situation would have perhaps looked entirely different to an outsider, two elderly women standing and staring at each other outside a new building in the dimming sunlight, a large, rather fierce-looking wolf beside them.

Sylvia broke the menacing silence with a cough, "Couldn't I come in, just for a cup of tea? I do hate the thought of us growing apart, Wendy. It seems so futile. It's really the opposite of what Arthur would have wanted."

Wendowleen shook her head slowly, "Arthur knew what he wanted, and neither of us should trample on his memory by claiming we know his thoughts." Wolf's growl became audible. "Sylvia, you really cannot come in, not even for a cup of tea. Wolf here is not a fan of yours, and I'm afraid that he might rip you to shreds." She laughed, an easy-going and tinkling laugh that ran across Sylvia's spine, out of sync with the meaning of her words.

Wendowleen stepped to the side and toward the front door of her unfamiliar home.

"That step is awfully big Wendy, can you manage?"

"I am one hundred years old Sylvia, this is true." She turned and shook her head. "But I can climb a step. In fact, I can do many things. I can remember every single one of the lectures that I taught to my students. I can sense when someone is lying to me. And I understand when things are not quite what they seem."

Wolf flattened his body against the concrete floor, still watching Sylvia but signalling that she may pass him without getting bitten. Sylvia, in turn, rolled her eyes and tutted at the both of them.

"Wendowleen — you are so paranoid. It's a shame, really, what has happened to that once excellent mind of yours."

"Oh!" Wendowleen held a finger up in the air, remembering one last thing, "And I am excellent at holding a hammer too. Quite something."

With that, she pushed her key into the front door and stepped inside.

Once in the hallway, Wendowleen double-locked the door and peered through the peephole at Sylvia, who stood awkwardly in the space where the garden had once flowered and bloomed. Why on earth was she still standing there, and what did she want? Wendowleen touched Wolf's head absent-mindedly as she thought. Sylvia was obviously in touch with whoever knocked her house down, paved over her flowers and invited people into her space. She took a deep breath and let out a single bark.

"Bugger off Sylvia!"

Through the peephole, she could see Sylvia hesitate and blink hesitantly at the door. She held up her hands.

"I haven't anywhere to go, Wendowleen."

"Head back to the Finery."

Sylvia straightened up and shook her head. "I could die of exposure Wendy, what would Arthur think of that?"

"If you try and guess what my late husband might have felt about a current situation one more time, Sylvia, I will have no qualms in letting Wolf deal with you himself."

Sylvia sighed, rolling her eyes dramatically enough for Wendowleen to see. She turned and began to wander away from the building, and Wendowleen watched her until she had reached the road. When satisfied that she had finally left, she breathed deeply. It was time to prepare for her disappearance.

Wendowleen had around five hours until midnight. Relying on the darkness to safely disguise her leaving the house was one thing, but staying awake until midnight was entirely another. Since Auri had mentioned the word 'midnight', Wendowleen had worried gently about her sleep pattern – all she could do was hope that rest would be plentiful with the partisans. Wolf whined at his food bowl, and Wendowleen topped it up with dried biscuits for him, watching as he chewed them. Now – there was something she would need to pack, Wolf's food. And his dish. But wouldn't that need to be kept for the sake of appearances? And what about her favourite mug? Those little routines were a part of life, a gentle hand on her shoulder. The feel of heat from her morning cup, the ease with which it fit into her hands, was a joyful part of her day. And then, did anyone know that about her, really? And how much would the partisans prepare? Would they have all this information and copy her favourite mug and Wolf's food and understand the intricacies of their days together?

She sat down heavily on the new old sofa and stared at Wolf. These were questions she wished she had had the presence of mind to ask Auri before. Clothing was one thing she could think about. Shadowy colours...comfortable shoes...something to make her and Wolf blend into the darkness. And it was here, listening to the gentle chewing of Wolf's teeth, pondering what she should pack and how she might spend the next few hours above ground, that Wendowleen fell asleep.

Chapter Thirty-Four

Sylvia did indeed traipse back to the Finery, because she simply didn't know where else to turn. There was no hotel booked for the evening, no plans made beyond her being given the order to stay at Wendowleen's. She was ushered up to the Director's office by the groundskeeper this time, who seemed outraged at Sylvia's presence. He knocked on the Director's door and glared at Sylvia while he did so, muttering under his breath.

"It's not part of my job, this isn't. If I get into trouble for tracking mud in, I'm taking you down with me."

Sylvia glanced at his boots, which were not muddy in the slightest, and shrugged at the groundskeeper. He seemed inept. After a moment, a gruff voice from within the room beckoned them in, and Sylvia hustled past the irritated gardener with a silent apology.

The Director sat behind the table as he had before, seemingly unmoved, but with a glass of dark liquid before him. As Sylvia moved closer, she could see the knot of his tie was looser, lower than before. She smiled as she took a seat and nodded to the glass.

"I wouldn't say no to a glass of that myself."

The Director did not smile back but raised his eyebrows and took a small sip. "Well, that won't be possible at this time."

"Ah, I was only –" Sylvia began.

"Why are you back here?"

"Well, I don't have anywhere to stay – you knew it would be a bit of a risk sending me back to see her. She doesn't consider me to be family anymore – that whole Squid's Inn business with the camera…"

The Director's expression cut Sylvia off. She stared at him and smiled gently, hoping to dissolve the tension in the room with her good humour.

"I can try again tomorrow. It's just that it is getting late, and I really don't see what else I –"

The Director held his hand up and silenced Sylvia.

"Okay. You're ineffective, but I gave you a second chance because you're…well, you."

Sylvia nodded, understanding.

"We're going to move forward tonight, I suppose. You're her only remaining family – she won't let you in…what sort of people would we be to let an old, delusional and paranoid woman sit alone in that house? I want what is best for her, of course. We knew this day would come. Unfortunately, it is the price you pay for a long life."

The Director picked up the old fashioned phone on his desk and prodded two numbers with his index finger. As expected, it appeared that it was answered instantly.

"Yes. Case 258903. Tonight."

He placed the receiver on the handle and cocked his head to one side, nodding at Sylvia.

"Perhaps you should go with them, see if you can relax her, etcetera. I'll make sure a room is kept for you here – though I'll be honest, at this short notice, it won't be the luxurious heights of The Squid's Inn."

Sylvia nodded and stood up wearily. It had been a long day, and she longed for her bed, far from Finer Bay. And the evening was going to continue.

"They'll meet you downstairs, in the foyer."

Sylvia didn't respond but walked toward the door with feigned confidence. In all honesty, though, she was afraid. She and Wendowleen were of a similar age, and though she certainly wasn't a risk to the Director in the way that her sister-in-law was, there was a thought bouncing around her mind that concerned her. It wasn't hard to convince people that you were insane. It was impossible to convince them of the opposite.

When Wendowleen had owned a garden before it was concreted over, she had measured her years by the growth of the rheum. She didn't need to touch it and, apart from those days where she took its fruit for stewing and baking, hadn't pruned it in generations. The rheum had a definite pattern that Wendowleen took notice of, which matched the seasons. In the cold weather, it wilted, hibernating for a better day. As soon as there was the hint of something warmer, a whisper in the air, the greenery expanded over the lawn, its leaves bursting into the space and the pink fruit growing up to an inch each day.

When the sun was bright in the sky, Wendowleen would watch it bask and stretch, providing sweet treats and soft scents. And it never died. The snow could not quash it, extreme heat did not burn its leaves, the rain could not dampen its spirit. Wendowleen came to look on it as a type of friend, steady in the face of any adversity. Then, of course, it had been covered over. Perhaps it had been cemented down, cut up, chopped out. She didn't know. And, as she slept on the sofa, head tilted back and mouth open, she dreamt of the rheum. She felt its power beneath the slabs that stood where it once grew and saw it burst through manufactured fibres in her subconscious. In reality, its roots did lie beneath a paving slab, stopping it from reaching up high. As Wendowleen dreamed of this, there was a heavier weight on the very slab it sat beneath. It was the weight of highly polished leather boots.

Of all his clients, Wolf found Wendowleen to be the most like him. She was not fussy, as some of his previous clients were, and she was incredibly independent. Wolf wasn't really sure what he was required for, so he simply did his best to be available by trotting around after her, which seemed to be the right thing to do. All this recent nonsense made him feel uneasy. For a start, he hated settling into a new place, even if it was somewhere like The Squid's Inn, because the smells were disconcertingly different. He was used to Wendowleen's own brand of dusty, damp smell, sometimes with the scent of hidden biscuits in secreted pockets. The new place didn't have that dampness built into the walls, and he didn't like it one bit.

In the old house, he knew each room simply by scent, and if he chose to (which, to be honest, he didn't often), he could wander around blind from room to room, up and down the narrow staircase. At times, he might wake up in the middle of the night to find that Wendowleen was not warming the bed properly. Sometimes he would find her using the bathroom, in the kitchen making a midnight chestnut broth, or on the odd occasion, in the high upstairs part of the house to which they rarely ventured. He knew that house, its creaks and noises, the way the heating shuttled through the pipes and popped through the vents to warm his ears.

Wolf now lay at Wendowleen's feet as she snoozed on the new old sofa in the strange lodging that had been built for them. He sniffed the air and groaned quietly. It smelled utterly wrong. And then, there was a new sound. His ears pricked to attention, swivelling as he tried to gauge the direction of the noise. A key into a lock. He recognised that well enough. Footsteps over a newly carpeted floor. His head raised from his paws, and he stared through the darkness toward the door of their new, strange dwelling. A clear sound vibrated through it, a bang, bang, bang. It flew through the door and into the floorboards, vibrations creeping up Wolf's nails and through to his bones. He leapt to his feet and nudged Wendowleen's legs with his snout, growling very quietly. She stirred, and he nudged again, urgently.

Wendowleen raised her head and stared at him, blinking in the scene through the dim light. She frowned at him sleepily — Bang, bang, bang. The door went again. They stared at each other, both understanding. The partisan visitor they were waiting for would not risk the use of noise. Wolf nudged once more, silently, and Wendowleen awkwardly got to her feet. They had to get out.

Chapter Thirty-Five

The life of the partisans was a simple one. They had lived underground for so long that many could not even imagine the life that they occasionally watched through the eyes of their holograms. It seemed so unreal that some questioned the reality of it. What did these people that walked on the land really eat? Animals? How could that be true? The first partisans to step into the underground warren, when it was only a room, had given up meat immediately. Stories had occasionally drifted to their ears that should they decide to come back up to the ground level, a great feast would be put on for them, full of all the foods that they could only dream of below the soil. But this was a long, long time ago when there was an awareness of those who chose the partisan life. Throughout the years, the stories of their existence turned from fact to rumour, to myth, and then, it was simply forgotten. It is true that stories were written down when they first went underground. Those stories were now mostly abandoned, some locked within the restricted access section of the University of Finer Bay library, hidden beneath volumes of dusty nonsense that no student had cause to request.

The partisans ate well, fuelled by root vegetables plucked from the walls of the growing rooms. Each person was taught how to sew, grow and pluck from a very young age, instilling the importance of getting the proper nutrients into each mind that grew underground. The first partisans struggled with the lack of sunlight, testing and trying new implements that might quietly let in the outside brightness. The result was effective; a series of small mirrors, covered in thin silver leaf, hung throughout the warrens, taking the sun from its source and filling the spaces with natural light. Of course, the silver leaf came from above ground, and as such, few were allowed to touch the mirrors. Each smashed mirror caused a grieving period of one hundred sundowns. The culprit would be banished to the lonesome room for the entire period to think over their error and write and rewrite the sacred history books, including their mistake.

The partisans now looked different, as could be expected by such a change in lifestyle. Despite having the sunlight bouncing from room to room, their eyes had become accustomed to living beneath the soil, and had grown smaller over time. Their ears, as if to compensate, had grown larger and now sat prominently on each side of the heads. They could hear above ground very well and could be woken by a single footstep upon the earth.

Their nostrils had enlarged too, the scents of soil and growth filling their days. They could smell the entry of a new person into a room five warrens away. The scent of ailment was unmistakable, and anyone who had a deficiency was sniffed out immediately. In this way, they managed to avoid much disease by filling the patient with nutrients before anything truly took hold. They were all doctors, growers, writers, historians and the number of the group had reached around five hundred.

With new people came new challenges, always. There was the initial excitement of moving, as there always is. The new visitor enjoyed the first month or so, and learning was undertaken with passion and enthusiasm. And then, for most, the new member would become dejected. They would long for what they saw as a simple want – a walk outside, perhaps a picnic. To feel the elements on their skin, the wind, the air, the sunshine. They would talk of things that the original partisans had never experienced, such as iced cream and flavourful triangular tree fruits that filled the mouth with sweetness. The youngest of the partisans would grow weary very quickly with this shift in perspective, as it would cause feelings in them that they would rather not acknowledge. It would cause books to be removed from the book store that were to do with the outside world, and the youth would share ideas as small as recipes for pies that they would never eat, and stare longingly at a flower, wondering how it might taste.

After this period, the visitors usually settled. After all, there was little choice. There had been a few rejections of the lifestyle, which was to be expected. Those few had had their memories wiped and had gone back to their old life, knowing nothing of the underground warren they once experienced. The outcome for those people was always bad. The partisans welcomed visitors in danger only, and their predictions for the future were so accurate that it was never really a case of "hope for the best" for those individuals. So, the few that had rejected the partisan way of life had chosen the pleasures of the wind over life itself. Each lived for a varied amount of time, but never more than three hundred sundowns before they ceased to exist.

BANG, BANG, BANG. The knocking continued. Wendowleen stared at Wolf and reached for her coat, wrapping it about her as quickly as she could. She moved across the floor, sliding her feet, trying not to make the slightest sound.

"CRIPCOT! OPEN THIS DOOR IMMEDIATELY."

Wolf quivered at the yell but remained close to Wendowleen's legs, flattening his fur in fear. They reached the back door, quietly turned the key in the lock, and slipped out into the darkness. Behind Wendowleen's house had always been a very small garden, but now she blinked in confusion at the change. Where grass once grew, concrete lay. The patch of land was significantly smaller too. The new house backed onto the ends of the old houses around her, the gaps between them small, but, Wendowleen thought, sufficient for her and Wolf to squeeze through. She touched his head lightly and flattened herself against the brickwork of her neighbour's building, shuffling along the gap. Once at the end, there was another, similar layout. She did the same again. They scrambled and slid until they reached a proper alleyway, streets from her home. Once there, she looked at Wolf.

"We must reach somewhere safe. Somewhere they won't look." Her mind swam. She felt too close to the house. She thought of her options and then, without saying a word, began to trace the familiar back passages of the city, to the University of Rytter.

Those who had watched Wendowleen had indeed been taught by her, as Auri had said. They had maintained an interest in all that they knew above ground as a way of helping themselves cope with the loss of their previous life. The couple, who had met at university, had given up their lives for safety. They had produced their daughter underground, where she had grown and blossomed for a short while, and then they had noticed that something was different about her in comparison to the other children. She would spend longer watching through the eyes of the holograms, standing in the mirrored daylight and basking in its glow. Her parents had become accustomed to their new life and wondered why their daughter obsessed over small things. Chestnuts, for example, on her first time trying the (hard to get underground) broth. She would ask every elder she could find about them, how they were grown, where they could be sourced. To each answer, she would listen carefully and then ask further questions such as, "How long would a blade of grass be?" and, "Have you ever tried to bring the sunshine beneath the ground?"

The elders struggled to answer such questions, some of them having no experience of grass in any way. They would direct her to the extensive library they kept inside their warren, and suggest that she read more to try and find the answers for her inquisitive mind. But, this did not help. The more Auri read, the more trapped she felt. She didn't want to live a life underground, despite being with her parents, friends, loved ones. She would read stories, handwritten by her mother, of hanging washing out on the line on a warm and breezy day. Auri would close her eyes and imagine the scene, her nostrils filled with the phenomenal scent of imaginary blossom, the detergent whipping past her nose as she pinned up the damp clothes with fingers that tingled in the wind. The sun would beat down on the nape of her neck, warming her skin with each touch, and she would breathe in deeply. The fresh air that filled her lungs in her dreams made her desperate to experience it.

At seven years old she began to plan an escape route, one that would allow her to come and go as she pleased. It wasn't that Auri wanted to leave the partisan community, far from it. She wanted to live in two worlds, to experience all things.

Her parents began to suspect something was not quite as usual when soup was served for dinner one night. Each community member had their own set of eating utensils given to them at birth/entry, and each member was responsible for cleaning, maintaining, and bringing these to the table. This did many things, from teaching the children to care for their items, to limiting disease. On this occasion, Auri came to the table with a fork only. Her mother and father found this curious, given that she had not made such an error since she was two years old. Auri laughed in response and said that she would like to eat with the fork if that was permissible. It was not, said her father, and would she please stop delaying dinner time and go and fetch her spoon. She would not, she said. This continued all evening, each side getting more and more irate with the other. Eventually, the threat of limited library time was whipped from beneath the irritation of her father, and Auri left the table and returned with one very muddy and worn soup spoon. Her parents stared at it, confused. Her mother spoke first.

"What's happened?"

"Just a bit muddy."

"From what?"

Auri did not lie, and it was not in her nature to lie to her mother. She stayed silent instead, wiping her spoon awkwardly on her napkin.

Her father knocked on the table in front of her soup, raising his eyebrows when she finally caught his eye. "From...?" he prompted.

"From...digging."

It took a while to wean the entire story from Auri that evening, but they found out that she had been digging behind the bookcase in the library, planning her new route. Her father was furious, despite Auri's assurances that her tunnel took safety very seriously (indeed it did, on later inspection, her parents found that she had been using panelling to stop the sides and ceiling from caving in), and her mother was understanding. Auri talked of how she wished to hang washing on the line in the midday sun, of how her dreams involved goosebumps forming on her arms from cool breezes and her hair becoming drenched in the rain. She longed to feel the elements, she said, she wanted to touch the leaf that had fallen from the tree after the hot spells had ended.

Her mother and father winced at this, understanding entirely what she meant. That evening, they sat in bed next to each other, Auri now asleep in another room. Her mother turned to her father and shook her head.

"She has inherited our memories."

Her father stared at the wall and sighed. "She has not. She has read too much."

"No, it is more than that. She is not a partisan."

"She was born here."

"Yes. But she dreams of a different world."

"All children dream. She dreams of a life that we cannot let her have."

They sat in silence for a moment, and her mother spoke again.

"Perhaps she can have it. Our prediction skills are still poor."

"It's too big a risk – they might find out she is our daughter."

"Has anyone *ever* done what she talks of, lived a life in both places?"

"Only as holograms."

They both nodded together.

So it was that the parents of Auri went to three of the seventeen elders within the partisan community. The group of elders often split into smaller teams on a weekday, enabling more people to visit with queries. They asked for a prediction, worried that they may make the wrong decision. The elders were well-versed in the lesson of leaving. As soon as the dilemma was explained to them, the eldest spoke up.

"Of course, she is having these thoughts. What child hasn't? It is as normal in here as it is to dream of flying in the world outside."

Auri's parents listened and nodded. Another elder coughed slightly.

"Well, each decision must be made, considering each individual. One cannot decide an eternity based on the feelings of others."

"Ah," the final elder sighed, "but I suppose that you do not want her memories to be taken from her?"

Auri's parents shook their heads.

The elder nodded and continued, "and here is the problem. She either stays with you and is unhappy, or she goes and knows nothing of you."

The first elder spoke again, "She could be unhappy there too. There is much on the other side to cause grief."

They agreed in silence. Auri's parents stood patiently, waiting for the prediction.

After around ten minutes, one of the elders coughed again. He blinked rapidly at another and shrugged. The other elder widened his eyes in response and shrugged also. The remaining elder squinted slightly at Auri's parents and spoke.

"I don't quite —"

"Hush up!" was the response from the other elder.

The third, with the cough, coughed again awkwardly. "I think what my colleague is trying to say, is that we can't seem to get a grip on the prediction...."

Auri's parents had not heard this before and frowned in confusion. Her mother nodded.

"That's not usual, is it?"

"No, it is not," the cough said, spluttering into his handkerchief, "and I'm not sure exactly why this has happened."

"We could make something up if that would help?" ventured the first elder, a hopeful smile set on his face.

"That wouldn't really help, no," Auri's father said uncomfortably.

"Well."

"Hmmm."

"Yes."

Silence filled the room, and the five sat for a moment, uncertain as to what to do next.

The cough clapped his pale hands together, dropping his handkerchief into the dirt. "Your time with the elders is complete!"

Auri's parents left the room and closed the door gently behind them, but not before they heard the elders speak behind it.

"Well, that was a shit show, wasn't it?"

The lack of prediction material available for Auri was very concerning for all of the elders, and of course, her parents. It was most unusual that this should be the case. It had not been so for hundreds of years. All of the seventeen elders got together to discuss the issue and to pore over their history books.

"She is different," one said.

"She must be – I can always predict a life. Ever since I was a child, I would have dreams where-"

"Please, Rhapet, focus on the issue in hand."

A stern exchange of looks.

"I think we should bring her in," one said.

"For what, to talk?"

Nodding of heads. One shake, swiftly ignored by the others. Auri was beckoned in from her waiting place in the darkened hallway. She stood before the figures and bowed slightly, unsure of the correct procedures.

Rhapet smiled warmly. "You would like to leave the community, to live above ground?"

Auri nodded.

"But you realise," another elder began, "that this would mean erasing your memory?"

Again, Auri nodded.

"So, you understand what you would be giving up?"

Auri raised her hand awkwardly, requesting permission to speak. The elders nodded, almost in unison.

She began, "I understand, of course, that this is the way that things have been done in the past. However, after some discussion with my parents, I would like to propose a new idea to you."

There was a strange pause, Auri having practised her talk with one of the elders at least saying, "Go on..." or perhaps, "No, we don't do new ideas." As it was, they just sat and stared at her. She glanced at their faces and continued.

"I have spoken with my parents, and we have discussed the way that things happen now. When a member of the outside community is in danger, it is not always easy to convince them that life here would be safer. As you know, letters are passed to and fro, endangering our way of life. What if a letter ended up in the wrong hands?"

One elder held their hand up and shook their head from left to right. "I don't believe that this is possible; the letter would burst into flames."

Murmurs of agreement.

Auri nodded, "I understand that this is the goal; however, this does not always work – and there was that fire that it caused once, the blaze that took down those two houses."

Rhapet nodded solemnly. "Even so, that was predicted."

Another elder spoke, "Well, yes, there was a fifty per cent chance of that happening that day...we erred on the side of risk."

"But, if you allow me to go above ground, think of the work I can do for our community. I could take the place of the letter, answer questions, convince those chosen and explain our lives."

The elders sat, expressions of concrete, unblinking. Silence descended.

"Paper cannot be corrupted."

Auri nodded. "I understand. But, with respect, neither can I. This community is where I am from and where my family is. I would not put them in danger."

"You could not come back again. The risk would be too great. Few have gone before you, Auri."

"I understand. But you see, it would mean that I could talk to my parents while being free to live life above ground. I think that I would be gaining more than I am losing."

The elders stared again. One spoke. "I think that you are too young to know what the outside world is like."

Auri smiled. "With respect, I don't believe that anybody in this room has any real experience of the outside world."

Rhaphet nodded. "She has a point, although she probably shouldn't have made it."

"It shows courage," said one.

"It shows rudeness," said another.

There was a long silence.

"We need to consider the future. If we cannot predict successfully, we must try something else. You will have your answer by the end of seven sunrises."

Auri nodded solemnly and left. She felt strange as she stepped out of the room into the murky corridors. It was a feeling she matched with reading her favourite book, a turning of age magical romp, in which the main character experienced the world beyond her farmhouse for the first time. And yet, something was disappointing there, holding her back. Her parents. How would she cope without them? Would the sunshine resting on her skin really be the life that she had envisioned for herself, everything that she had hoped it might be? She wandered back to her room slowly, weaving in and out of warrens, taking long routes and twisting her feet through the dirt. With each step, she imagined the floor was covered in the green sprouting matter that she had read about in her science books, the scent of which some likened to warm and lengthy days outdoors. She knew that she was right to try for that life, that taking deep breaths of the outside air would be akin to reading ten beautiful new books underground. As she reached the door of her room and turned the handle, she already knew the outcome. If the elders refused her offer, she would leave anyway.

That night Auri slept fitfully. She dreamt of climbing through dirt, toes scraping through mud. Each breath she took seemed to catch in her throat, and each time she reached the top, her reward was not the sunshine and luscious grass of her daydreams, but more mud and filth. By morning, she was exhausted. She sat on the edge of her bed, breathing deeply. Her mother joined her, holding a cup of warm broth in her favourite mug. She sat beside her carefully.

"Did you know, Auri, that up there you can watch the sun rise above mountains in the morning, and tumble into the sea in the evening?"

Auri took a sip of her broth and smiled at her mother, unsure of the meaning of the conversation. Her mother wrapped a long, slim arm around her shoulders and squeezed.

"Did you know that there are at least twelve types of horse that can carry you to caves filled with glittering rocks, renowned for their beauty?"

Auri shook her head.

"The point, my love, is that your father and I already know that the decision is made. The elders don't control your heart. They make the decisions for this place, and of course, we are grateful to them, but you must leave." There was a pause as Auri stared into her mother's eyes. "For I have seen your future. You are to do great things that cannot be accomplished underground."

Auri nodded, knowing better than to ask for details. Her mother stood and kissed her firmly on the centre of her forehead. She walked to the door and turned as she placed her hand on the handle. "Tonight."

Auri had spent the day quietly organising her things, unsure of how she was to leave. Aside from her mother's morning visit, her parents treated her much the same as any other day. Even as the hours wore on and it became time for bed, they acted as usual. After dinner, her father swept her into a huge hug and kissed her hard on the cheek.

"Go and get ready for bed, Auri."

She nodded, unsure of how ready to get, exactly. She returned to her room and hovered around her pyjamas, reluctant to put them on if she were to be ambushed into leaving soon. Eventually, she decided to wear them and climbed into bed as she would any other night. She waited. Nothing happened. In time, she drifted into a fervent sleep.

The first thing that woke Auri was the sensation of dampness. She squirmed and shivered, a strange feeling of coldness climbing up her pyjama leg. She reached automatically for her duvet to find that it wasn't where she had left it, wrapped about her body. Uncomfortable, she opened her eyes, blinking a few times in the darkness. Her nose tingled and flared. The air was so cold and unfiltered that it shocked nostrils into sneezing. She sat up sharply. Her eyes were adjusted well to the darkness of the underground, but this wasn't the same kind of darkness. There was a source of light, a large, grey-blue sun, creating shadows in the nighttime. Before her were tall, thick trunks, their limbs holding fluttering pieces of paper that rustled in the air. She shivered once more; the air blew around her as she had never experienced, catching and pulling at her clothes and hair. She put a hand on the ground, sharp beneath her, and stood awkwardly. The tall objects around her seemed to grow ever bigger, looming.

Auri took a step forward, her foot nudging something in front of it, bare toes hitting canvas. A bag. She opened it desperately, for she felt afraid, hoping for some answer. Inside were the items that she had organised earlier. There was only one difference, and as her hand hit it, she felt a flood of relief. She knew what it was the moment she felt the soft fabric. Her mother's housecoat. She pulled it out graciously, causing other items to fall to the floor, and wrapped it about herself, breathing in the scent of home. Despite knowing that this was her destiny, and furthermore, her own choice, she couldn't stop the tears from falling. She dug her hands deep into the housecoat's pockets and felt the sharp edges of a piece of paper. Auri opened it carefully, squinting to read in the light of the moon. She could not. With a deep breath, she dried her cheeks and re-packed her bag, securing the paper in her pocket once more. She thrust her bare feet into socks and then boots, the only items of footwear she had brought. Already she was starting to feel warmer, and with the warmth came bravery. She stared at the ominous figures about her and thought back to her books at home. Oak trees. Nothing but oak. Auri grinned. She took her first step forward into her new life.

Auri walked through the night, unsure of where she was going. Her step was steady, but her heart was uncertain. The housecoat kept her spirits high, as though her mother were holding her hand throughout the journey. After walking for three hours, the sun began to rise. At first, she noticed it as a strange, warm orange glow that hovered in a straight line before her. Though she walked toward it, she was afraid. Her first thoughts were of fire, terror, and nothingness. How could there be anything on the horizon? It seemed so blank and bare. Only trees stood in the line of the thin glow. The cool air began to lift, and eventually, she stopped to take off the housecoat, folding it carefully into her bag. As she stood, she noticed that the horizon she had been watching had begun to change shape. Suddenly, there appeared to be pinpricks of small black shapes appearing, and in between, a large bright ball began to rise. Auri threw her bag onto her back and began to run toward the blinding light, laughing. It was the sun! It was the sun that she read about in her books! It was the essence that they talked about underground, the delicious light that filled your bones.

The closer she got, the quicker the sun seemed to rise. She'd never had the space to run like this, without any limit or boundary, and the boots that once traversed the mudded wood of the partisans' home now thudded with abandon through leaves and soil. Finally, the sun had risen. Auri stopped and tilted her head skywards, closing her eyes. She felt its warmth, her skin prickling and tingling. She began to feel warm, truly, as though the rays were reaching into her core and heating her from within.

"You all right there, miss?"

Auri's eyes snapped open, and she stared at a young boy, his face dirty and clothes marked. She blinked at him, nodding slowly. He gave her a strange smile, accompanied by a frown.

"Where are we?"

The boy smiled awkwardly. "We're in Towen, miss. Just arrived?"

"Oh, yes," answered Auri. "Thank you."

The boy shrugged at her, paused as if waiting for another comment, and wandered away. She watched him walk toward a small town, those tiny black pinpricks now large wooden buildings, winding their way into the distance. She began to follow him slowly, not wishing to draw attention to herself. Her tingling skin was quickly forgotten, and she watched the town around her springing into life in the early morning sun. Large tables were being set up as far as Auri could see down the main dirt floor street, umbrellas balanced precariously above them. Stall owners laughed and jeered with each other, readying themselves for the hustle of the day.

Each stall brought a new adventure, and Auri stepped slowly through them, letting her senses soak up everything the town had to offer. Her taste buds experienced the unknown with each penny that she handed over. She tried nuts roasted in a hot fire, covered in sweet crystals. There were caramelised soft segments of a small red vegetable that she had to stand in line for, waiting behind excited children. Auri didn't realise that, to the townspeople, she too was a child. She felt as though she were fully grown, witnessing the society from an experienced mind. When Auri reached the chestnut broth bar, her heart ached for the first time. The scent of the smooth, salted and yet sweet liquid dragged her mind home. She sat down clumsily in one of the chairs that surrounded the bar and felt, for the first time since she had woken up, exhausted. The trip had made her limbs ache, but she hadn't noticed until now. She leaned back and sighed. A girl, wearing a clean yellow apron, strode up to her. She looked a similar age to Auri, and Auri smiled.

"Would you like a broth, miss?"

Auri nodded, watching as the girl went behind the bar and returned, handing her a flagon. She clasped it to her and closed her eyes, before taking a sip. It tasted ever so slightly different to the one at home, though she couldn't say precisely why. There was a sour note beneath the sweet. Auri thought of the last time she had drunk some, sitting on the edge of her bed with her mother, and then she paused. Why could she remember that? If people left the underground, their memories of it were wiped. She tested this, thinking of the route to the library or the kitchen. She could think of them all. The elders. They had not approved this. Auri still had no idea how her parents got her out – that was the only section of memory that she was missing. It must have been on purpose; perhaps they foresaw a desire in her to return. Her eyes remained closed, and she continued to sip the warm liquid.

"Are you okay?"

Auri's eyes snapped open. The girl who had bought her the broth stood in front of her, hand on one hip, head cocked to the side. Auri sat up slightly and nodded.

"You look awfully pale."

Auri blinked. Did she? She glanced at her arm and then back at the girl. She was right.

"Are you sure you're not ill?"

"No, I'm fine, thank you."

The girl nodded, and her cocked head changed sides.

"I've never seen you at school."

It wasn't a question, so Auri said nothing, but just gave an uncomfortable smile.

"In fact, I don't recognise you at all. Who are your parents?"

Auri leaned forward and rounded her shoulders. She wished that she had sat with her parents and come up with some sort of plan of action, some reason for being anywhere above ground, the simplest of backstories. But, there just wasn't time. She smiled firmly at the girl.

"I'm not from round here. My parents are dead."

The girl hesitated, her hand falling from her hip. As though checking that no one else had heard, she glanced around her and pulled up a chair beside Auri.

"You can't be all alone," she said quietly. "Isn't there anyone who looks after you?"

In a flash, Auri remembered the square piece of paper in the pocket of the housecoat. Suddenly, she had a firm assumption of what might lie within it.

"I'm not all alone. I'm on my way to see my uncle, who lives in a different town."

Auri didn't have an uncle, or at least, not one that she knew of.

"Where does he live?"

"I have it written on a piece of paper in my bag. Anyway, that's where I'm heading."

The girl sat back in her chair and shrugged. "All right. Do you want to join my family and me for lunch?" She checked a strap on her wrist, which held a small circular disc. "It'll be in half an hour. We're having fish today."

Auri winced. She'd never eaten meat. Underground there was no option for anything other than root vegetables. But she had read about meat, fish, and how those above ground ate living things. She shook her head.

"I don't eat that."

The girl laughed. "Oh! We have other stuff. I'm sure my dad can rustle something up. He's a cook."

Slowly, Auri agreed. She was tired, desperately tired. She needed some normality, some essence of home. She told the girl that she would wait for her until her shift was finished and sat squarely in the chair until half an hour had come and go.

Eventually, for it seemed like a long time to Auri, the girl came and collected her. They walked side by side down the main street, their feet kicking up dirt, until they reached a small, dark alleyway. The girl seemed not to notice the change in light, and walked ahead of Auri fearlessly. Though Auri followed, she did so with trepidation. This girl was just a child, but Auri was suddenly aware that she was the only person responsible for her own safety. The girl stopped at an old wooden door about halfway down the tiny, dim street. She turned the handle and pushed it open, welcoming Auri inside. Scents poured out. Auri wrinkled her nose as a robust and tangy smell met a deeper, musty aroma. The girl turned.

"What's your name?"

"Auri."

"I'm Hona," she said softly before turning and bellowing through the thin hallway. "MOM! I BROUGHT A FRIEND BACK FOR LUNCH."

She led the way through the hallway into a kitchen at the end, larger than Auri had expected. It was sweltering in there. A big round wooden table sat in the centre, in the middle of which burned a lit fire, a large metal cauldron suspended above it. A short, squat woman bustled in from the garden, hands clutching various wild herbs. She gave Hona a hard kiss on the cheek, and Auri a hard stare, before throwing the herbs fully formed into the bubbling liquid.

"A friend from school, are you?" she asked, her accent dipping and waving in ways that Auri had never heard before.

"No, I don't go to school."

The woman frowned at Hona, a look that seemed to ask a question that Hona knew to answer.

"She's on her way to her uncle's, mum. I met her at the market just now." Hona glanced at Auri and then loudly whispered to her mother. "She hasn't got any parents."

The woman hesitated, her frown softening. She looked at Auri, and her head cocked to one side, in the same way that her daughter's had earlier in the day.

"Is that true? Are you an orphan?"

This was not a lie that Auri was comfortable or happy with. She nodded, opting to stay silent.

The woman sighed begrudgingly and pulled a chair out for Auri, motioning that she should sit. "We're having fish stew. Hona, fetch your brothers."

Auri stared at the bubbling liquid in the pot, and swallowed. She didn't want fish stew. Was that the sour, sharp scent that filled her nostrils? Small, bulbous eyes appeared in the pot, and Auri noticed, in mild horror, that they were attached to a fish head. Hona's mother stirred the head back in with a wooden spoon and nodded to Auri as though she had asked her a question.

"Gives it that extra bit of kick, the heads do."

Auri nodded and tried to smile. Hona reappeared just then, a small boy balanced on her hip, and another, older, two behind her. They all inspected Auri from afar, surprised at the stranger sitting at their dining table. Hona and her mother worked in a pair, sitting everyone down and handing out bowls. The stew was then slopped out with a ladle, small splashes hitting the surface of the table without notice.

Everyone began to eat immediately. Auri grasped her spoon and hesitantly dipped it into the broth, seeing, with dismay, that she had gotten the fish head. She closed her eyes and brought a full spoon to her lips, sipping carefully. Her taste buds waited for the horror to begin...but, she realised with surprise, it wasn't so bad. It was salty and savoury, reminiscent of the scent of the mineral-filled mud that clung to the walls underground. She swallowed and opened her eyes. The three boys, Hona, and her mother, were all watching her with interest. The smallest boy spoke up.

"You got the fish head," he said.

Auri stared at the floating, detached, being and nodded.

"That's good luck," said another boy.

There was a moment of silence.

"But only if you eat it," said the final brother to speak.

They all stared, a strange excitement in their eyes, and Auri felt the atmosphere pop with suspense.

"I think...you're joking," she said, trying a smile.

The family burst into boisterous laughter, the boys slapping each other on the backs and grinning wildly. Hona's mother reached over and patted Auri's hand, giving a slight shake of her head.

"Ignore them, child. They're daft as anything."

Now that the initial first bites were had of the stew, and stomachs settled with the promise of food, the family began to chatter to each other. Auri let the talk wash over her, comforting a part of her that she would not allow herself to acknowledge – homesickness.

"Auri – where does your uncle live?" Hona asked suddenly. Auri snapped her attention back to the present. She thought of that square of paper and smiled awkwardly.

"I have the address written on a piece of paper in my bag – but I haven't had a chance to read it yet."

Hona's mother raised her eyebrows and cocked her head to one side again, a clear family trait. "Well, you ought to do that now child, once lunch is done you might have to find somewhere to stay for the night."

Auri nodded and opened the bag that sat between her feet. She fished for the sharp edges of the paper and then rose, triumphant. She opened it, and read the address, instinctively only providing the last words.

"Finer Bay."

Hona's mother let out a low whistle. "Now that's a journey. That'll take you at least a night. Hona, you better finish up here and take her up to the cart bay. The sooner she gets going, the better. Can't have a child wandering the land of Rytter all alone. Auri, eat your stew."

Auri responded to the command immediately, spooning the broth into her mouth with abandon. She ate as Hona left, and then accepted a second dish while she waited for her return. She was back quickly and clapped Auri on the back, making her dress stick to the sweat that had formed on her skin in the heat of the kitchen.

"There's a chap that'll pick you up in an hour, Auri. He'll take you to Finer Bay. He was quite pleased actually – you can always get a good fare for that. There's two types of cart, but I didn't know which you'd be having."

Her mother rolled her eyes noisily and tutted. "You didn't know which cart she'd be having? You daft child, who wants to travel in an open-top cart overnight?!"

"I *chose* the one with a roof, *actually*," Hona responded huffily.

"Good. Will your uncle be paying for the journey, Auri?"

Auri pushed her empty dish to one side and pulled a small coin purse from her bag, shrugging. Though she understood currency and had learned about it in her history books, she had no idea of how much things actually were. Hona's mother placed a steady hand on Auri's shoulder and peered into the coin bag, exclaiming quietly under her breath.

"Right. You'll be all right, Auri. Come with me for a second."

She led her into a small room, the shelves lined with cans, and produced a little leather pouch from inside the folds of her dress. She emptied it into her palm, and carefully placed the money on a shelf beside her, then handed over the pouch.

"Auri, you're carrying around that sort of money in your bag, so I'm guessing no one has ever taught you this particular lesson before. You have to split it. Keep only a small amount in a purse like that – keep the rest, the larger amount, in a pouch like this – against your body. Keep it in a place where you can feel it against your skin. If it were missing – you should know about it. Now give me your purse."

Auri hesitated for a moment and then handed it over. She watched as Hona's mother counted out the large coins, leaving only smaller, silver ones in her small purse. Auri dropped the large ones into the pouch and pushed it under the neckline of her dress, resting against her heart. Hona's mother nodded firmly.

"Don't you let anyone – not *anyone* – know that you have that there."

Auri nodded. They left the cupboard tiny room and went back to the kitchen, where the boys sat playing with the fish head, shrieking with laughter. Hona handed Auri her bag and smiled.

"We should go. I'll show you where the cart bay is."

Hona dropped Auri off quickly, saying that she had to be back at the chestnut broth stand. She gave her a strange, hard stick of sugar 'for the journey' and shook her hand very firmly. The cart driver was a bit rough-looking, with only one tooth hanging in his mouth, but smiled kindly at Auri and made her feel comfortable. In the cart, she watched the world go by behind the flimsy glass windows until dusk began to fall, and her head started to bob. She slept then, though not solidly, sometimes waking to check her surroundings, sometimes being lurched from slumber by a bump in the road. At those times, the driver would shout, "Sorry, miss!" and she would murmur something in response, drifting back into sleep with the background sound of horse hooves comforting her.

It was the noise of the cobbles that brought her round fully. The horse's gait had changed to a staccato walk, and each step brought a bump through the carriage that shook the coins in Auri's borrowed pouch. She glanced out of the window at her surroundings. The light was a strange mixture of reds and yellows, bouncing from cobble to brick. They were moving slowly down a street now, and it seemed to Auri to be a fragile sort of dwelling, the houses slim and tall, battling for position both next to and opposite each other. Auri's stomach began to make strange noises, and she sighed, thinking, to her surprise, fondly of the fish stew from the day before. Was that the day before? It seemed long ago now. She closed her eyes and began to indulge in the thought of the food she might eat back home for breakfast. Pickled eggs. Raw cocoa yeast treats. A bang on the roof of the cart shook her back to the present.

"Miss?"

Auri opened her eyes and hesitated a response, "Yes?"

"We're in Finer Bay. I don't know whether you have an exact drop off point, but if it makes no difference to you – my sister lives here, so I'd like to drop you off."

She nodded, though aware that the driver could not see her, grabbed her bag and climbed out. The driver dipped his hat and grinned his one-toothed smile, then held out his hand. Auri stared at it for a moment, and then shook it firmly, as Hona had done with her earlier. There was an uncomfortable pause.

"That'll be sixteen."

Auri focused on the words and suddenly felt embarrassed when she realised their meaning.

"Of course." She removed her coin purse from her bag, and counted out sixteen coins into the driver's hand. He watched her do so, and then climbed down from his seat atop the carriage and moved a little closer to her.

"This coin is bigger than the others, you see, miss? That one is a ten. You're fine to give me that ten, and six of these smaller ones. I won't be needing the rest. You use those to get some breakfast." He carefully handed back nine of the coins and then paused. "Breakfast, depending on where you go, shouldn't be more than two of those coins. Okay?"

Auri nodded, wishing that she had asked more questions about currency when underground. She dropped them back into her purse and stepped away from the driver, watching him climb into his cart and trundle away.

Left alone in the small street, she carefully began to walk on the cobbles. They were challenging, her shoes kept slipping into the cracks, and she felt the rounded shapes beneath her thin soles, her ankles feeling like string. She noticed the light begin to change, the warms of the reds and yellows merging into a colder brightness.

The higher the sun climbed, the more alive the city became. It danced around her, and she, in turn, danced with it. She swayed for the carts that trundled through the centre of the street, deftly sidestepped the doors that flung open without warning, and dipped beneath the low-hanging signs of the shops. It was as though her body knew this dance well, and she let it take the lead, her mind taking a backseat to the mayhem of the city. She closed her eyes and let spice fill her nostrils, the scent of roasted chestnuts giving her a sense of home.

"AIN'T NO BROTH FINER IN FINER BAY!"

Auri's eyes snapped open to find a woman with a cart standing right in front of her, yelling this repeatedly. Strangely, she kept looking at Auri as though she were there for her benefit. Auri nodded and winced with each yell. She produced her purse. At this, the vendor grabbed a tankard and grinned, scooping the steaming broth to the brim.

"WILL YOU TAKE A DIPPER FOR A PENNY MORE?"

Auri flinched, nodding, unsure of what a dipper was. She watched the woman produce a long, inch thick, stick and place it into a paper bag. Auri handed the money over and watched the woman trundle away, though her voice didn't seem to trundle with her.

Auri wandered from the centre of the square to one of the tables and sat, placing her broth and bagged up dipper before her. She took the long stick out and stared at it a moment, before taking a bit of the end.

"Hmmmmfffghhh," she moaned, removing the stick from her mouth, her teeth exclaiming with disdain at the threat against them. It was solid. Had it gone off? Had she been sold expired goods?

"Oh bless your heart, child. You're supposed to dip it in your broth – didn't you wonder why it was called a dipper?"

Auri glanced to the table next to her, at two older women. She wasn't sure which had spoken but thanked them, making sure to nod to each. She tried again, this time holding the stick in her broth for a moment. Aware that the two women were watching her, she took a bite. This time, the dipper crumbled beneath the weight of her teeth, filling her mouth with both the delicious tastes of the chestnut broth and light cocoa. It was, she thought, the single tastiest thing she had ever eaten. She glanced at the women, who had, she noticed with interest, gone back to their discussion.

"Suka broke a tooth once on one of those, don't know how she got a hold of them."

"Hmm, well, that doesn't surprise me. They can reach anything once they set their minds to it."

Auri sat and finished her broth and dipper, listening all the while to their chatter, finding it a strange, distant comfort.

That evening Auri sat on an old wooden bench on a street corner, her bag beside her. She stared at the now crumpled piece of paper with the address on it and sighed. She had tried all afternoon to find the place, and it seemed impossible. The street to her left had the same name as the piece of paper held. She had walked up and down both sides at least twenty times and couldn't find anywhere at all called Seneca. Her eyes began to sting, and she blinked furiously. There was no time for that, she admonished herself. Pull yourself together.

The sun began to bob in the sky, the moon started to rise, and Auri watched as they greeted each other briefly. It was a moment she had only dreamt of. She pushed her bag to one end of the bench and laid her head on it, pulling her feet up to her chest. She closed her eyes and – ouch. What was that? Something prodded and poked at her ear from within the bag. Auri sat up and pushed her hand inside until she found the culprit, a smooth, wooden box. She pulled it out and stared at it, and then opened it carefully. A note lay on top, written in her mother's writing. She smoothed the paper with her fingertips and read aloud.

"Auri – if in doubt, ask the cards. Your Mother."

Auri kissed the note and folded it carefully, and then examined the cards before her. There were ten in the box, and none of them had a clear image. They were covered in faint outlines and randomly placed dark strokes. Auri held them gently and breathed in. She wasn't sure how to ask the cards for help, but she needed it.

"I um…" she cleared her throat, "I'm having trouble finding Seneca…."

A strange wave of calmness suddenly enveloped her, and she opened her eyes carefully, placing the cards on her lap. The lines on three of them began to dance, moving in time with each other, merging and dispersing. Auri stared as the cards settled on an image. It was of a short glass filled with dark liquid. She licked her lips thoughtfully. It reminded her of the drink her father used to enjoy on special occasions. Malt? As soon as her mind arrived at this word, the image throbbed. Auri carefully placed them back into the box with the note, and pulled her bag from the bench. She began to walk down the street once more, paying particular attention to each number or shop sign. Suddenly she stopped. There, on a sign protruding from a building, was the same glass of liquid. She ran to the door, breathing deeply, and read the name of the shop.

"The Malted Mash."

A wonky wooden sign read *Open, If you can pay* above the handle. Auri opened it and stepped into the murky bar, squinting in the dim light.

"Hello?" she ventured.

A barman looked up from his book and grinned widely. "Auri," he said approvingly. "You found us then."

Auri walked hesitantly up to the bar and nodded. "I think so. Your name is?"

The barman grinned and held out his hand. "I'm Seneca. Your parents told me to expect you. I'm the only person you'll meet above ground who knows about their way of life, and you'll not find a more trustworthy individual in these parts. Chestnut broth?"

Auri nodded silently and sat on a stool as the drink was made for her. There, she had the first sip from the mug that would, from then on, be her own.

Seneca would regale her of stories from her parent's youth, when they too had found their home in The Malted Mash. There Auri grew taller, braver, and smarter. Over a matter of years, Auri changed much about the world in which she and Seneca lived. She created a complicated machine that translated words to code, meaning that the letters that once travelled to and fro, sometimes causing fires, were no longer needed. She could finally talk to her parents in real-time. Over this machine, she was taught to improve the few holograms that had once been created, and longed for the day she might make her own from scratch.

Her parents often mused about her accomplishments, and apart from the rare occasions when Auri was not operating the code machine, and their messages of love disappeared in the air — they knew they had done the right thing in letting her go.

Chapter Thirty-Six

Plans often came to the Director in the early hours of the morning. He found that as he aged he needed less sleep, which amused him. Sometimes it felt as though the less rest he had, the better he was at making final, excellent decisions. This one had him reaching for the phone and dialling quickly into line two (phone line one being held for emergencies – on the off chance that Sylvia might once again mess up and need more assistance than the couple of officers he had provided).

"Yes. It's me."

"Good morning, sir," the mayor murmured into the receiver, trying to shift any sleepiness from his voice. In subtle contrast, he really did need eight hours a night to function properly.

"We're going to hold an election. You'll announce it tomorrow."

The mayor paused, heart hammering. His term was far from over.

"Did you hear me?"

"Yes, I did. But I haven't finished my term – I haven't –"

"Ah, and you still may! The people may still vote for you."

"Well, who would I be going up against?"

There was a silence on the line. It answered the mayor's question perfectly. His stomach convulsed.

"I see..." he said, wiping his quickly dampening hands on his pyjama trousers.

"You are extremely important to me, Mr Mayor. I will always take your policies into account. And in fact, should I win, you'll be as important to me as I am to you in your current role. But there's a, somewhat confusing, spread of power at the moment. Don't you find? The people are confused. They need steady leadership under one name only. You aren't seen to be a member of the Finery."

"Well, that's because I'm not," the mayor said quietly, irritated with himself for having to fight back tears.

"Join me for breakfast in a couple of hours, and we'll sort out the details."

The Director hung up the line, leaving the mayor sitting on the edge of his bed, clutching the handset. The checked pattern on the mayor's pyjama trousers warped before his eyes. He'd always tried to be an honest man. He'd tried to do things properly, by the book. He'd wanted to help people, for goodness sake, that was the point. His wife turned over and touched his back, causing him to flinch.

"There's going to be an election."

She frowned. "But your term isn't even halfway there yet."

He sniffed. "Yes, it is."

She nodded slowly. She understood.

When the mayor arrived at the Director's office only a few hours later, he was surprised to find other people there. As well as the usual uniformed members of the Finery, members of his own team were standing awkwardly, hands clutching glasses of ruby red liquid. There was a buffet, exotic bright fruits jostling with thick golden pastries and, the mayor was confused to see, a lot of bunting. The team began to clap as he entered, led by the Director, who grinned and smacked him on the back.

"Someone get the man a drink!" he exclaimed jovially. A member of his own staff hurriedly passed him his glass, and they stood, staring at each other for a moment. The Director laughed heartily.

"Well, I'll lead the cheers then! Just a little early breakfast buffet to celebrate a conversation that the mayor and I had in the early hours of the morning. I appreciate it's short notice, but the fact that you are all here means a lot to both of us." His hand squeezed the mayor's shoulder firmly. "We've decided that another election is in the interests of the city and its people – and what better time than at Artomia? They need to know that their leaders are a team, that the people who keep them safe on the streets at night are the same people that make the decisions in the offices. And this man," another loud clap on the back, causing the mayor to spill a little of his drink, "has done such a *fantastic* job. The people, ourselves included, are undoubtedly grateful. To the mayor."

The group lifted their glasses and repeated the last three words. Those who were members of the mayor's team did this with a little hesitation, thinly-veiled confusion on their faces. Was this an election or was the mayor stepping down? The mayor lifted his glass and nodded his head in thanks. To him, it was clear.

Chapter Thirty-Seven

Wolf led the way to the university. He'd never been there before, but Wendowleen was as taut as a wire, practically humming. Each time they reached a corner, a paw in the wrong direction would be met with a twang of tension, crackling through the air between them. He began to slow when they reached the large intricate gates of the facility. An old man sat in a small hut beside them. He glanced up as they came along and smiled wildly.

"Is that Prof Cripcot?"

Wendowleen smiled briefly and glanced about her in the darkness. "That's right, Ralph."

"Ah, back for a trip down memory lane, are you?"

"Something like that. All right if I pop through?"

Ralph glanced at Wolf and shrugged. "I don't see why not. Odd time though, isn't it? I'd have thought you would be prepping your festivities." He leaned forward conspiratorially. "I've got a half bottle of malt in my hut. Keep that between us now."

"I will, Ralph, of course," Wendowleen said, hurriedly gesturing to the gate. Ralph smiled and stepped forward with his keys, unlocking the gate and allowing the pair to slip inside. He watched them move swiftly toward the library.

The Director steepled his hands before the mayor and smiled.

"So, the campaign. It won't be much of one – I wouldn't worry. We won't go big on this thing – there are so many more *important* places for our money to go."

The mayor nodded silently.

"For example, you and I think very differently about money. Funding, for example. Your funding of the University of Rytter is little to be desired."

"With all due respect, Director, this is the only university in the land."

"Of course, of course. But the money could be better spent – the people are asking for a firmer hand at the wheel – more *responsible* spending, more houses – you know the details. As for your campaign – well, you offer what you like. I'm not going to tell you how to do your job."

The mayor stared at the desk in front of him and tried desperately to suppress a sigh. "Will my campaign...will it make any difference to the end result?"

The Director chuckled and spread his hands, long fingers stretching before his face. He shrugged gently. "I'm a confident man. I mean, of course, your campaign could have a real impact. It is certainly possible that you might be voted back in. But, I'm a very confident man. Well!" He leaned back in his chair, giving a tight smile. "You must go and get yourself ready, I suppose. I'll see you very soon."

The mayor nodded and stood quickly. As he left the room and closed the door behind him, he breathed a deep breath of stale, office building, air. What campaign had he? What hope did he really have? The world from his eyes looked bleak and bare. He thought of his wife, of the bottle of champagne that they shared when he had been named the mayor. Slowly, he trudged his way down the staircases, and out of the building.

To the average person, the world looked much the same as it did an hour before. To the mayor, the streets were grey. The flowers, the trees, the greenery, had wilted. His feet took him in the direction of home slowly, scuffing the toes of his once shining brogues. He noticed some Finery youths on the street as he stepped, crowding around one lamppost and then marching over to another in a group. He paused and then hauled his heavy feet toward them. They were putting up posters, he noticed, with dim interest. One of the youths turned to him and nodded.

"All right, sir?"

"Hmmm. What's this?"

The youth thrust a piece of paper at him and then turned back without a word. How quickly they lose respect, the mayor thought to himself. How quickly you cease to matter. He stared at the paper. It was purple. A photograph of the Director took up the whole middle section. It was covered in promises.

MORE HOUSING, MORE FARMING, MORE FOOD. FREE FARMING EQUIPMENT, FREE FARM ANIMALS, FREE LAND. VOTE FOR A BETTER FINER BAY, A BETTER RYTTER, AND A BETTER WAY OF LIFE. VOTING BEGINS AS ARTOMIA STARTS.

The mayor nodded. No one had asked him a question; indeed, no one really cared what he thought of anything, but the poster itself seemed to deserve a nod of recognition.

Before he could realise what was happening, the mayor found his feet leading him into a nearby pub, and scooping themselves around the wooden legs of a barstool.

"Well, hello, if it isn't the mayor of Finer Bay, gracing my bar with his presence!" The barman grinned, filled up a large glass with dark, treacly liquid, and swiftly placed it in front of the mayor.

"It isn't," the mayor uttered gloomily, taking a deep sip.

"It isn't what?" The barman frowned.

"It isn't the mayor gracing you with his presence."

The barman stared at him for a moment, brow furrowing. "You look awfully like him. You could be one of those look-alikes. People could hire you for parties and things."

A man at the bar swivelled to get a better view. "Oh yes," he said, "oh, you do look like him. My cousin is an agent, you know – I reckon she could get you lots of gigs. Ivan's the name."

He held out his hand, and the mayor shook it weakly.

The barman whistled through his teeth and nodded, "It's your lucky day coming in here; you're set to make a fortune."

The mayor breathed out slowly and took another long sip, "I was the mayor, but I'm not anymore."

The barman and Ivan glanced at each other. Ivan pulled his stool closer to the mayor.

"Since when?"

"Since tomorrow." He handed them the purple poster, now crumpled. Ivan took it and read it with interest.

"Free land? Is that right?"

The mayor shrugged despondently. The barman leaned over the sticky bar and glanced at the paper.

"*Free* land, though? Never mind the animals and that, the equipment, but there isn't much land to be had in Finer Bay. Even if you own a bit, it's just a small bit."

"That's right," agreed Ivan. "I don't know where they'll be getting that land from. And what does it mean, free land for *everyone*? How the hell is that supposed to work?"

The mayor dropped his head into his hands. "I have no idea.""Listen, Mr Mayor," Ivan clapped him on the back, "People in Finer Bay are pretty smart. After all, we've got the most educated folk in all of Rytter, what with the university being here. We can see through false promises."

The mayor lifted his head and glanced at the two men, who were both nodding enthusiastically. "I know you can tell the difference, lads, and no one has more faith in the population of Finer Bay than I do. I'm just scared that it won't make a blind bit of difference now."

"We'll vote for you. Won't we, Ivan?" The barman swept the glass from beneath the mayor's nose and topped it up. Ivan nodded firmly.

"Thank you," responded the mayor, his eyes glassy with tears. He blinked awkwardly.

Ivan looked back at the purple flyer. "Voting begins as Artomia starts. Well, that's...an odd time to start...people will be beginning their celebrations, won't they?"

The mayor nodded. "They will, Ivan. They certainly will."

continued hurriedly, "what I can do is see what the book is…ah here it is – Essays of Plagiarism – book 1129. Oh…is this to do with an appeal of some kind?"

Wolf whined beside the pair, bored of the waiting. Wendowleen glanced down at him and then smiled warmly at the librarian. "It is, my dear, that's exactly what it is." She was suddenly determined to find out precisely what this book was. She hadn't plagiarised a day in her life!

"Well…" the librarian looked around again and paused thoughtfully. "I can't see the harm in that. After all, an appeal has its deadlines too. What I'll do is give you the pinakes, but please be as quick as you can possibly be." She traced her finger along the front of her clipboard. "It's P.E.C. 2678."

Wendowleen thanked her kindly and gestured to Wolf to follow. They walked into the dim room behind the librarian, eyes adjusting to the poor lighting. Wendowleen steadily checked the end of each large iron bookcase until she reached her reference, muttering under her breath. "P for Plagiarism, E for Essays, C for Cripcot." There. There the book sat, a layer of grey dust decorating the spine. She pulled it out and held it carefully, its weight significant. The index gave her the page. And there it was. She breathed a breath out of her nostrils sharply as she read the words, as they were indeed her own. Each and every one of them. She flicked through the pages until she reached the end of the essay, and there she paused. The name was familiar, but it was not her own. *Cripcot*, yes. *Ayin*, no. *Ayin Cripcot* stared back at her, a challenge in written form. A red stamp lingered beneath the name, the ink blotted and old. It read: *Expelled*. She frowned, glanced around, and then tore the essay pages from the book and secreted them into her coat. She pushed the book back onto the shelf.

"Wolf." He glanced up at the voice of his owner. "Come."

In Rytter, the colour black exists, as it does elsewhere in the world. But there is also a colour that few know, a distant cousin of black. This is the absence of colour. In the darkest corners of Finer Bay, you might find, if you ask for the right people, someone willing to sell you paint in this colour. However, it's only made in small batches, and this is mainly because the person making the stuff painted the front of his house in it, and – to put it bluntly – it's now a bloody bugger to find (even for them on a cloudy night).

Auri knew of this colour. She flicked her reigns and moved at speed through the streets of Finer Bay. The coach that she sat atop had been coated in the absence of colour. With care, they moved through the darkness. Passers-by paying great attention might notice something, for a moment, on any other night. But tonight, Artomia was the focus of everyone's thoughts. Though more people were lining the pavements than on a usual evening, those people were paying plenty of attention to their pints and not much to the traffic.

Auri drove the coach carefully past Wendowleen's house and saw the presence of three Finery officers in her concrete garden. She silently urged the horse on, aiming for The Malted Mash. As she left the street, one of the officers turned. The moonlight seemed to flicker strangely over the houses before him. He blinked a couple of times and then turned back to his colleagues.

"She's not in. What time do we clock off for Artomia anyway? My throat is awful dry."

Chapter Thirty-Nine

Wendowleen had left the library in a hurry, Wolf patiently bearing with her, despite the fact that he was pretty sure some treats should be due right about now. Wendowleen led the way this time, the hood of her old coat pulled up, the evidence of plagiarism burning through her pocket, her feet moving as quickly as possible. She knew the rough way and occasionally paused to look at signposts, an act that caused Wolf to whine in a way that filled her irritation.

Once they began to near The Malted Mash, Wolf quickly took over the guiding, his mind full of the treats he had received on their last visit. As they neared the door, Wendowleen held her breath and checked around her. Lamps dimly lit the street, but not many revellers were to be found. She turned back and knocked gently. The door creaked open immediately, and she followed Wolf into the bar.

Auri closed the door behind her and helped her visitor to a chair. "Wendowleen. I am grateful to see you. I passed your house – the Finery-"

Wolf gave a low howl and pawed at Auri's cloak, interrupting her speech. She glanced down at him and quickly pulled a handful of biscuits from the folds of material, dropping them onto the floor.

"Yes, I assumed that it was them at the door," Wendowleen responded in a quiet voice.

"Listen – no matter. You are here. I have a coach ready. Seneca will drive you."

Wendowleen sighed, noticing the barman standing in the corner of the room. He waved, and she nodded at him. "Thank you."

"All right. Let's go." Auri beckoned the three to hurry. She went first, checking the street outside the bar for people. She was grateful to find it quiet. Wendowleen came next, followed closely by a purring Wolf. Wendowleen blinked at the street and then at Auri's arm, noticing with confusion that it was held in front of her, fingers curled around thin air.

"This is the coach," Auri hissed quietly, "trust me. Step up."

Wendowleen grumbled to herself. It was quite enough, really, to step into an average coach. She closed her eyes and picked up her right foot, placing it in front of her. To her surprise, it found a step. She held her hands before her face and felt the edge of a door and then fumbled herself into the back of the coach. Once in, she could see the red velvet seat, and sat doggedly in it, pulling Wolf in after her. He wasn't too fussed by the illusion himself, just grateful to see the velvet. Auri's face appeared in the doorway.

"I leave you here. Seneca is trustworthy, and he will look after you."

Wendowleen nodded. "Thank you, Auri."

"Wendowleen – give my love to my parents."

With that, the door closed, and the windowless box began to move through the night. Wolf licked Wendowleen's hand happily before walking in a little circle and settling down for an overdue sleep. Wendowleen watched him for a moment and then closed her eyes, happy to do the same. The land slipped effortlessly into the beginning of Artomia.

There are three types of people on the first morning of Artomia, and they can all be distinguished by the way that they react to the warm air of the sunshine creeping through the bedroom window. Some roll over, pull the blanket over their head, and curse their celebratory post-midnight merriment. There are those who cheer, having not yet gone to bed. And, there are those with children, who cheer in midnight and then fall gratefully into the pillow, and awake with excitement the next day, ready to welcome the weather and warmth.

The mayor was the first of these. He squinted at the light and cursed under his breath. A strange tension appeared to fill the bedroom, and he turned to see his wife drinking a cup of chestnut broth in a way that could definitely be described as 'haughty'. He clumsily sat up, propping the pillows behind him, and leaned his head back onto the wooden headboard.

"My head," he said without much thought.

"Hmmm," his wife responded. The mayor watched her take another sip of her drink. Yep, definitely haughty.

"Happy Artomia, my love," he said experimentally.

"Is it," she murmured.

Ah-ha! Thought the mayor, I *knew* it. "You're annoyed," he said, stating the obvious.

"Am I," she responded.

The mayor noticed that none of these statements had question marks after them. He shifted about uncomfortably. "You're annoyed because I stayed out."

His wife rolled her eyes and took another sip. The mayor nodded, encouraged by this reaction.

"You're annoyed because I didn't spend the start of Artomia with you. And I understand, I do. But I had rather a trying meeting with the Director, and voting started at *midnight*, and I just found myself in a bar and time sort of...."

"Disappeared," his wife said slowly.

The mayor nodded and closed his eyes for a moment. The moment turned into a nap, quite unexpectantly.

The Director sat in his office, listening dully to the click-clack of Sylvia's knitting needles, which seemed to be interspersed with the occasional, "Oh bugger", and, "There goes another one". He stared at a card on the desk. A deer was playfully trotting through a field beneath the words *Happy Artomia* on the front. It was from his head of staff, who had signed the card 'Bob' instead of his title, which seemed a little familiar and unprofessional to the Director. He'd have to think about that one further. You couldn't have people going around and calling themselves Bob, as though titles didn't really matter. For example, he really had had no idea who the card was from for at least half of the morning, and that sort of thing was just irritating and irresponsible. His concentration was broken suddenly by a tentative knock at the door.

"Enter," he murmured.

The door swung open, and the room quickly filled with the scent of boot polish. Two officers marched in and stood squarely before the Director's desk, their eyes focusing somewhere in the distance behind him. He noticed one of them glance at the card and then back again.

"At ease."

The officers relaxed. The one who looked at the card offered him a strange sort of smile.

"Happy Artomia, Director."

The Director sighed slowly. "I'm sure it will be, with the good news you're about to present to me."

The officers appeared to swallow in unison. One spoke up.

"Actually, Director, Cripcot wasn't at home. We forced entry, sir. She wasn't there. No sign of her or the wolf. There was no sign of her having left for good, though—all of her clothes were still there, the wolf's bowl was still half-empty."

The Director stared at the pair and nodded, and then picked up a pen on his desk and began to write. There was an uncomfortable silence. The men glanced at each other nervously.

"So we'll...we'll..."

The Director glanced up, "Yes?"

"We will…head back to check again?"

"She is a century old. How far do you think she could have gotten? Check her haunts. Do some research." The Director paused for a moment and then put his pen down, smiling. "Check the university library."

The men glanced at each other again, and one cleared his throat. "Sir, it is customary that we might have at least one of the evenings of Artomia off, and-"

The Director seemed not to have heard this and smiled wider still. "On second thoughts, I'll come with you."

Chapter Forty

A thump shook Wendowleen from her slumber, and she opened her eyes blearily. Wolf gazed at her in the dull light and gave a big yawn, displaying all forty-two teeth. She smiled at him, stroking his warm fur with fondness. Suddenly, light filled the box, and the two blinked at the appearance of Seneca in the doorway.

"Hello, both. It's morning. Got to stop and get the horse something to eat – thought you might be after some breakfast?"

Wolf's ears pricked up at this word – he knew it well, and he gave a short bark of agreement.

Seneca smiled. "We're in a place called Towen. Usually a market on down that way." His head jerked left to indicate the direction. "We're not far off mind, but you'll be all right here for an hour."

Wendowleen nodded and accepted his helping hand out of the coach, hesitantly placing one foot down on the invisible step. Wolf bounded down after her, wholly unfazed.

Seneca showed the pair where he would meet them after an hour, by a livery yard near the centre. Wendowleen watched him take the horse and wander off and closed her eyes for a moment. It was a pleasure, really, to be in a new place. Of course, the Finery had bases throughout Rytter, but she would be able to walk among the people without worrying about who was watching for an hour. The air seemed sweeter, honeyed, and with a firm sniff, she opened her eyes and strode purposefully in the direction of the market.

It took almost no time to reach the first of the stalls. It seemed they had been open for hours. Wendowleen smiled at the people as she wandered through the market.

"Happy Artomia, mam!" an older man yelled, holding the tip of his cap. Wendowleen paused and shook her head.

"My goodness, I'd completely forgotten."

"Forgotten about Artomia? Well, it don't come that often I suppose."

Wendowleen stepped forward to inspect the wares on the man's stall, admiring the large wedges of filled bread carefully laid over gingham cloth. She pointed at one that looked particularly interesting, brimming with sausage and pickles, and then sat on a bench near the market. She took a deep bite. The bitterness of the pickles settled among the burst of fruit pips, and she closed her eyes as jam followed through with a hearty tang. Her skirt began to feel tight. She opened her eyes to see Wolf with his teeth around the end of the material, pulling and growling.

"Oi!" she scolded. A couple of passers-by glanced over with interest. Wolf sat and let out a single cry.

"All right. You can have one sausage," she said firmly, fishing out the desired object and placing it on the floor before him. He greedily set about eating it, and Wendowleen felt a pang of guilt. He must be hungry, too. With care, she pulled out another sausage and dropped it beside him. After that, he got his own pickle. Together, they finished the sandwich and enjoyed the sweet tastes of meat and freedom.

The mayor walked hazily through the decorated streets to his local polling station. His wife had voted already, she said, and he had listened to this with interest. If she had voted when she was mad at him past midnight, perhaps other people had actually voted too? He began to walk a little quicker and reached the door of the nominated hut. It had a big sign on it.

"Voting now closed…" The mayor breathed in sharply and growled.

The Director and his two officers arrived at the university and rattled, loudly, on the large, iron gate before them. Ralph's head popped up quickly from his hut, and he staggered out before mock saluting and falling into a heap of giggles. The officers stepped forward quickly, but the Director held up a hand and paused them.

"Good morning. Enjoying the festivities of the season?"

Ralph grinned and held up his bottle of malt as evidence. "That I am."

"So I see. The university is closed today?"

"Ah," said Ralph, hiccupping, "It is only closed to those who don't have the key."

The Director stared at him and raised his eyebrows. "Of course. And you have the key, don't you?"

Ralph nodded enthusiastically.

"Indeed. So, please open the gate." He indicated the lock and stepped aside with his men.

Ralph fished out the correct key and stepped forward, and then at the last minute, paused. "Who exactly is wanting to get in?"

"The Finery," responded one of the officers.

"Ah. Okay." He deftly turned the key in the lock, and pulled the gate aside, nodding to the visitors.

"Been a busy night, has it?" The Director asked, with an air of absent-mindedness.

Ralph shrugged. "Not too busy really, no."

The Director nodded and paused. "Oh, just out of interest, do you allow care wolves into the library? We had a report of a dog in the area earlier — just wanted to check it out."

"Oh, you mean Cripcot's? Oh yes, nothing wrong with

that. An old friend."

"Wonderful. You are accommodating." The Director smiled tightly, and Ralph noticed with interest that the corners of his mouth seemed to turn down instead of up.

Chapter Forty-One

The Director and his officers strode up to the library with such purpose that the doors swung open as soon as they arrived.

"Search the study halls," the Director instructed the officers, who clumsily went to look at a map of the building so they could work out where the study halls were.

The Director, on the other hand, knew exactly where he was going. He stormed up the steps and swept into the doctoral research room. It was empty. There, before him, was the door to the restricted access library. He stared at it in disbelief. There was no one staffing it. He flew through the room and stared at a hastily handwritten note pinned to the oaken door.

Restricted access. Please fill out an application form. Thanks! Happy Artomia. Xxx

The Director looked at the kisses on the end of the sentence with such menace that they might have flown off the page. He tried the handle. Unbelievably it was open. What was the point, really? What was the point in passing laws, in working hard, in trying to *protect* people? They were all basically idiots. And being an idiot is absolutely fine, if you can follow orders. That's really the ideal, but being an idiot who can't even follow orders is like having a nose and sneezing through your teeth.

The Director walked into the room and let his eyes adjust to the light.

"P for Plagiarism, E for Essays, C for Cripcot," he said aloud as he stalked the bookshelves.

There, exactly where it should be, was Essays of Plagiarism – book 1129, with a spine that was curiously not as dusty as the others beside it. He pulled it open on the index and then flicked to the correct pages. Or rather, he flicked to where the pages should have been. He stared at the ripped remnants of paper and closed the book, replacing it on the shelf.

"Oh, Mother," said the Director quietly.

Despite their hourly deadline, Wendowleen and Wolf sat a little longer on the bench, enjoying the sunlight. Now and then, Wendowleen fancied that someone might look at her a little strangely. In turn, she watched the passers-by with interest. Perhaps some would only stare because she was staring at them, she told herself. Wolf sat patiently by her, waiting. Suddenly, the scent of boot polish filled Wendowleen's nostrils, and she paused, turning her head. A member of the Finery was standing behind her. The uniformed woman walked steadily around the bench and looked at Wolf, and then at Wendowleen.

"Nice wolf," she said.

"Oh, him? Yes. He's a caring wolf," Wendowleen responded, standing with a bit of difficulty.

The woman frowned slightly. "That's not a Towen accent you have, is it?"

Wendowleen stepped away slightly, shaking her head.

"Where are you from?" The woman stepped toward her.

"Me? Snorington."

"Ah."

"Anyway – must dash." Wendowleen clicked her fingers at Wolf, and they hustled together back through the market. Wendowleen was careful not to turn around.

Seneca was waiting patiently, his back warming against the horse's haunches, eyes closed in the sunshine.

"I'm sorry you have to work on Artomia, Seneca," Wendowleen said.

He started, his eyes opening suddenly. "Oh no, don't worry about that," he said gently. "Find yourself something to eat?"

Wendowleen nodded, and with the barman's help, stepped into the back of the coach once more.

"It isn't far now."

The door closed, and Wendowleen and Wolf yawned together, stomachs full and minds racing. Well, Wendowleen's mind was racing. Wolf's mind was focused on not losing the taste of sausages.

The party atmosphere had not dropped in Finer Bay. Whatever celebrations had happened the night before, the town was ready and willing to give it their best all over again. The Director and his men arrived back at the headquarters quickly, only one of them lagging slightly as he watched others celebrating. The Director turned to them at the front of the building, and both men tried desperately not to look hopeful.

"Go and check on the vote. The counting should be almost finished."

They both dipped slightly at the shoulders but nodded and saluted. The Director turned and walked to his office. Sylvia sat there still, not much further with her knitting. She glanced up as he came through the door.

"Any luck?" she asked.

"No," the Director responded. "Where could your sister-in-law be? You must have some idea."

Sylvia stared at her knitting and then the ceiling, saying nothing. The Director sighed wearily.

"Sylvia – I don't know why I've kept you here."

She nodded in response, blinking rapidly. "It does feel time to go home."

"No, that's not what I mean at all."

There was a pause of silence as Sylvia tried to understand this comment.

"We're family," she said into the stillness.

The Director ignored this, and sat heavily in his chair. He thought for a moment and then lifted his phone, dialling quickly.

"Yes. Dispatch the wolves. Get the scent." He placed the receiver down.

Another silence crept into the room, unnoticed by the Director. Sylvia coughed, and he lifted his head to look at her.

"Ayin. They'll kill her."

His body flinched as she said his first name. He smiled tightly. "They may not. And anyway, who better trace a wolf than a wolf?"

Auri sat in The Malted Mash alone, watching the clock behind the bar. Where would they be at this point? She reached inside her pocket, at the same time as a knock at the door came.

"Are you open for a drink?" someone shouted through the lock.

"We're closed."

"But it's Artomia!"

Auri rolled her eyes and said nothing, eventually hearing them mutter crossly and wander away. She pulled out her mother's cards and laid them on the table. The shapes of three shifted and battled before settling into the silhouette of a coach. She viewed this with mild surprise.

"Shouldn't you be there by now?" she whispered.

The air around The Malted Mash remained unmoved, and the clock continued to tick onwards. Auri breathed out. She was waiting for the howls.

You may be forgiven for believing that all wolves were created equal. This is not the case. Where Wolf was bred, among others, for his gentle nature and mild intelligence, Finery wolves were bred for their cruelty. When man decided to own dogs, much the same was considered. The kindest wolves were bred with each other, and then as kind wolves sired gentle pups, those too would become parents to even kinder beasts. The Finery wolves were bred using the opposite ideals. There was, on occasion, the type of wolf entirely wrong for a caring role. It might be that they were easily bored, unable to take direction, or, on occasion, aggressive. If the cause of this aggression was not physical (a wolf with a sore tooth is bound to be a little grumpy, after all), they were sent away to the Finery. The Finery bred exceedingly intelligent wolves for all sorts of projects.

There were those who could smell contraband, who would be stationed in the dingy and dark areas of the cities throughout Rytter, sniffing and waiting. Those who were bred for speed could run and leap over fences quicker than any robber. And, there were those bred for tracking, who could hold a scent within their noses for hours on end and could often run faster than the being possessing the odour.

A member of the FWT (Finery Wolf Team) was showing the wolves around Wendowleen's empty house. There were five in total, and the officer watched with satisfaction as they sniffed the air, not one of them taking the opportunity to have a bit of Wolf's food, still in his bowl. Now that, the FWT officer thought to herself, is training. After around five minutes, she blew a sharp whistle, and the wolves quickly huddled into a formation. The FWT officer set her timer, for data's sake, and blew another long whistle. The wolves left at pace, paws thrashing through earth and over concrete. They didn't require any human assistance from this point on. They would find their mark, as always, and then would bring them back alive or dead. There was no telling which.

Chapter Forty-Two

"Results, results!" the Director enthused at the mayor as he sat down before his desk. The mayor stared at him in mild surprise. He had never seen, or heard, him be so authentically stimulated.

"So, the results are in?" the mayor asked quietly.

The Director tapped an envelope on the desk and grinned widely, "I had my head of staff put the results in this envelope – to create a bit of tension. Would you like to?" He motioned the envelope in the mayor's direction, who shook his head curtly.

"Very well. Drum roll…" he said, picking up a short knife and slicing open the future. He pulled a piece of paper out and read it quickly. "Well, Mr Mayor – you did very well, considering."

The mayor sat up in his chair quickly and leaned forward. "I won?" he asked hopefully.

The Director raised his eyebrows, surprised. "Of course not, man. You didn't even put up posters. No, no, I won with 86% of the vote. So you did well."

The mayor sagged back in his seat and sighed.

"You mustn't be too hard on yourself. The world has this funny way of telling us when to move on. In your case, it's me verbally telling you to move on. But – not before I've presented you with…." He put his head down into a desk drawer for a moment, and the mayor listened to him move items around. "…this watch!"

The mayor reached over, took the loose, gold watch from the Director, and nodded, thanking him quietly. He turned it

177

over briefly and noticed an inscription on the back.

"Oh, you had it inscribed!" he said.

The Director paused and frowned, and immediately the mayor wished he hadn't said anything. The inscription read: "For my beloved." There was a silence between the two men as the mayor realised where this watch most likely came from.

"So, should we need anything in the near future, handover business, I'll be in touch." The Director nodded briskly, the physical display of 'You've taken up enough of my time.'

Auri stood at the window at the top of The Malted Mash and watched the street below through the netted curtain. She had checked the cards again, and still, they were in the coach. The predictions of the partisans were powerful and more often correct than not, but they were not fool-proof. And then, just as she had feared, came the skid of twenty paws. They halted immediately outside The Malted Mash, and Auri watched as they paced for a moment. She thought of Wolf. Had these wolves been of a similar personality, she could have simply lined the street outside with biscuits, and they would have had no more trouble. The wolves suddenly sniffed the air and turned into a disappearing blur as they galloped away.

"Off to Towen," Auri whispered into the air.

Wendowleen yawned in the dank light of the coach and placed a hand on Wolf's head. He had begun to whine gently in the last ten minutes, and she watched him curiously. Perhaps it was the sausages? The coach came to a sudden stop, and both blinked as the small room filled with light again. Seneca nodded at the pair.

"We're here."

Wendowleen accepted his hand once more and stepped out with care, unknowingly leaving the handcrafted whistle from Towen on the seat behind her. The view that welcomed her caught the breath in her throat, and she blinked. They were in a forest, a vast lake before them. Mountains formed a backdrop, the smallest of which sat front and centre, its base diving into the water. The reflections made the scenery seem never-ending.

"My goodness," she murmured.

Seneca stood beside Wendowleen and nodded. "It's a wonderful place."

Wendowleen glanced at him. "So, how do I get to – ?"

"Well, first of all, you'll be needing this." He pulled a small, clear, textured bag from his pocket and handed it over. "Put anything you don't want getting wet in there – it's waterproof."

Wendowleen laughed a little and stared at the lake. "You're not serious."

"Do you have any papers or anything that you don't want to get wet?" Seneca responded as though Wendowleen had never spoken.

She patted down her pockets and then remembered the pages of the library book. She pulled them out and placed them carefully into the bag, allowing Seneca to seal it for her.

"All right. You must go to the lake – both of you. The current is strong. You must swim down as though you are trying to reach the bottom. Swim toward that mountain." He pointed at the smallest before them. "There will be a large dark circle. Swim toward it. Take deep breaths. Let your body settle for a moment when you enter – the water is cold."

Wendowleen stared at Seneca with disbelief and then at the lake. When was the last time she had gone swimming?

"Wendowleen," Seneca said slowly.

"Yes, I know." She knew what he meant by the tone of his voice. He meant that there was no time. She stepped forward, Wolf by her side, and into the waters. They were cold, yes, and they greedily covered her clothes and body, soaking into Wolf's fur and pulling the two down. When she could still touch the ground with her toes, Wendowleen turned her face to the shore and saw that Seneca was no longer there.

"Wolf. I know that you don't understand, but you must hold your breath."

She demonstrated breathing in, puffing out her cheeks. Wolf watched curiously, paddling water. And then, she took one huge breath of air and went under. Wolf stared at the rippling water and copied.

Beneath the stillness of the reflections lay murky greenness, and Wendowleen did her best to keep her eyes open and her heart steady. She swam down as hard as she could and then, when she eventually reached the sandy floor of the lake, stared ahead. There was the dark circle. She had done it right. Her heart filled with hope, her mind trying to force out the impenetrable chill of the water. She steadily began to swim forward but found herself lagging. Her foot refused to move, and she kicked with both legs firmly. It was tiring, ever so tiring, more activity than she had done in a lifetime. She kicked again, used her arms and hands to propel herself forward, but was stuck. Her right hand found Wolf, his fur floating around him in the mire, and she grabbed on steadily. *You mustn't close your eyes*, she told herself. *You must stick with this.* But, sometimes, we only tell ourselves these things when the inevitable is happening. Wendowleen closed her stinging eyes and felt Wolf's teeth close about her arm. The pain it caused slowly drifted away as she spoke to herself calmly; he doesn't mean it. He is only trying to help.

Above the surface, gentle bubbles popped. The mountains knew nothing of the lake's troubles.

Chapter Forty-Three

The wolves reached Towen in record time. Seneca had taken the coach on a different route home, all too aware of the dangers he could find on the usual path. Their twenty paws pounded through the market square, and they sniffed and strayed from between the stalls, trying to work out a fuller picture through scent. The sun was still hot in the sky, and the early afternoon crept in, filling the marketplace with more and more people. Eventually, a new scent was found, and they leapt into action, streaming past passers-by. The whistle seller turned to a customer and tutted.

"I don't know what this town is coming to. I have never seen so many wolves in all my life as I have today."

The customer, an elderly woman, nodded. "Oh yes, it's not like it used to be. When I was young, you could go a whole lifetime without seeing a wolf. And that was proper, that's what we called proper."

The two stood and mused over this for a moment, murmuring noises of agreement.

The Director clicked his fingers and rolled his shoulders back. The old mayor had been dispatched, and he was now the ruler of Finer Bay, and, he mused to himself, practically Rytter. He stared off into the distance for a moment. He was like a modern-day King in a way. Of course, royalty hadn't existed for hundreds of years – not since the Great Revolution of the Fire Swamp – but even so. King had quite a ring to it. A knock at the door interrupted his thoughts.

"Enter."

In bustled the Vice-Chancellor of the Rytter University, leaving a shocked officer standing at the door alone.

"WHAT'S THE BLOODY IDEA YOU ABSOLUTE –" the Vice-Chancellor roared, his black gown swishing about him with every word. The Director placed his hands in the air and frowned at the Vice-Chancellor gently.

"Sit down, Vice-Chancellor, let us talk like human beings." He glanced at the still shocked officer and nodded to him curtly, indicating that he leave them.

The Vice-Chancellor sat down before him and leaned over the desk with menace.

"I have just received a hand-delivered letter of closure." His words fired out like bullets, each an individual piece of fury. "You cannot close the only university in Rytter. It is senseless."

The Director smiled calmly. "I understand that you are angry, VC. Do you mind if I call you VC? Vice-Chancellor is rather a mouthful." And one, he thought, that you won't be hearing again. "However, it is not senseless. Education, in the wrong hands, can be a hazardous thing. It can lead to *terrible* things; of this, you must be aware."

The Vice-Chancellor opened his mouth to speak, but the Director ignored this and continued.

"For example, I have data that proves that in the land of Rytter, and in particular Finer Bay, where we suffer for having the university, we are short of *essential items*. I'm talking about food – VC – clothing. The people are suffering."

The Vice-Chancellor tutted loudly, "That's absolute –"

"And jobs, too," the Director interrupted. "We need more people doing worthwhile jobs. The things that bring actual money and items of value into the cities. Farming, import, the creation of items in this land is more important than higher education at the moment. And, we need people for the Finery.

182

There are many great and important jobs in this land where education would put people at a disadvantage."

"Education will never put people at a disadvantage," the Vice-Chancellor growled.

"You are wrong. And that is okay; you are allowed to be wrong. I am in charge of a great many people, and they entrust me with their help."

"As am I, Director."

"Indeed, VC. But there's a difference, isn't there? Because I don't have anybody above me, and you, unfortunately, have me. Oh, and the Chancellor of the university, of course."

The Vice-Chancellor narrowed his eyes. The Chancellor was a mere title handed out to a wealthy person, occasionally brought out to cut a ribbon. It changed every few years, and currently, it was Lady Montgomery, a woman who, despite having inherited more money than belonged to the entire university, seemed only to be interested in claiming more.

"The Chancellor has been most helpful, and she is a wonderful and insightful woman. She entirely agrees –"

"You paid her off," the Vice-Chancellor said sharply. There was a pause in the discussion, which shot through the air like electricity. The Vice-Chancellor shook his head. "What powers do you have, anyway?"

"Ah, well, you haven't heard the good news. There'll be an announcement in around half an hour. I'm no longer just the Director of the Finery. I'm the Mayor," he ensured the capital sat firmly at the start of the word, "of Finer Bay, and by extension, Rytter." The Director smiled warmly.

"And by extension, Rytter? In what world?"

"It was in the contract. It was part of the offer, for which was voted by 86% of the city. Didn't you read it, VC? I am surprised, a man of intelligence, not giving something his full time and consideration."

"Closing the University of Rytter is going to impact the entire land."

The Director raised his eyebrows. "I am fully aware of that. And VC, did I say that it would be forever? I did not. We shall see how it goes; I am nothing if not flexible and reasonable. However, as you can expect, I do need to prepare for my announcement, so if you could take your leave." He pressed a button beneath the desk firmly, and two officers marched into the room immediately.

The Vice-Chancellor stared at him for a moment and then stood slowly.

"You're not going to get away with this."

"And it is comments like that, VC, that I'll ask you to consider carefully, moving forward. History is full of people like you, who choose the wrong battles to fight in and find themselves written out of all memory."

The Vice-Chancellor slammed his fists down on the desk. "There are hundreds of books in libraries across the land with my name on the spine. Try all you like, but you will never write me out of history you –"

"Take a breath VC, or it'll be your last." The Director motioned to the left of the Vice-Chancellor, who turned his head to find himself staring down the barrel of a gun. He paused, and stood up carefully, and then marched out of the room. The officers turned to the Director for instruction. He shook his head briefly.

"Oh, leave him. He'll just go and get drunk, no doubt. We can always catch up with him later."

The wolves stood at the edge of the lake, pawing the ground and trying to find the continuation of the scent. Eventually, one leaned toward the water and then paused, seeing something floating on top. They waded in and began to swim through the chilled liquid, eyes focussed on their prize. The other wolves whined in anticipation. In a short time, the prize was dropped onto the shore of the lake, and the wolves crowded around it. The scent was strong. The wolves looked at each other momentarily, each understanding the situation in turn. The smell had come to an end. This was all that was left. One of them picked up the item: papers in the sealed waterproof bag, and then they turned in unison to begin the gallop back to Finer Bay.

Chapter Forty-Four

Throughout Finer Bay, speakers crackled. Radios buzzed, songs switching into crackling silence. Televisions faltered, white noise and darkness overlaying the usual stories.

In The Malted Mash Auri sat at the bar alone and started with surprise when the radio on the top shelf suddenly buzzed into action. She squinted at it. How long had they had that?

"Hold on for an announcement from the Director," a crackling voice buzzed into the room. Auri's eyes narrowed as a long beep followed the voice.

"Good day Rytter. It is a great pleasure to be talking to you as your new Mayor. Long have I kept you safe, looked after your loved ones, fed your families. I know that times have been tough, and I am here to improve life for all of you. You voted for more jobs, more food, more land. I *will* deliver. Of course, to be the Director and the Mayor of Finer Bay and all of Rytter means having to face personal sacrifice. I am prepared to do this for you alone. In turn, I ask that you, too, make small sacrifices for the greater good. What form this takes will be different for each of you, but rest assured that every expense at your door will create a stronger Rytter. Every patch of land given to a neighbour so that they may eat as well as you do will strengthen ties.

We are set to become a land of plenty, and with your help, we will get there quickly. There may be a few changes in your immediate future, and I ask you to face these modifications with faith, bravery and wisdom. Have faith in your government because we think of only you and your future. Be brave in the path of change, for you know that you alone can make a difference to your companions' lives. Be wise in your battles, because to fight with your own kind is treason.

Today I ask you to embrace one small change that will have a tremendous and positive impact on the nation.

Tonight, curfew begins. At sundown, we shall expect you to retire to your property. This is a small ask and one that I do not doubt you will excel at. This will give you peace of mind – no longer will you wonder where your child has gone to. It will provide you with a more restful evening – the quiet of the street after sundown will send you peacefully into slumber. Inevitably, it will create a better workforce, as rest and relaxation are at the pinnacle of hard work. Of course, officers will be on the streets tonight, ensuring that the curfew is adhered to, but I don't want you to worry. Everyone understands that any change takes a short while to get used to. The Finery are there, as ever, for you and your loved ones protection.

It is, as it has always been, a great honour to serve you, Rytter."

The crackling voice faded into nothing, and across the land, shows sprang back into life. Auri stared at the dusty radio, now in silence. Throughout Rytter, thousands did the same, blinking slowly at the information given. Some nodded heartily at each other, saying things like, "Well, that all makes sense to me. I shouldn't mind a better night's sleep." Others frowned and shrugged and said, "I thought Rytter was a great land anyway… when did this vote happen?", and some, the old mayor included, wept with their heads in their hands, overwhelmed with feelings of confusion. Their collective thoughts were made up of similar fears; "This has crept up on me, and now I don't see how I can fight it."

Few people recalled the vote taking place.

The clunk of pottery on wood jerked Wendowleen from her sleep. She stared at the mug beside her, blinking slowly. The hair on her head felt damp, and she touched with hesitation, noticing then a white bandage on her forearm.

"Professor Cripcot."

Wendowleen blinked again, noticing a woman sitting on a chair beside the bed. Her features were soft and recognisable. Wendowleen squinted. "Auri?"

The woman shook her head kindly. "No, but the chestnut doesn't fall far from the tree. Auri is my daughter. I am Elegwet. You taught me at university."

Wendowleen did her best to recall, but the images of all those she had taught were hard to distinguish between. She pulled herself up on her good arm, propping the pillows behind her.

Elegwet smiled and handed her the mug from beside her bed. "I'm glad to see that you are recovering well."

Wendowleen noticed Wolf then, curled up and sleeping at the end of the bed, as though nothing had changed. She glanced around the room. The walls were dirt, yes, but intricately decorated with patterns and motifs, and painted in bright yellows and mustards. The bed she sat in was also made of clay, but was as firm and as comfortable as her own. The scent in the air was damp but fresh, like a freshly-cut lawn on a bright sunny day. Perhaps the only thing that was different to above ground was the lack of windows and sunlight. A bulb hung from the centre of the brightly-coloured ceiling and filled the room with warmth.

Elegwet followed her gaze. "Solar-powered. It gives us more than light, of course, we get the goodness now also. Auri worked that out from above ground. She is exceedingly clever."

Wendowleen smiled. "She is."

"How are you feeling?"

"I am not sure. I see my clothes are dry, but –" Wendowleen glanced down at the strange grey tunic that she wore beneath the covers, "Also that they are not my own. What happened?"

Elegwet glanced at Wolf. "He saved your life. The entrance to the welcome tunnel is beneath the water, through the dark circle. As soon as Wolf saw that you were trapped, he swam in to find help. He found us. We haven't had a wolf wander into the partisan's network *ever*. It was not predicted; his barking took us quite by surprise! Anyway, Auri's father swam out to get you. You were unconscious but still alive. You coughed up the water, but we could see that you needed rest."

"In that case, I would like to thank you all. And specifically, Auri's father. Where is he?"

"He is in the kitchens at this time, enjoying a 'celebration beverage'." Elegwet mouthed the word Malt and winked. "You will see him later. I don't doubt it. You must get your strength back first, of course."

Wendowleen took a sip from the mug and raised her eyebrows as the earthy sweet taste filled her mouth. "It's much sweeter than the one above ground."

"That's because we keep our chestnuts in sugar. It stops them from going off so quickly beneath the soil." Elegwet straightened her shoulders, her expression dropping. "Wendowleen, you are here because the Finery is searching for you."

Wendowleen nodded in response, "Yes, I know."

"Do you know *why* they are searching for you?"

"Knowledge is a dangerous thing."

"Yes. It is. But at this time, the knowledge that you hold, specifically, is of great danger to them."

Wendowleen frowned and shook her head. "I can't think what I know that could cause so much trouble."

The wolves tore beyond the borders, and through the earth of Rytter. Finer Bay almost lay on the horizon. Nobody paid the blur of paws and howls much care.

Auri stared at Seneca as he came in and stood quickly. She rushed toward him and then paused hesitantly. "You made it there before the wolves found her?"

Seneca pulled up a chair at the bar and nodded. "Yes. I tried to buy us some time by stopping at Towen along the way. Wendowleen had no idea. Wolf probably knew something wasn't quite right, but he was happy all the same."

Auri sat beside him. "I have not had news from my parents yet. But, they say that no news is good news. She must have made it."

Seneca nodded. "Follow me to the workshop. I want to show you something."

Together the pair stepped into the back of the building, and behind a small staircase, Seneca pushed open a door to the cellar. They both climbed down the steep and thin steps steadily. The light flicked on automatically, sensing their arrival. Seneca pulled a large object covered in a sheet out from the corner and revealed it slowly, the dusty air causing his nose to wrinkle and flare.

Auri blinked slowly and stepped forward. "Seneca, you finished it?"

He nodded silently in response, and the two stared at Wendowleen's hologram with interest. Auri touched the face gently, firm beneath her touch, and the image flickered and then stilled.

"It's good. But we can't release it. They're after her. It'll end up behind bars, or...worse."

The two stared at the fake Wendowleen, who blinked back at them from rest mode.

The man leaned his head against the table and tried to suppress a yawn. His eyes were heavy, and his eyelashes brushed the pages of the book beneath his face. Artomia was not the time to be studying. And, it was his own fault, he knew that. He shouldn't have spent all night up with his friends, or at least, he should have got this essay finished first.

"Right," he murmured into the stale air, lifting his head weakly. He stared at the sparsely-occupied study room of the library. "The War of the Fishmongers," he said aloud.

A young woman at a nearby table glared at him and held her finger to her mouth. He stuck his tongue out in response and waited for her reaction. But it wasn't the reaction he expected. She sat up in her chair and frowned. He put his tongue back in and grimaced back, confused. A hand suddenly weighed heavy on his right shoulder and glanced up to see a member of the Finery standing beside him.

"This establishment is closing in five minutes," the officer announced loudly.

The man tried to move from his grip and coughed. "Excuse me. I have an essay —"

"You have five minutes," the officer responded, resting a hand at his belt. The student followed the movement, stared at the gun, then gathered his bag and queued with the rest of the students to get out of the room.

Outside the university gates, the street seemed to be heaving, despite the holiday season. Students squashed alongside teachers, who stood beside confused caretakers. All stared at the large iron gates as they were closed shut and locked firmly with Ralph's keys. Ralph stood in his hut, door locked against the world, unsure what to do. People yelled and shouted, jeering each other on, some spitting on the ground in protest. Officers watched in dismay. Eventually, one stepped forward, grabbed a bin and turned it upside down. He stepped up and stood on it, staring into the crowd.

"The University of Rytter is closed for the foreseeable future. Anyone who has not dispersed from this place within ten minutes will be arrested."

More jeers flew from the crowd, some words flying through the air easier than others. The officer in charge stared back, and did not flinch as 'asshole' reached his ears. Instead, he smirked, pulled his gun, and fired just above the crowd in one smooth and unjustified moment. They stood shocked for a moment. In the silence, the officer spoke again, but his voice was at a much lower decibel this time. "Disperse."

The people did just that, and moved away from the area at a pace. At the back of the crowd stalked the man with the unwritten essay, striding away with purpose. He turned to the stranger next to him and growled, "No-one even did *anything*. Bunch of bloody cowards!"

Chapter Forty-Five

The wolves were nearing Finer Bay, their paws tingling from the run. Their focus was unlike anything a human could imagine. It was as though they were staring down a microscope, at the end of which a prize was waiting. For each wolf, the prize was slightly different. It was food-based for four of them, at least, but the wolf who held the papers gently in his mouth craved and saw something different. That wolf saw status. The others would not have been able to comprehend such a complex idea.

The elders stared at Wendowleen from their seats, hoods clouding their faces. Wendowleen stared back and nodded, pleased to see some people her age for once. The chair that she was sitting on was hard and clay, yet surprisingly comfortable. Wolf sat patiently beside her.

One spoke, "You had your life saved by a wolf." A couple of glances were thrown Wolf's way, and he sat and wagged his large fluffier-than-usual tail. Some of the partisans had bathed him after his swim, and he was looking a little more like a teddy bear than a wolf.

"Yes, this is my care assistant wolf. Though I know you do not usually allow animals here, I appreciate that the rules have been changed for myself and Wolf."

A few nods from the elders. One spoke, "He won't...do his business anywhere unsanitary, will he?"

"Absolutely not. However, it can make good fertiliser."

"Can it really?" One leaned forward excitedly, "I had heard of horse dung but —"

A few coughs from the other elders finished the sentence, and there was calm once more.

One smiled. "You are safe here, Wendowleen, and welcome."

"Thank you. Yes, life above ground was getting a little stressful."

One nodded. "Your ties with the Mayor were putting you in danger."

Wendowleen frowned and laughed gently. "No, I shouldn't think so. The mayor is ineffectual at best. My relationship with him is a sort of administrative annoyance."

There was a pause in the air, and one of the elders glanced at another.

"We are talking about the new Mayor. The Director of the Finery."

Wendowleen's brow knitted into a complex pattern of wrinkles, and she cocked her head to one side. "Is he the new mayor of Finer Bay? Well, that's a shame. But regardless. I have no real ties with him, his rules are despicable, and his actions are worse, but if I'd met him, I'd be surprised. It is education that he fears. He is, I don't doubt, running every professor the University of Rytter has ever seen out of Finer Bay."

A few nervous coughs filled the room, and one elder murmured in another elder's ear. All seventeen seemed suddenly uncomfortable.

One leaned forward, as though they might pat Wendowleen on the knee had they been closer. "It easy to forget, perhaps, what one once had, when in such trying times."

Wendowleen stared into the partially-hidden face of the elder, and her ears began to burn. "I'm not sure what you mean."

The elder shifted their chair forward slightly and spread their hands. "You know the Director's full name, of course. His real name. Ayin. Ayin Cripcot."

In that instant, the room lurched suddenly to the right, the very foundation of the chair that Wendowleen sat on falling from beneath her. She clutched for the seat in an attempt to stay upright but fell hard against the dirt floor. Wolf stayed low and close to her, whining softly in her ear.

She closed her eyes, her mind flashing with images and bright lights. The empty frame on the landing in her house. The frame she always dreamed of filling. It had once been filled, and she saw it now as clearly as if she had been standing in front of it again. She saw the image. The tables at Artomia, always set for three people. Arthur. And Arthur. Arthur helping her through the door with the shopping, pulling the pram in from the garden, the wheels mudded and brown. Arthur playing in the garden with…Wendowleen's eyes snapped open.

Two elders beside her helped her to the chair and squeezed her hands. Elagwet hurried in, a glass of water in hand, and helped her to sip from it, pulling up a stool so that she could sit beside her. The elders settled in their seats once more.

"There are many potions in the land that can cause illness, forgetfulness, and the like. None is so strong as the power of disbelief. As we age, we become wiser. Our minds clear. We are the oldest of the partisans, and thus we excel the most at predictions. There are thoughts and memories, I'll warrant, coming back to you, that have been slipping for some time. This is something that Ayin expected, though perhaps he did not know you would live so long as to rid him of his power."

Wendowleen stared at the group. "He is my son," she said quietly.

One said, "He is. Do you remember?"

Wendowleen nodded weakly. "He was intelligent."

One agreed. "He was. He still is. But he was not able to handle the rules. People telling him what to do. He stole some of your own work, but it was found to be plagiarised fairly quickly. You tipped off the relevant authorities."

Wendowleen put her hand to her forehead, the memories coming back as though they were being tipped into a sieve and shaken into her mind. She remembered rage. "He said we weren't his parents. Arthur tried to restrain him, but...." She fell into silence.

Elagwet reached out and held her hand gently.

An elder spoke, "Yes. He hurt Arthur. And after that, Ayin found a safe home among the Finery. They love recruits like that – so malleable, so angry. And we think, when Arthur died, following that awful day, you pushed it so far from your mind that it could no longer be found."

"Because I believed it was murder," Wendowleen murmured.

One nodded. "For just cause. But now, when his power is at its greatest – Ayin is afraid. He is afraid that you will remember, come after him, and out him. Out him as a cheat, a liar, a university scholar, and a killer. Perhaps his power is not so finite that he could survive this, for you have the proof. They lie in the restricted part of the library."

Elagwet coughed slightly, and stared at the elders, and then back to Wendowleen. "No, I'm afraid that you do not have them. They weren't in any pockets of your clothes. You must have lost them in the lake."

Wendowleen stared sadly into the dirt ground before her and, for the first time in many, many, years, began to cry. Wolf joined in beside her, resting his head on her knee.

The letters had been prepped, typed up, signed and sent out before Artomia. The Director had planned it carefully, so that they would land on doorsteps after his speech. Indeed, they had actual times printed on them for when they should be dropped through the letterboxes. He smiled. He was feeling better than he had in a *long* time. The world was finally listening. The great things that he would do, that he always knew he *could* do, were finally coming to fruition. The letters would be the first step to creating a happier and more united country. Yes, he expected some angry phone calls (of course, he wasn't a stupid man), but he would simply explain the pros of the situation to the farmers. And that reminded him! He grabbed the receiver of his phone and spoke to his assistant.

"The Rytter post, editor." There was a click.

"Hello?" A tinny voice clambered through the mouthpiece and into his ear.

"Editor Rice, it's the Director."

There was a pause and then a slight cough. "Can I help you?"

"You may. What is your headline for tomorrow? I would *love* to know."

Another pause. "Well, to be frank, it's *You Can Keep Your Curfew*."

The Director grinned. "That won't do. I have something better in mind."

"Yes, I thought you might."

"I think you need to be a little more positive. After all, don't you get some funding from us?"

"Hmmm," the tinny voice said quietly.

"I think something about our streets being safer would be fantastic. Actually, that would be great on the second page. The front should be reserved for the new farm initiative."

"Go on..."

"Oh, I'll let you work out the finer details, Rice. I'll get my assistant to send you one of the letters we've sent out. Essentially, it's this: Everyone – and that includes you – gets a half an acre of land."

There was silence on the other end of the line and then a breath. "I thought there was a housing crisis."

"Yes. There was. That's because of people buying up land and keeping others out. We are offering the farmers a very fair package in exchange for their co-operation. We are offering a six-month delay on their monthly bills."

"A delay?"

"Yes, an interest-free delay. Think of it — land for every person. Land to grow your own food on, keep livestock on — and the like."

"Right. What if they don't want to give up their land? What if I, for example, don't want my half an acre?"

The Director leaned back in his chair and sighed. "Rice, there are times in life when you're given an option, and it's best not to think of the alternative. Not because the alternative is worse, but rather because it would be ill-advised. Do you understand what I'm saying?"

"Yes. I'm afraid I do. And, just so I'm aware, what if I take my alternative option, and go for my original issue of the Post tomorrow?"

The Director sighed. Why did people always try to vex him when he was in a good mood? He shook his head silently and then spoke. "How are your children, Rice?"

The answer was immediate. "Got it."

The Director placed the receiver down and laughed gently. People were so amusing. The things that they could create in their heads could go above and beyond the realms of anything he himself could ever say.

The letters did reach the farmers at the time specified on the envelopes, though, as can be expected, they were not all read immediately. The news reached some before they had even got to their letters, and there was a couple who walked home slowly after talking to the next farm over, hoping and praying that the letter would not be sitting on their mat when they opened the door. All were asked to give acres of their land to someone else. Of course, there were many types of farmer, as there are many types of people, each with their own views. Ruskin, a man in his late sixties, sat beside his husband in the kitchen of their farmhouse and stared out over the seventy-acre land.

"This land has been in my family for generations."

His husband nodded slowly, clutching the letter, but said nothing.

"The thought of looking out of this window at strangers. What do they know of farming? What do they know of grain?"

His husband wavered and shrugged. "They each know something different, I suppose."

Ruskin put his head in his hand. "And the horses. That hurts me most. Ten acres for them alone. We can't give that up – it is essential."

"Not according to this letter, Ruskin. Not according to this. Here – listen – the grazing of non-farm animals is not a legitimate use of an acre." He passed the letter over, and the two stared at it.

"Where will they live?" Ruskin said quietly.

"The horses or the people?"

The two stared in the distance again in stunned stillness. In the gloom, the question turned from being a genuine question, to a rhetorical one. Eventually, Ruskin shifted his chair and broke the muted calm.

"We could protest."

"Hmmm. We could. Burn the barn?"

Ruskin grinned. "That's right. Destroy the land. Burn the barn. But all that's later stuff, right? First things first, we'll write a letter."

A scoff filled the air. Ruskin raised his eyebrows at his husband.

"First letters, first words. Then fire." He stood and strode out of the room, returning quickly with a typewriter in his hands. He placed it onto the large oak table, then sat down before it.

"Okay. So, we begin with the niceties. To Whom It May Concern…"

Ruskin's husband watched him type and nodded.

"We were concerned to receive your recent letter regarding our farmland," Ruskin continued, speaking the words as he typed.

"This farm has been in my family for hundreds of years, and we work hard to improve the local economy and the land with our produce."

"That's right."

"We will not allow our land to be –" Ruskin stared at his husband and frowned. "To be…"

"Divvyed up?"

"Hmm. *Shared amongst strangers.*"

"Yes. And if you do not change your policy, we will come for you, Director."

Ruskin nodded. "Yes. I might leave that bit out for now, though."

"Put it in. Let's find out how serious he really is."

In the towns around Rytter, other letters were beginning to arrive. These were letters with coordinates on. The Director had ensured that the farmland was already diverged, so that once the inevitable questions from farmers came rolling in, he could tell them precisely what was happening with the nation's land. As with the farmers, the letters were being reacted to in varied ways. Some were excited, willing their try their hand at toiling in the field, working the soil, and had always fancied owning a goat, now that you mention it. And, didn't your Aunt Patricia still have that sheepdog she was trying to get rid of? That sort of thing could be helpful on a farm, that could.

The letter landed on the desk of Rosalie, a local teacher in Snorington. She had just put down the phone after a chat with her nephew about the University of Rytter being put on 'hiatus'. Rosalie knew that this was her nephew's word and darkly suspected that the closure was more of a permanent fix.

Her stomach dropped as she thought of her little school and the five hundred students she helped to teach. She ripped open the envelope in one movement and read it carefully.

Rosalie saw, as many did (and many did not), the real meaning behind the words. Had she put it into a letter for her nephew, she would have changed almost all the content to say what it really meant, they are taking people's possessions, land, and homes. They have given me a section, a responsibility which, I suspect, may surpass the one at my school.

Rosalie stared at the small plant that sat dying in her window and breathed in.

"And I, who does not know how to grow a thing, who does not understand about the quality of soil or the processes of farming, am to be given this. What sense does it make?"

She reread the letter, and, this time, focussed her attention on the words. They would provide her with some limited farming equipment and seeds, to begin with. As she reached the end of the letter, she realised that there was an accompanying page. She turned to it hastily. It was a graph. Data set out expectations for growth and danced across the page. There was a tonnage of grain that her land was expected to provide to the government 'and the people'. Surely, this wasn't right? She picked up the receiver of her telephone and quickly dialled the operator.

"Hello, yes. I'd like to speak to Snorington Mayor, please."

There was a buzz and a click. "Good day, Snorington Council. How can I help?" A voice drifted down the line.

"I'd like to speak to the Mayor, please."

There was a pause of uncertainty. "I'm afraid that you have come through to the wrong place. The Mayor resides in Finer Bay, and can be reached on the following —"

"No, Snorington Mayor."

"I'm afraid that the person you are referring to no longer works here." Then the voice suddenly dropped in professionalism and turned into a whisper down the line. "There is only one

Mayor now. Finer Bay."

The line went dead. Rosalie placed down the receiver and stared back at the dying plant.

"What are we going to do?" she hissed at it. It didn't respond.

Chapter Forty-Six

The wolves had reached the Finery headquarters and sat in front of the Director's desk, a member of the FWT next to them. He stared at the papers that had been presented to him and nodded.

"So – she is dead?"

The FWT officer nodded. "Yes. The wolves do not return until they have done their duty."

"I see. You are dismissed."

The officer blew a short and sharp blast from her whistle, and the wolves stood and trotted to the door. The Director shivered. That wolf at the front had given him the creeps. He was staring at him in such a way that made his blood harden. He knew that the wolves were highly trained and would never just attack for no reason, but there was something in that wolf's eyes. Ambition. A lack of fear. You needed a lack of fear to deal with his mother, he thought. Those cold, grey eyes were the last to see her. He saw her then, a flash of memory, preparing for Artomia before his father came home. She was excited, her short, squat frame lingering over the steaming pot in the kitchen, the heat wilting the paper decorations hanging from the cupboards, laughter dancing through the dusty air. He felt his mouth twitch at the corners, hearing himself chatting beside her. Excitement, joy, the feeling of removing his winter socks and placing his warm feet alongside hers on the tiled kitchen floor. "When Artomia comes, Ayin, we'll open all the windows." A simple pleasure they both rejoiced in, moving through the house among a gentle warm breeze. The Director, pulling himself from his dreamlike state, pushed the image of his mother far away. *Bury it. Bury it with paperwork.* There was nothing inside the Director that could be referred to as 'remorse'. Rather, it was his complete lack of empathy for others that had enabled him to gain, and hold onto, his position in life. Numbness. That was the gift he had been given, and the gift that enabled him to thrive. Memories of good times occasionally came, but there was no longing that accompanied them. A longing for a cold, tall house with two of the 'educated' watching his every move? There was nothing desirable there.

The Director sat in his chair and then picked up a paper on his desk. Updates about the recruitment drive. It was going well, it seemed. He had decided to reduce the age of admission, and this had been a popular move. Children loved to be a part of something, especially when it had uniforms. He leaned back and thought of his childhood again, of staring out of the window at officers, longing for the long leather boots to be his own. His mother would never let him play, never let him have ambition. And his father. Both the same. Any life without a university education was a life wasted.

Auri sat at the bar, watching Seneca gaze out of the window. There was a feeling in the air and on the streets that made everyone feel uneasy. It was a strange pulsing throughout the land, a type of anticipation merged with fear, an iota of excitement dropped in for good measure.

She turned to her cards, laid them out before her, and smiled. The lines merged and switched and then settled into the shape of a key. Auri turned back to Seneca.

"Wendowleen is safe," she said.

Seneca turned and smiled sadly. "I am pleased. There is a strange sight on the streets, more Finery than usual."

"Yes. The curfew begins tonight. They are there to make sure everyone knows about it."

Seneca rolled his eyes and pulled the heavy curtains across, causing the room to dim. "Adults told when to go to bed."

"That's right. And during Artomia too," Auri agreed, reaching across the bar for a bottle of malt. "Still," she said, "it isn't like we go out all the time. We rarely go out, do we?"

Seneca watched as she poured small amounts into two glasses and sighed. "It isn't the going out, to be honest, it's the being told we *can't* go out. It makes me want to throw a street party or something, go dancing, paint the town red. All the things I usually avoid."

"That's exactly it." Auri held a glass up for Seneca, and they clinked the two together lazily.

Wendowleen sat with Eglawet in her tiny kitchen, shifting dried nuts and vegetables around her plate with a fork. Elagwet had tried her best to lift Wendowleen's mood, but it remained heavy.

"Do you know, I've had these peculiar thoughts for such a long time that I just thought it was a type of madness? Phrases just swimming around my head, day after day. Like "There has been a murder." – That used to pop into my head at the strangest times. And it turns out that it was a different sort of madness that I was experiencing all along. A madness of forgetting. Of choosing to forget. How could I do such a thing to Arthur?"

Eglawet placed a hand gently on Wendowleen's arm. "You did what you had to do to protect yourself, to keep going. It wasn't your fault. And he was your son. Arthur surely would have just wanted you to stay safe."

Wendowleen shook her head. "I should have gotten help. Had Ayin arrested. And how did I bring up a child to have such a hatred for his parents?"

Eglawet sighed. "These things are not always linked to the way someone is cared for. You need to forgive yourself. You tried your best." She stared at the peas on the plate before her. "There is no way of knowing what goes on in somebody's head. We can only be responsible for our own actions."

Wendowleen looked at Eglawet sideways. "Do you know what it is that the partisans have predicted for his future?"

Eglawet nodded. "I do. Truthfully, Wendowleen, there are two dominant schools of thought, and the elders are divided over each. I cannot go into too much detail. You have already been through a lot today. Perhaps it would be best to take a rest."

Wendowleen stared at the uneaten food before her and then picked up the plate and carefully put it on the floor beside her. Wolf stood immediately and began to chew on the leftovers. Vegetables, while not his favourite, would still do. She paused and then glanced at Eglawet. "Oh – I hope you don't take offence. That's quite normal for us."

Eglawet laughed, "Oh no, just be yourself. This is your home too, now."

"What a funny thought. Eglawet, you must tell me if there is anything that I can do to help. I brought Ayin into this world. I am responsible – whatever anyone says – for the mess that he creates."

"You are not responsible for him any more than I am, Wendowleen. Auri and Seneca will be finishing your hologram. And once that's done, you can step into the world once more, but safely. What you can do to help the land of Rytter, I do not know. Only time will tell how much needs to be done."

The partisans had indeed foreseen two futures. One was a future similar to the past, a tale of how their forefathers and foremothers had lived. This was passed down through partisan books and songs and recalled by the eldest of the elders as a memory, although none of them had ever lived it. The songs were sung at Artomia, the most popular being *And lo, the grass is growing.*

As Wendowleen lay in bed hours later, she heard the song drifting through the walls and along the corridors. She had never heard it before and watched as Wolf pricked his ears back and forth to the rhythm of the lyrics.

The fire you built is dying down,
The frost laden branch is bowing,
The earth is welcoming your embrace,
And lo, the grass is growing.

The time has come for planting seeds,
The river swift is flowing,
Of winter, you will find no trace,
And lo, the grass is growing.

So rush out you, go rush, go rush,
For nature is bestowing
Her gifts to you, her greenest grace,
And lo, the grass is growing.

Wendowleen closed her eyes to the gentle singing and breathed in deeply, the earthy scent of her room still not familiar enough to disappear into the known. She drifted off to sleep, Wolf by her side, and dreamed of the sprouting buds of Artomia.

The other future that the partisans had seen was not one of songs and joy. It was a future that they had been hiding from for a long time and one that had been predicted at the start of their way of life. Indeed, it was the very reason they lived underground. Persecution happens the lands over, in all sorts of societies and creations by humans. The one that they saw in Rytter was no different to many. Darkness was predicted, and the weight of the prediction rested on the shoulders of all of the elders. They saw the Director smiling in his high office, the people of the land wailing in the streets below, begging for the simple pleasures of life: food, independent choice, to love whom they chose to love. These things taken for granted were soon to be whipped away, and those who saw it coming were powerless to combat it alone. And there, the partisans saw, was the problem. If each person felt alone in their discomfort, nothing could be done. They needed to come together as a unit. But these things are not organised easily, especially with the watchful eye of the Finery hanging above you. Some predictions said that it would take years for the courage to build, for the people to find a way to come together. Some predictions said it would take a lifetime.

Wendowleen slept, not knowing any of this for sure. Of course, she had her suspicions. But she had something else too. Wendowleen had a knowledge of the people that the partisans did not, and her faith in them was unwavering.

Chapter Forty-Seven

In The Switched Dragon, the favourite haunt of university staff and students alike, the Vice-Chancellor stared at his malt and breathed in, hard. He'd had that job for the last eight years. That was nothing to sniff at. He sniffed again, despite this thought. A student sitting beside him glanced over and sighed, nursing her own drink in her hands. The barman stood between them, cleaning a glass distractedly.

"You two are a chipper pair of chaps tonight."

"Hmmm?" the Vice-Chancellor responded, eyes lifting slowly.

"Is it to do with the curfew? Because let me tell you, informing a bar with one day to go that there will be no customers after eigh –"

"No. The university has been closed down," interrupted the student sullenly.

The Vice-Chancellor nodded and took a long sip of malt.

"Is that right? Today is a bad day for all, then," the barman grimaced.

"They're crooks," said the student.

The Vice-Chancellor shook his head. "No, they're following orders. He's a crook. The Director. He's the crook."

"Well, they're not bloody welcome in this establishment from now on," said the barman, "and believe me, we get enough of them in here."

"But this can't be the end, can it? The end of a university education? I mean...that can't be the evil in the world. It's education," the Vice-Chancellor murmured.

"My cousin is in the Finery," the student said quietly, embarrassed at her admittance, "and he *hates* the education on offer in Rytter. Says it's all the wrong stuff."

The barman continued to wipe the glass in his hand, despite it being as dry as the earth outside. "The wrong stuff. So what's the right stuff?"

"Farming and that," answered the student. "Animal breeding. And politics."

The Vice-Chancellor rolled his eyes. "We teach that stuff."

"Yes. But you probably don't teach in the way the Director wants it to be taught," the student said.

"Well, I could tell you some stuff about him," the Vice-Chancellor responded loudly.

"You might want to keep your voice down, sir," the barman hissed. "There are ears everywhere." He shot a warning look at the pair. They sat in silence for a moment, the smell of malt crackling around their nostrils.

The curfew was starting in half an hour. Shining boots patrolled the pavements, the heavy click of heels sending children scattering into their homes, where their guardians stood, watching the streets with interest. A few of the officers had loudspeakers and occasionally yelled into them, negating their point. On Wendowleen's old street, the neighbours stood in their gardens, watching curiously from fences and walkways. Everyone wanted to know the same thing; just how serious was this curfew business anyway?

Wendowleen's immediate neighbour wandered idly over to his own neighbour on the other side, and nodded at a member of the Finery marching past.

"What do you think of this then, Clowder?"

"Not much Keuy, not much at all. You?"

"Oh no." Keuy shook his head and then paused. "Well, I say oh no, but then there is a bit of me that thinks, "Well, at least any ruffians will be kept away.""

"Ruffians," said Clowder, trying on the word for size. "You sound older than your years."

Keuy sniffed and raised an eyebrow. "Well, we can't all think the same. My old mother used to say, "A garden of awatoprams would be boring.""

Clowder glanced sideways. "I think it'd be quite nice, all that gold. Anyway, no one grows awatoprams like the Professor over there. Before she had her garden paved over anyway. Odd decision. You seen her lately?"

Keuy shifted slightly in his shoes, feeling uncomfortable. He hadn't told anybody about his last conversation with Wendowleen, especially the neighbours. They were all guilty of doing the wrong thing, as far as he could make out. He glanced at Clowder, who was now giving him her full attention, including a good dose of hands of the hips.

"I don't know anything," he said eventually.

Clowder stared at him. "I haven't seen her for a long while, now that I think of it. A good long while. In fact…"

"What?" Keuy asked suspiciously.

"I'm going to ask this officer chap to check on her now."

Clowder stepped to the front of her garden and raised her hand, waving it in the air. "Officer! Officer! Could you help us please?"

The Finery member turned and strode toward them, heels clicking on the pavement. He arrived and saluted, a move that made Keuy unexpectantly want to giggle.

"Officer, would you do us a kindness and check on our elderly neighbour? We haven't seen her in a while, and we're a little concerned."

The officer glanced between the two neighbours, face unmoving. "You don't have long to be out, you know."

Clowder rolled her eyes. "Yes, officer, I'm aware of that. Are you able to check on her or not?"

"What's her name?"

"Professor Cripcot. Just that house there, next to Keuy."

The officer shrugged and strode over to the house in silence. Keuy and Clowder watched from their gardens. He knocked sharply on the door and called out, "Miss Cripcot! Are you in?"

Clowder rolled her eyes again and hissed at Keuy, "I don't know what on earth is wrong with those people; they can't force themselves to use an academic title in any circumstance."

After a moment, they saw the door open. The officer stood in conversation for a minute and then saluted once more. He strode back to the neighbourly pair with purpose and authority.

"That was one of her lodgers. She's moved away."

Clowder started. "She's moved away? But Prof has lived in that same place for…oh well, as long as my own mother can remember."

The officer stared at her with a look of disapproval, his eyelids heavy and low. "You have one minute to get back into your houses. Enough gossiping. This is the very reason a curfew has been given."

"I thought it was to keep us safe from ruffians," said Keuy, matter of factly.

The officer frowned. "From what?"

"From ruffians, he said," responded Clowder.

The officer stepped up to Keuy's garden fence, until they were almost toe to toe, apart from the wooden divide. "You're using a word that I don't know, and I take that to be an insult."

"You're insulted by words you don't know?" asked Keuy, trying not to let amusement slide across his face.

"That's right. Now you ought to step back into that house before I reach for backup."

Keuy saw the officer's hand move to hover over his right hip and stepped back automatically. He nodded and turned to the house, walking quickly. Clowder stepped back too, moving a little slower, glancing behind her at the officer the entire time. One safely in their houses, Clowder dialled Keuy's number.

"I *told* you not to use the word ruffians."

The Vice-Chancellor had begun to slur his words. He had just finished his third malt, and the barman's worried warnings were no longer being listened to. He checked his watch and leaned toward the Vice-Chancellor.

"Listen – everyone has left to adhere to this bloody curfew. I'm happy to stay open because – guess what – I live upstairs, so technically, I am breaking no rules, but you, sir, should be aware that they'll be coming in at any minute. Try and keep it together; that's all I'm asking."

The Vice-Chancellor glared at the barman and shook his head. "It's eight in the evening. That's barely even the beginning."

The student, slightly less drunk but certainly not sober, glanced around the room. "Everyone's gone. The beginning of what?"

"Evening," said the Vice-Chancellor.

As the barman had predicted, the door of The Switched Dragon burst open. In strode two officers. They stared around the empty tables and chairs, the dying embers on the fire, and then focused on the three figures at the bar.

"There's a new curfew – this bar must be closed immediately," said one of them, striding over.

The Vice-Chancellor spun around wildly on his stool and pointed his glass at them. "You and your bloody men!"

"Oh, it's the VC!" one officer said to the other, grinning. "It's the VC. Here, shame about your job, isn't it?"

"That's right," said the other officer, clicking to the other side of the bar. "What'll you do now, VC? You could get a job with us if you hadn't a degree. Perhaps you'll have to do something *menial.*"

The VC growled as his eyes followed them and then bellowed to the group. "Your own bloody Director came to our university – you do know that don't you?"

The officers stared at him, amused. The barman reached a hand over to his shoulder and patted him gently. "He's had a bit much to drink, that's all. We don't need any trouble."

One of the officers frowned and stepped closer toward the Vice-Chancellor, hand hovering over his left hip. "He did not attend university. That's a lie."

"He bloody did! Kicked out for being stupid enough to plagiarise from his own mo –"

As quickly as the student and the barman could blink, they saw the Vice-Chancellor fall to the floor. The officer closest to him twirled the long baton around his hand and then glanced at the red smudge on it, wrinkling his nose. He stared at the two curfew breakers that remained and asked, "Anything to add?"

The barman, having dealt with many fights over the last few years, and knowing when to cut his losses, shook his head firmly. He tried to encourage the student to do the same with his eyes but instantly sensed that she wasn't going to. He saw it happen in slow motion. She stood up, squaring her shoulders, and opened her mouth to speak. No sound came out. There was a dull 'thunk' as the baton made contact with her head, and she fell onto the tiled floor.

The barman put his head in his hands and breathed out the words, "Oh gods."

He knew before he had even begun to move, the danger of what he was about to do. And yet, there was something within him that couldn't seem to stop. It was as though the world was momentarily moving at a lumbering pace, and he was only watching his actions, as opposed to being in control of them. His hands dropped to his sides, and he stared at the two men, who stared back. He leaned against the bar, giving the pair an apologetic smile, his right hand resting just beneath. He began to say something, and what it was he couldn't quite make out, something mundane about curfews and laws, the words spilling from his lips in slow motion. His hand touched the barrel of the cold metal first, and he grabbed it firmly. He stepped back, pulling the hammer of the pistol back with his thumb. He aimed it at the officer with the baton, but stared at the other.

"I will shoot you if you reach for your weapons again."

The officer with the baton stared. "I have the power to kill, sir, in the face of disobedience."

"I will shoot both of you before you can even think of it. I've got awards." He gestured upwards with his head, and the officers glanced up quickly, to see a row of trophies above the bottles. "Those are my shooting trophies. Best in Finer Bay."

The officer beside the bar glowered. "You are in so much trouble."

"Funny that, I'm the one holding the gun. Give me a minute," said the barman. "MAMA!" he yelled, causing the officers to glance at each other.

A voice came singing from another room, "Yes, love?"

"Come in here a moment and help me, will you?"

An old, grey-haired woman with rosy cheeks appeared at the door. She was wearing pyjamas. She stood and surveyed the scene.

"Well, this is a bit of a mess. Let me fetch my gun," she said merrily, shuffling back out again.

The barman winked at the officers. "It was Mama who taught me how to shoot."

Chapter Forty-Eight

There were a couple of seconds across the entire city of Finer Bay that coincided with the barman's decision that were unlike other seconds. They stretched into more prolonged periods of time, as though a second and a minute had no variation. People stood behind their doors, wondering why they were suddenly inside without that pint of cream they had been on their way to get from the shops. Some sat in pyjamas on their sofas, and felt a sudden and overwhelming urge to stand up, and leave the house. Others watched their cats trot out of cat flaps, intrigued by this turn of events that meant that their pets had more freedom than they did.

A woman dressed in her coat and shoes was standing at the front door, just about to pop out to get a loaf of bread for the morning. Her husband came thumping down the stairs and paused.

"What are you up to?"

"Oh, popping to the shops before they close. We're all out of bread."

"Well, you can't. The new curfew starts tonight."

There was a silence as the woman remembered this. She frowned. "Well, what are we supposed to do for bread?"

"I don't know." Her husband shrugged. "We'll have to get some tomorrow instead."

"That's an absolute faff. I want my toast for breakfast."

"I don't know what to tell you," said her husband, continuing his thud down the steps and walking past her into the kitchen.

"Well," sniffed the woman to the empty hallway. "Sod that."

She pulled open the door and poked her head out curiously. The street seemed empty enough, and despite knowing that the shop would probably be closed under the new rules, there was just a slight feeling that forced her to step out into the world. She moved quickly up her driveway and glanced around, and then noticed someone across the road doing the same. She grinned and then tottered over.

"Hello! A little bit naughty, aren't we!"

The neighbour stood with their arms crossed, brow furrowed. "I'm not having it."

"No!" said the woman, enthused, "Neither am I."

"I'm not having it either!" A voice flew past them, and they turned in unison to see another neighbour striding toward them.

"Well – that makes three of us. So let's wake up the street – what do you say?"

The Director sat at his desk before his head of staff and smiled broadly.

"Good," he said, "I'm pleased."

"Yes, sir, the entire city has taken the curfew in their stride. A few of the younger officers are out checking on the pubs."

The Director's grin dipped slightly, and he frowned. "A few of the *younger* officers are dealing with the pubs? Is that wise? Who had that idea? I don't remember saying that."

Bob coughed awkwardly. "We don't predict any trouble, sir. We thought it would be a good experience for them. Also, it shows the people in general that any officer is to be listened to."

The Director shook his head briefly. "I want an immediate check on the pub closures. You do understand what goes on inside a pub, don't you? The *first* night of curfew – the first night – requires some very careful treading. That's what I told you, isn't it?"

"Yes sir," Bob gulped noisily, "but I did think —"

"When people drink, their confidence rises. They forget all those silly little things like laws and rules and who is in charge. I cannot comprehend your stupidity. And WHAT," the Director's volume suddenly shot in the air, causing Bob to jump in his chair, "ARE YOU STILL DOING HERE?"

Bob scattered out of the room, leaving the Director staring at the desk before him, eyes lit with rage. The stupidity of his staff left much to be desired. He pinched his nose with his forefingers, closing his eyes. He could see it now, crowds of drunken louts arguing with young recruits. And the young recruits were always trigger happy. Always excited to be in uniform, desperate to show off their newfound power. He thought that there might be some trouble tonight, expected it really, as anyone with half a mind would. He hadn't suspected the problem would result from the ineptitude of a high-ranking member of his own staff, though.

"Ahem," a soft voice murmured from the doorway. The Director opened his eyes to see Sylvia, poking her head around the corner.

"What do you want?" he said sharply.

"Just wanted to ask you something." She walked into the room slowly. "So sit down. I don't have much time."

"All right." Sylvia sat on the chair before the desk, noticing the warmth that Bob had left behind. "It's about Wendowleen. Has she been found at all?"

The Director stared at his aunt and nodded. "Yes. She has gone the way of my father, I'm afraid."

Sylvia stared at him in silence. The silence filled the air in the room so completely that the Director gave a slight shudder as though that might break the spell. He matched Sylvia's stare and then cleared his throat.

"Is that all?"

"Ayin," she said softly.

"Do not call me that," he growled in response.

"Your parents loved you. Tell me that you know that your parents loved you."

The Director stared at Sylvia in disbelief. She raised her eyebrows in a challenge, and he shook his head.

"You have some nerve."

"Well," she said, spreading her hands calmly. "We share the same blood. I told myself that if you informed me that Wendowleen had passed, I would no longer be afraid of your threats. That was your mother. You said that she would be taken into a care home. You said that once I had checked on her and made sure her memory was okay, she would be taken care of."

"She was taken care of," the Director responded, his eyes hard and glaring. "And if you continue to speak to me in this manner, as though you have forgotten who I am, I'll deal with you in the same way as I did your brother."

Sylvia's eyebrows crumpled, and she leaned forward. "Arthur died of a heart attack."

The Director paused, and then nodded slowly. "I have tried to be fair," he said in a low voice. "I have done my best to be as thoughtful as a nephew might be to an aunt, despite your best efforts to thwart every situation in which you may have helped *me*."

Sylvia fluttered her hand as though waving away a fly, signalling that his words meant nothing. "Ayin. Arthur died of a heart attack. Didn't he?"

The Director glowered at her, his top lip curling in anger. "You don't listen to me, do you, Sylvia? I told you to stop calling me that. That is not my name. That name belonged to somebody very different."

"I know it did," said Sylvia, plainly. "It did. It belonged to a young boy who used to be excited when I visited his house. It belonged to somebody who had respect for their elders, who cared that his mother and father worked hard to provide him with everything he wanted. They *loved* you. You have no idea how much they *longed* for you. When you arrived, every day was Artomia. You were their glory, Ayin; you were everything."

The Director shook his head slowly, his right-hand quivering. It moved quicker than Sylvia could comprehend, and in a flash, produced a pistol. He stood, aiming it at her head.

"I asked you not to call me that."

Sylvia stared into her nephew's eyes. She raised her eyebrows and took a breath. "So what are you waiting for, Ayin? You'll only kill your last surviving family member."

The Director's finger didn't hesitate over the trigger. Sylvia fell as the last syllables sprung from her mouth. Blood washed over the floor, and the Director turned away, picking up the receiver of his phone.

"Yes. Code 4, my office."

He slammed the telephone back down and stared at the wall. He had asked her, he thought to himself, not to call him that. If one person shows power over you, you eliminate them from the equation. That was the simple mathematics of leadership.

The three neighbours re-joined in their empty street, this time armed with pots and pans. One of them had strapped a wok to his chest and wore a saucepan on his head, while clutching wooden spoons. They stared at each other and nodded, and then in silent agreement, began to bang their collective kitchen apparatus.

"No Curfew for Us!" one shouted, and the others glanced at them in approval.

"Join Us Against the Curfew!"

Windows began to open, at first in irritation, but then in curiosity.

"Here, here!" an old man yelled from the top of a house.

Residents cagily began to move out of their front doors, pots and pans in hand. Children leapt out of bed, grinning from ear to ear, excited at this astonishing turn of events, and the authorisation of misbehaviour. A crowd formed quickly, and they began to march down the street, shoulders squared and chins high. The noise of the ruckus seeped through the populace of Finer Bay, crept between the cracks of their front doors, and in no time at all, the crowd grew larger and larger.

Chapter Forty-Nine

"He's a bit of a jobsworth him — but I'm not so much," the officer said with a grim smile, blinking apologetically at the barman and his mother. His wrists were beginning to ache from the twine wrapped around them, his shoulders sore from his arms being pulled back and secured behind a chair. He glanced at his colleague, who sat in the same situation, and frowned.

"Your mate is quick to denounce you, isn't he?" said the barman to the quiet officer, interested.

There was no discernible response, just a hard sniff. The barman's mother took a sip from her glass of chestnut sherry with her free hand, the other on a rifle that was pointing at the two members of the Finery. Once she had come back with her gun, it had been relatively easy for the barman to secure them. They had turned into 'docile youngsters', as his mother had put it. The barman knelt beside the Vice-Chancellor and the student, checking their pulses.

"You've knocked them out," he said, "but I think they'll be all right. I've dealt with enough bar fights in my time." He stood and moved toward his mother before sitting on a barstool.

"So, you've chosen a life of indiscriminate skull smashing. Is that what you wanted to be as a child?" he asked.

The officer who had done the smashing grunted and stared at the floor. The other officer, who had already declared himself not to be a jobsworth, cocked his head to one side, considering this question.

"Do you know," he said, "I always fancied being a vet, actually. Loved animals. Still do. We had all sorts back home when I was growing up."

"Oh?" said the barman's mother. "Well, it's never too late to try. After all, I retrained as a midwife after I had him. And I had him when I was forty-odd."

"That's right, that's right. So you did," said the barman.

The ambitious officer shook his head and shrugged as best he could with his arms tied behind the chair. "Nope. Once you join the Finery, you can't up and leave. That's one of the rules. There are plenty of rules, but that's one of the most unbreakable, I reckon."

"So, if you wanted to be a vet, why did you join the Finery?" asked the barman, leaning forward with genuine interest.

"Couple of things, I suppose. First of all, my dad was sick. My mom's salary was a pittance, really, given that I've got nine younger siblings. My dad couldn't work anymore, and times were getting a little tight. And then a Finery recruitment drive came to my school one day, and they said they were accepting anyone aged fifteen and up, so I figured that everyone could benefit from that. I send my wages home to the family, back in Towen. And the Finery give you board and meals and things. It's not so bad, really."

The barman's mother shifted the muzzle of her rifle from pointing to him to aiming at the surly jobsworth and smiled kindly. "Oh, so you're a good boy, really. Sending your wages home like that. What you coming in here and shooting your mouth off for then?"

"Well, it's part of the job, ma'am. I don't mean to be rude or anything. I'm sure if we met under altered circumstances, it might be different, but intimidation is part of the training. Some of us," he glanced sideways at his colleague, "take to it better than others."

They all stared at the jobsworth for a moment in silence. He raised his head and stared back at the barman, then muttered, "Keeping an officer against his will is punishable by death."

The comment hung in the air like a polluted wind, and the barman raised his eyebrows and yawned slightly. "Being a vet would be an interesting job, I reckon, meeting a different animal every hour."

"Oh yes," the officer said enthusiastically, pleased to move on from the unfortunate comment his colleague had uttered. "I've high hopes for my little sister, actually, in that field. She's very smart. She'll be able to get the right grades at one of the new schools."

"At one of *what* new schools?" asked the barman's mother.

The officer opened his mouth and then closed it, frowning. He stared at the glass that held the woman's sherry. They all followed his gaze and watched with interest as the liquid began to pulse from the centre, sending ripples and waves flowing to the sides of the vessel. The clean mugs stacked together on the bar started to clink to the same rhythm.

The barman stared at his mother and frowned. "What on earth is that noise?"

Auri and Seneca had gone to bed early, in need of some rest. Seneca had, of course, not slept during his delivery of Wendowleen to the partisans, and Auri had stayed awake should she be needed at any time. Both rested in their beds uneasily, looming threats and predictions preying on their unconscious thoughts.

Auri was the first to hear the noise. The dull wave of thudding and clanging shook her from her slumber, and she blinked into the darkness. It continued, getting louder by the second. She swiftly got out of the bed and hurried to the window. There she saw the first of the crowd, moving through the street. The windows in the houses opposite The Malted Mash sprang open, and Auri watched her neighbours consider the furore. She pulled her own window open and stuck her head out, feeling the cool breeze wind around her ears. Doors began to open down the street, and figures launched themselves into a march, joining the protest.

"DOWN WITH THE CURFEW!"

"RESPECT OUR INDEPENDENCE!"

Shouts reached Auri's ears, and she grinned widely. She turned, grabbing her cloak and wrapping it around her. She pulled open her door and stepped into the dim hallway.

"Seneca!"

He came out of his room almost immediately, coat already on.

"You have seen?" she asked him.

"Yes. Let's go."

"Ah, but first," she said excitedly, "we fetch the hologram."

Together they took to the stairs, winding and flying downwards at speed until they reached the workhouse. Auri dragged the sheet from Wendowleen's hologram, and they stared at it for a moment.

"She hasn't logged in yet," Seneca shouted, trying to make himself heard over the din from outside.

Auri nodded. "No, but she will. I think we should still take it. I have a feeling."

Seneca smiled. "You have predicted something."

"I have. But we mustn't dwell on it right now." Auri lifted Wendowleen's hologram up by the arms, indicating that Seneca should do the same. "Except to say," she continued, "that it is as predicted."

Seneca took the other arm, and the two picked the fake Wendowleen up and pulled her up the steps, and to the front door. They stepped out sideways and stared at the protesters. There seemed to be hundreds. They heaved through the street, making space for each other, laughing and grinning. There were people with children on their shoulders, children holding their pets, adults in pyjamas, and smartly dressed proud folk in their best clothing. Some ate popcorn as they walked. Others held up banners and signs, as though they had had all the time in the world to prepare for this moment. Their marching fell into a rhythm, the pots and pans banged continuously. Auri smiled excitedly at Seneca, and the three joined the throng, the eyelids of Wendowleen's hologram falling and opening with each step forward.

Chapter Fifty

The farmers dropped the typed letter addressed to the Director into the post box down their road at around twenty past eight in the evening. They weren't too worried about the curfew; officers, and in general, people, weren't often seen down their street. It was farmland for miles. They sauntered back up the country road to their house, silent in nature. The sun was dipping in the sky, the familiar sound of cricket legs rubbing together enhancing their steps.

"That bit we wrote at the end of that letter. We might be in a little trouble over that," said Ruskin.

"Hmmm," his husband responded, non-committedly.

They continued the short stroll in quiet, and as they reached the farmhouse, Ruskin paused. The telephone was ringing from inside, tinny trills that sent panic through his legs.

"Bit late for a call," his husband said, confirming Ruskin's own thoughts exactly.

They rushed in through the door and pushed it open, Ruskin grabbing the phone.

"Hello?" he said, breathing a little quickly.

"Ruskin! It's your aunt down the way – now listen here, they're marching on the headquarters in Finer Bay!"

Ruskin raised his eyebrows and turned his mouth down at his husband, quietly mouthing the words he had just been told.

"Ruskin! Pay attention!" a screech came down the line.

"Yes, aunt."

"They're starting to gather here – in the main square. So just you come and pick me up! I'm not missing out on this."

"Well, we're not driving to Finer Bay, not at this hour."

"No, no, you daft – no, they're flouting the new curfew, that's what it's about. And let me tell you, I didn't fight to be single my whole life just to have a man tell me what time to go to bed! That's the *very* thing I've always been against. So get your butt in that cart and Pick. Me. Up."

The line went dead. Ruskin laughed and took his husband by the shoulders.

"Let's tack up Jessie. We're off to town!"

Wendowleen woke from a deep sleep in one sudden movement. Her eyes blinked open slowly, and stared at the earthen wall before her.

"Wendowleen," said a man's voice beside her. She turned to see the speaker and was surprised to find a strikingly familiar man standing beside her bed. Wolf yawned beside him, seemingly no longer frightened of strangers.

"I am Auri's father, Eglawet's husband. My name is Reuel."

Wendowleen shifted herself into a sitting position and smiled kindly. "Hello, Reuel. I have wanted to meet you. I must thank you for saving my life." She touched her bandaged arm absent-mindedly.

Reuel smiled and bowed his head, saying nothing in response. Wendowleen hesitated.

"Can I help you at all?"

"Yes, I am sorry to disturb your slumber. The elders would like you to log on to your hologram – it appears that there is some activity before the eyes, and it would be immoral for them to view it alone without you."

Wendowleen did her best to stifle a yawn and nodded. "Of course. Yes. I'll just need a minute to right myself. Which way will…?"

"I shall wait for you, outside the door." Reuel gave a short bow of the head and left, closing the wooden door behind him.

She pushed her legs out of bed and did her best to dress quickly, Wolf watching her sleepily the whole time. She stared at him for a moment before lacing her shoes.

"We'll not get a minute's rest, will we Wolf?"

He whined quietly in response, his ears flattened, as though the very act of pricking them forward was far too much to deal with at this moment in time.

Reuel was, as he had promised, waiting for Wendowleen outside her door. He led her down the winding walkways, filled with their colourful paint and scent of grass, pointing at various turns on the way and explaining briefly what each led to.

"It is a rabbit warren when first you arrive, that's true enough. But you soon learn the way. Shortcuts are hard to come by, I'm afraid. There is either the way, or there is not."

Eventually, they reached a large oak door, and Reuel knocked on it once. A muffled voice from within allowed them access, and he pushed the heavy door open with some effort, motioning that Wendowleen should step forward.

She did her best not to exclaim aloud when she saw the beauty of the room before her. A giant oak tree filled the centre, roots spreading throughout the tremendous circular room and creating different elements. Some roots had shaped into armchairs, and a few of the elders sat in them, reading. Other roots held books in lines, as though the tree had understood the purpose of a bookshelf and really wanted to help. Around the walls, picture frames were held in place by branches and roots, curled around the edges of the image. And there, in the middle of the tree, was a series of screens, before which sat three elders, murmuring to each other beneath their breath.

The three elders turned around and ushered Wendowleen in-between them, offering her a chair formed of roots. She sat down before the screens and smiled awkwardly. The screens burst into life before her, all being used for the same single image. It appeared to be a crowd, but the picture kept dipping and diving, going blank and then springing into colour. Wendowleen leaned forward in interest, as an elder handed her a soft rubber hat, covered in sticky purple circles. Her attention was briefly taken from the screens, and she stared at it.

"Put it on your head, and you will be able to control your hologram," the elder said softly.

Wendowleen followed her orders and pulled the strange textured cap over her hair. It stuck onto her forehead and reminded her of swimming as a child. She looked at the screen again. Almost instantly, the picture straightened, the image clear. Before her was a crowd of people, backs and heads, moving in time. An elder flicked a switch before the screen, and sound filled the room, wrapping around the viewers and the tree alike. Suddenly, Auri's face came into view, and she stared at the screen as though she was looking straight through it into the room. She grinned widely. Reuel suddenly appeared at Wendowleen's side.

"Ah, my daughter!" he exclaimed excitedly. "Wendowleen, they no longer need to hold you up. You are wearing your controls. You simply need to will yourself forward, as though you were walking down the hallways here. It is the same with talking. Try and say something."

Wendowleen nodded and opened her mouth, hesitating slightly. "I um, I am walking..." she said. Auri laughed on the screen, and gave a thumbs up.

"You got it, Wendowleen. We're going to try and let go of you now – okay?" Auri's voice said, springing from the branches of the oak tree.

Wendowleen nodded and imagined that she was walking forward. She did more than this; she strode in her mind as though she were marching through the tree. On the screen, Auri clapped her hands together once. "No one is holding you up.

You got it."

The three marched onwards, the crowds around them growing ever bigger, the wider country of Rytter marching into their future with confidence, not knowing what it could bring.

Chapter Fifty-One

The Director sat in his office after the clean-up; his mood soured substantially. He hadn't wanted that to happen with Sylvia. It reminded him of his father. He hadn't wanted anything to happen there, either, not really. He focused for a moment on a freshly-scrubbed piece of floor, closed his eyes, and did something he rarely allowed himself to do. He cast his mind back to that fateful day.

The rain had been falling hard, the weather heavy in the sky. From the moment he had woken up, his head had pounded, as though the weight of the clouds was pressing in on him, pushing him into the earth. There had been no university that day. He knew that well. It was the day after he had been expelled, the day after that woman, his own mother, had dobbed him into the exam board. He hadn't even wanted to go to university. That didn't factor into his life goals the tiniest bit. He had tried to explain that to both of them, that the thought of going to the University of Rytter, even early, as they had planned, was not something that he was proud of. They had been sitting together around the small circular table in the kitchen months before, a meal of mackerel and potatoes before them, and he had explained it all through the strong scent of fish.

"I don't want to go to university. I want to see Rytter, to be my own man. I want to join the Finery," he had said, holding words before him on a piece of paper, having planned the sentence carefully the night before.

They had laughed. They had laughed at their only son. Arthur had dismissed it as a mere flight of fancy.

"You don't know what you want," he had said, eyes dancing. "You'll be best off getting an education *first*, and then, if you truly want to join the Finery, you can do that afterwards."

Ayin had shaken his head. That was impossible. Youth without a university education was the only type to join the Finery. And he had a good chance; he had spoken to a career advisor at his school about it.

Wendowleen had remained silent until she heard this and then steadily put her knife and fork down, mouth tight and straight. "No child of mine is to join an institution like the Finery. Ayin, you do not understand what they stand for. You do not understand how restrictive they are. You are too young to comprehend their history. You will go to the university and do it as planned – only 0.6% of fresh starters are aged below eighteen years old. Understand the gift you have been given, and speak to us no more about your Finery dreams. You'll thank us when you're older."

Of course, it must be mentioned at this point that the Director believed this conversation to be verbatim. His memories of it were exact, but this does not mean that they fit hand-in-hand with the actual history. Wendowleen's memories of this conversation, though lost for many years, were quite different. She did not think, for example, that she had been so curt. Ayin, on the other hand, she remembered as smashing a plate against the floor. Oh, and she recalled kippers, not mackerel, beside the potatoes.

And so, to Ayin, it had proved to be true. He had been forced to attend university early. His classmates had wished him good luck in front of the teachers, but behind their backs, they belittled him for being a 'smarty pants' and a big 'swot head'.

Although he only spent a couple of months in the dusty book-laden classrooms, university was a significant challenge.

Due to his indecision, he had been forced to take his mother's subject, and sat quietly in classrooms of older people, learning philosophy. But Ayin had, of course, been at the end of some of these discussions his entire life. Though Arthur's profession was in woodwork, his passion was philosophy, and he had also studied the subject at some length. Wendowleen and Arthur would have great debates and discussions at the dinner table, encouraging Ayin to join in from the time he was only just able to talk.

The classes that Ayin found himself in were dull and embarrassing. He was bored by the youths' conversations and found the ease in which they got off topic infuriating. The mere explanation of an ethical dilemma could send them into an hour-long trip down memory lane, causing them to bounce between philosophies and, Ayin's greatest irritation, to wonder what dead philosophers would have thought of their mundane life choices. The embarrassment came purely from his mother, whose voice boomed across the classroom even when calm, and who occasionally nodded to the fact that they were related by bringing him treats or wrinkling her nose in pleasure when he answered a question correctly.

It was incomprehensible. He couldn't possibly continue. When the first marked essay was requested, he did the only thing he could think of – he copied his mother's work, and handed it in as his own. He had expected a certain series of events to take place. First, his mother would mark it, of course. She would recognise her own writing; the phrases she used and conclusions would be all too familiar. She would then return home and be cross with him about it. Of course, he expected that. This would lead to an honest discussion of *why* he didn't want to study, and she would finally listen to him, allowing him to leave and pursue his own dreams.

Of course, this didn't happen exactly as expected. Yes, Wendowleen recognised her work, as predicted. However, instead of returning home to discuss this with her only son, she lifted the phone and directly called the Vice-Chancellor. She then turned the essay over to the exam board, which had resulted in a swift expulsion for Ayin.

You would be forgiven for thinking that Ayin would have been pleased with this result, for although a different path had been taken, the final goal was achieved. But he wasn't. When his mother came home that night, she burst through the door like a howling wind. She rained insults down on him in a fury, and it was all he could do to protect himself from the endless blows. Of course, this is how Ayin remembers it, a story woven into the Director's growth, and stretched and pulled to create a hatred of his family.

Eventually, Ayin stood and declared to the couple that stood before him that they were not his parents. They, who had longed for him, bore him, and cared for him, were not his. And at this, Arthur shook his head.

"Should you step out that door tonight, you are not welcome back. I will not have you speak to your mother that way, not now, and not ever."

Ayin saw red. This he could admit to himself, even at the darkest times. Before his eyes fell a dark cloak of vehemence, and he began to gather his belongings with force. He snatched his books from their shelves, caring not for the remainder that he sent cascading to the floor. He tore images of himself from the wall, ripping them from their frames and smashing the glass underfoot. He threw his mother's heirloom vase against the tiled floor, and it was then that his father stepped forward to stop him. A wrestle ensued. Arthur was strong, his arms built from years working with wood, but Ayin had a rage within him that could not be quelled. In a single moment that stretched before all three, Ayin struck his father in the chest. The punch paused Arthur's heart for a moment, before it continued its steady beat. Hours later, when Ayin had left, Arthur died. The news travelled through to Ayin days later, from a man in the street. And it occurred to him then that maybe it wasn't his fault, not really, and how heartless of his mother to cast him aside this way, how cruel to not even tell him the news. His shoes turned in the street, and he marched straight to the Finery, signing up for duty within the hour.

The Director sat back in his chair, watching the dim reflection of the lamplight in his office battle with the brightness of the moon. A knock came at the door, and he rolled his shoulders back and sat up straight.

"Enter."

Bob walked in at a pace that concerned the Director, as though he was skidding as well as walking, his gait laced with panic. He came to a halt before the Director's desk and cleared his throat theatrically.

"Let me guess — a fight has broken out in one of the pubs," said the Director, his eyes sharpening into a point.

Bob shook his head briefly and paused, his gaze resting on a pencil that lay on the Director's desk. It began to judder before them, suddenly accompanied by the noise of the glass in the window, shaking in its frame. The men looked at each other.

"Is that thunder?" the Director said, eyebrows furrowing.

Bob cleared his throat again and took a breath. "No, sir. That is the people of Finer Bay. They have broken curfew and —" the noise was steadily becoming louder, their closeness drawing in, "and they are marching towards the Finery Headquarters."

The Director's mouth set in a perfectly straight line, his nostrils flaring. "Okay. Release the wolves."

Chapter Fifty-Two

The thunderous noise had been shaking the glasses and mugs of The Switched Dragon for at least fifteen minutes now. The officers sat, heads lowered, both silent. The jobsworth was now entirely quiet and still, no further threats sprang from his lips, and no rolling of eyes came forth. The ambitious officer had long since stopped talking about his life goals and was instead thinking about how he might get out of this situation. Either he could sneak out of here while their backs were turned, or, and this was the more likely case (he thought), he was toast. He pursed his lips and considered this. If he *could* sneak out, was there anywhere he could hide while all of this took place? Maybe he could stash his uniform behind the pub, and sort of join the crowd in his pants, pretending it was a type of protest. After all, he wasn't really a fan of the curfew anyway. The thought process of his colleague was very different. The jobsworth was, as one can imagine, loyal to the cause. The curfew, he thought, was a fantastic idea. Long had the rabble of the country needed to be controlled. He had grand designs on his own future, too, and whereas his moronic companion seemed privately to dream of curing a cat of the common cold, he was destined to be the Director. He knew this. He had planned it all out. The rise to power simply meant walking a taut tightrope, the perfect mixture of loyal and conniving. For example, the second they got out of here, his colleague was to be reported for behaviour disloyal to the cause, fraternising with the public during work, and maybe even intention to abscond. All he had to do was overpower the barman. The old woman would be no trouble. The second he got his hands free, he would be able to reach for the gun that sat before him on the bar, and take her out. His eyes moved up slightly, and he stared at the barman, who beamed widely at him.

"All right, I'm not missing out on this. Mama, you want to join in the march?"

She wrinkled her nose and laughed, "I don't see why not."

"So, what about these two?"

The barman and his mother stared at them for a moment. There was a murmur suddenly, and all four glanced downwards at the same time to see the Vice-Chancellor coming to. He sat up slowly and put his hand to his head.

"What the?" he said fuzzily, staring at the scene before him. The student beside him began to rise also and blinked slowly.

"Bloody OUCH!" She stood up shakily and gave the jobsworth a sharp kick in the shin. He didn't respond. "Ouch!" she said again, "You can't go around whacking people over the head for nothing, you absolute —"

"Okay, okay," said the barman, lowering his gun slightly, "let's all just take a breath here."

The Vice-Chancellor stood up using the bar for support, and then paused. He stared at the steadily clinking glasses and then turned to the window, where the heavy velvet drawn curtains hid the march. "Is that my concussion, or is that real?"

"That's a protest. They're marching toward Finery Headquarters. We're about to join them, if you're interested in coming, Vice-Chancellor?" the barman's mother said, in a honeyed voice.

"What about these two?" the student said, glaring at the jobsworth, who stared back, seemingly unaware of the thin trickle of blood running down his leg.

The Vice-Chancellor put one hand on his aching head and breathed in slowly. "I've got an idea. It's an experiment we used to have some of our first years discuss. Do they have guns?" he asked the barman.

"They did. I took them away. They're there, on the bar." He motioned with his head in response.

"All right. So, we're going to join the foray," he said to the officers, picking up the guns. He slid both of them into his coat. "Aside from smacking us over the head, have either of these chaps shown themselves to be worthy of forgiving?"

The barman's mother spoke up. "Oh yes, this young'un wants to be a vet, sends money home to his struggling mother and all."

"Does he now?" said the Vice-Chancellor. He stepped around the ambitious officer and knelt briefly, pulling a short knife from his boot and cutting the twine with it. The officer pulled his hands out and remained seated, waiting to see what might happen next. The Vice-Chancellor moved to stand before him and cocked his head to one side. "Now then, I know you must be a little scared. After all, it's hardly what you signed up for this, is it?"

"No, sir. It isn't, to be honest. I was supposed to clock off at —"

"Exactly. So, I'm going to give you this gun back." The Vice-Chancellor handed the gun to the officer, who took it with trepidation. "And we're going to step out of here. This man," the officer motioned to the jobsworth, still tied to his chair, "is a menace. He needs to be reported for his behaviour. I'm sure that the Finery has rules for that sort of thing, doesn't it?"

"Well, sir, it does, but more often than not, we don't actually report officers because —"

"And the point is, that we know that you know the difference between right and wrong. We have faith in you to do the right thing." With that, the Vice-Chancellor stepped back, and waved his hands at the barman and his mother, gesturing that they should lower their guns. They did so, reluctantly. The jobsworth watched this with interest, a slight smirk dancing across his lips.

In silence, the troop made their way out of the oaken door of The Switched Dragon, pulling it shut behind them. The street outside was heaving with people, as far as the eye could see. The noise surrounded their ears, the sound of boots and shoes crunching through gravel, stepping over stones and clipping on pavements. The ringing of bells filled the air, clashing with the various clangs of pots and pans. As they slipped into the crowd, not one of the four heard a new noise over the din. The sound of a single gunshot rang through the busied air surrounding The Switched Dragon, and nobody paid it any attention at all.

In market squares across the entire land of Rytter, people began to gather. Even the smallest village, Tanka, which had a disputable residency of around sixty cows and seven people, appeared to fill the entire square, pots and pans and placards waved around for good measure. Finery officers and officer figures were definitely lower across the smaller venues of Rytter, but they were still present. They strode around the squares, observing the people, waiting desperately for information from headquarters. Head officers checked walkie-talkies repeatedly. The tension in the air contributed to their confusion, and they were fully aware of what could happen if they weren't careful. One false movement, one accidental gunshot, and the protest would swiftly turn into a riot. Many of the officers in the smaller towns had lived there all their lives, and had grown up among those now protesting. They stood before their former teachers, their mother's best friends, and tried to maintain an air of authority.

In the larger village of Towen, one officer leaned toward another and murmured quietly, "I don't blame 'em. Who wants to be sent home early?"

The other officer watched the crowd and nodded slowly. She agreed, though she wouldn't dare to say it. She felt as though she was very much on the wrong side of the line. Unbeknownst to her, this was a feeling that was spreading among the other Finery members across the land.

Chapter Fifty-Three

The wolves were released, fortuitously, at the same time as the front of the crowd (which now spilt out at a distance of ten streets), reached the gates of the Finery Headquarters. Those on the front line paused and stared at the beasts, whose slathering jaws dripped with anticipation. Behind the crowd, in the second street along, Auri, Seneca and the fake Wendowleen were shuffling forward as best they could. There were shouts from the front that moved swiftly along the crowd, telling them their predecessors had reached the gate of the Finery Headquarters.

Auri tried to peer over the heads in front of them and stood on her tiptoes.

"We'll need to get to the front," she told the pair.

The three stared at the crowds and paused. Seneca shrugged, "Perhaps if we split up?"

Auri shook her head, "No, we shouldn't leave Wendowleen out here alone. Come on, let's see what we can do." She tapped on the shoulder of the person in front and smiled warmly as they turned around, doing her best not to focus on the pan that sat on top of their head.

"I'm terribly sorry, but would you mind if we squeezed ahead? We need to get to the front of the queue."

The person with the pan on their head raised their eyebrows and sniffed. "Well, we're all trying to get to the front, aren't we? We all want to give the Director a piece of our mind. You'll have to wait."

"Yes, I'm aware of that," Auri tried again, "however, we –"

"I am the Director's mother," said Wendowleen's hologram clearly. Auri and Seneca blinked at each other, surprised, and then turned back to the person with the pan on their head.

"*You're* the Director's mother? Well, what are you doing here?" they said, leaning forward with interest.

"I don't support his decisions, that's what. I'm going to give him a bloody good talking to," Wendowleen's hologram responded.

The person considered this for a moment and then laughed loudly. They turned, raising up on their tiptoes and shouting clear across the people in front. "Make way for the Director's mother! She's going to give him a piece of her mind!"

People began to swivel slowly, staring at Wendowleen's hologram in surprise. Her hand waved in a type of royal sentiment, and Auri and Seneca began to move forward on either side, marvelling quietly at the success of their creation. No one seemed to question the reality of the hologram at all. The crowds continued to part, some turned with a frown, and others with a smile, but all cleared the way for them to get through.

Wendowleen led the way, watching from the roots of the tree with the partisans. She had confidence she had never felt before, hidden but visible. She felt truly alive and able. As they reached the gates, those at the front turned and moved aside. The three glowered at the wolves who lay low to the ground, growling and spluttering, ready for attack.

Wendowleen stepped forward and stared at them. Behind the screen, she sat with Wolf beside her, his ears flattening with each growl that travelled through the speakers.

"They'll just be descendants of care wolves – too naughty to cut the mustard," she said softly to Auri, who nodded with uncertainty. Wendowleen cleared her throat and stepped forward again, watched by a hushed crowd behind her. "SIT!" she barked at the wolves, squaring her shoulders. They sat quickly, their growls dying down, all except one. The wolf that stood front and centre raised his haunches, his lips retreating from his sharp teeth. He glared at Wendowleen through yellow eyes and readied himself for the attack. This, though unknown to the three at the head of the protest, was the wolf that had ambition, who had led the party to complete the supposed destruction of Wendowleen.

And then, in a split second, his ears shot forward on top of his head. He raised himself from his low vantage, standing not in attack, but retreat. Auri and Seneca watched in amazement as he retreated backwards, tail between his back legs. Wendowleen's hologram stood still, and Auri placed her hand on its shoulder.

"Well done, Wendowleen. Truly, you have a way with wolves."

However, none had seen precisely what the wolf had seen. He had watched the eyes of the old woman change suddenly into a wolf's eyes. The noise that sprang from her lips was not a sound that he had ever heard fall from the lips of a human. It was a low warning rumble, almost indistinguishable from a hum to the human ear. To see the old woman turn into a wolf this way had truly spooked him. Long had he tried to learn the ways of the humans, not imagining that they might be able to understand the ways of the wolf.

Behind the screen, of course, it was Wolf that had leapt from the floor and onto Wendowleen's lap, taking up the entire screen and growling in defence of his owner. He sat beside her feet again now and happily tucked into a biscuit that had appeared from within one of the elder's cloaks. Such a reward was undoubtedly necessary.

The Director surveyed the crowd from his window with growing interest. Bob stood just behind him, watching from his shoulder. They stared at the wolves backing down in silence.

"Where are the troops," the Director asked.

Bob noticed that it didn't sound like a question, but rather a demand for information. He coughed nervously. "They're supposed to be on the streets, sir, enforcing the curfew."

"Yes," said the Director. "I can see a few of them off the edges of the crowds there, but they're not doing anything."

"That's right. In such a time, it pays to be cautious. There could be a riot if we are not careful."

The Director turned to his head of staff and viewed him with distaste. "What do you call this?" he asked bluntly.

"I see what you are saying, sir, but it is the gracious handling of such an event that secures you as a leader," Bob said the last few words more quietly than the first, his heart thudding noisily in through his ear canals.

"Secures me as a leader? I am the leader, you cretin." The Director grabbed the walkie-talkie from his inept head of staff's label and brought it to his lips. "Fire once into the crowd – we'll show them who is in charge."

Bob hastily laid a hand on the Director's arm and shook his head, "I beg of you sir not to take that action."

The Director shook him off and stared once more from the window.

The crowd in Finer Bay were growing anxious. The officers that had been, on the whole, absentmindedly staring at the protesters while awaiting further orders now began to load their guns with purpose. Though there were those, as there always are, who had no intention of following orders, there were also those who had seen what took place in the darker parts of the Headquarters. These were the people who knew what a Finery punishment meant, who had spent time exploring the gloomy caverns of their souls in the night and had risen the next day certain of who they now were.

The officers who could no more fire into a crowd than they could send someone to the dungeons, stepped backwards and lowered their weapons. Those loyal to the regime beyond all else took a step forward and fired once through the heavy air.

The gunshots rang through the street, and Auri turned as the gunpowder scent reached her nostrils. The crowd was silent for a moment, minds assessing the damage, waiting for impact. And then, the moment came. Screams and shouts fell from mouths, the volume of Finer Bay expanding into the air.

People turned to each other, checking for harm, for loss, for hurt. And then, a strange realisation occurred and spread from person to person. Those hit had been protected by the pans that sat on top of their heads. There was a peculiar moment of mirth that danced through the crowd. Auri watched the people in their realisation and saw the individual faces turn from surprise into anger, faces twisting and dropping. The crowd began to split before her, groups forming quickly and at speed. Almost immediately, the officers who had fired were lifted off their feet by the protestors and charged rapidly toward the Finery Headquarter gates. Auri, Seneca, and Wendowleen's hologram stepped aside hastily as the officers were flung into a heap before the heavy iron entrance. Some hurriedly got to their feet, clinging to their weapons but not daring to fire once more. Others simply lay, silent, hoping that the worst of the crowd's wrath was now over.

"The emblems!" Auri said to Wendowleen over the din. "The emblems on their jackets will open the doors for us."

And so, it proved to be. The gates juddered open amid the confusion, and the tightly-packed group of protestors stood before it, eyes blazing. Wendowleen stepped forward and strode once more to the front. She glanced at an officer, who sat on the ground by the now open gate, eyes focussed on his shoes. "You. You will lead the way to the Director's office."

The officer lifted his head and shook it steadily, and Wendowleen smiled warmly in response. "Come, there is more to be scared of down here than up there. Trust me on that." This was a line that Wendowleen would look back on for the rest of her days, in regret.

The crowd was pulsing, desperate to heave forward into the headquarters, and Wendowleen motioned to them with her hand. The officer glanced around the angry faces, blinking in their outrage, and then steadily climbed to his feet, breathing in slowly.

Wendowleen held her hand up to those at the front of the gates, and smiled.

"So, we cannot all go up there. Four of you will join the officer and I up to the Director's office. That will be sufficient."

Whether they teach an evening class or at a university, the voice of a teacher has a depth to it that is world-renowned. They can command a room, and, what's more, can settle an argument with a baseline of authority. Those at the front glanced at each other, and then ten protestors stepped forward at once. Wendowleen nodded, her bravery now tinged with nerves that she was choosing to ignore, "That's fine, we'll all go."

Bob watched the gates open in silence. The role of a sidekick, a second in command, a dogsbody (and the like), is a tricky one to own in a time of crisis. Bob found himself in two minds. He could surrender and tell the Director that really he wanted nothing to do with this situation, which might incur the forgiveness of the people but the wrath of the Director. Or, he could stick by the Director, do his job, and hope that some semblance of control was regained. He stared down at the small figures of protestors and squinted his eyes.

"Hang on. Director, that's…Cripcot."

The Director leaned forward and also stared, narrowing his gaze. "It can't be. She's dead. And she has an entirely different gait. The woman is one hundred years old. She hasn't moved that quickly in years."

"Right you are, sir," Bob responded, opting to keep his opinion to himself. He stared at them as they came closer to the building, raising his eyebrows. It was Cripcot, he thought to himself. He had twenty-twenty vision, and that was her. "They're coming in, sir. What would you like me to do?"

The Director smiled widely. "Let them up. I'm not afraid of a small group of people led by an old woman, for goodness sake. The others appear to have halted, anyway. The human fears the bullet, above all else."

Bob turned his attention to the failed Finery officers gathered near the gate and sighed. They appeared to be ignoring all their training. Although he thought to himself, the training section on riots had been sparse. It was more preventative than reactive. A few of the officers were actually running away from the crowd, guns flying on straps behind their backs. Others were sitting on the floor, heads in their hands. And others, bizarrely, had taken their tops off and were now standing next to the protestors, as though they had been there all along.

The Director turned and marched away from the window, taking a seat behind his desk. He sat up smartly, shoulders rolled back and nodded at his head of staff.

"Get the door."

Bob hesitated for a moment and then pulled it open and stood back. He could hear the rioters climbing the steps, their heavy shoes and zealous murmurs. He stared as Wendowleen's hologram climbed the stairs with efficiency, overtaking the officer who had shown them the way and nodded at her.

"Miss Cripcot," he said steadily, attempting to warn his boss of the arrival.

The hologram gave him a blunt stare and walked past him, stating clearly, "It's Professor Cripcot to you."

The Director rose slowly from his desk as she stalked through the door, blind to those behind her. He hadn't looked upon the real face of his mother in years. And this was his mother, there was no doubt about that, and yet she looked strange. Her aged skin was almost glassy and smooth, her eyes were clear, but there was something wrong with them, something nondescript.

"Ayin," she said clearly, stopping before him, and raising her hand to the small crowd behind her.

The Director watched them halt under her command and smiled bitterly. "You've still got various ne'er-do-wells under your charge, I see, Mother."

Bob coughed nervously and took his place beside the Director. He privately acknowledged the fact that the Director had called her mother, and did his best not to let his face show his surprise. The face of the head of staff should remain blank at all times.

"I could say the same to you," Wendowleen replied, glancing at Bob. He frowned in response, uneasy in her presence. There was something very odd about the way she looked, but he couldn't quite put his finger on it.

"I am surprised to see you, I must admit," the Director said.

"Yes. Because you thought I was dead," Wendowleen retorted.

There was a silence between them, a string of pure tension ready to snap. Auri glanced at Seneca, sharing a look at the same time as the others in the room did. The atmosphere felt tightly-packed, from floor to ceiling. The officer who had led the way took this opportunity to shift toward the door quietly, and the Director's eyes suddenly snapped from his mother to the uniformed coward.

"Halt," he said, in a clipped tone. The officer paused and then stared down at his feet. "What is your name?" the Director asked him.

"Connel, sir."

"Connel. Do you have your gun?" The officer flinched at the single syllables spat out in a staccato fashion.

"I do, sir."

"Then use it," the Director responded, gesturing to the fifteen or so people he now found in his office.

The officer shook his head and raised his eyes, sighing. "I cannot, sir."

The Director's eyes narrowed, and his hand moved to hover over his hip. "And why can you not use it? Were you not trained?"

"It's...they're my cousins, sir." His eyes blinked steadily at a couple of younger men in the crowd and then glanced back to the Director, who in turn nodded silently at his head of staff.

"Yes, sir," Bob responded, and he fired a single shot into the heart of the officer.

The small crowd gasped collectively, and the Director raised his eyebrows.

"Refusal to cooperate will be met with —"

But the crowd never heard what it might be met with. Auri and Seneca moved wordlessly as one through the room, a blur of activity. Before the Director had finished his sentence, Auri had stripped the jacket from his shoulders, tying it tightly behind his back. She pulled the gun from his right hip and flung it to the corner of the room. Seneca, not one to be unprepared, pulled a cable tie from his pocket and secured the head of staff, twisting his wrists until his gun fell to the floor.

Wendowleen stared at the body of the officer and then stepped forward toward the Director. "You are not my son," she said slowly.

"I am aware of that," he threw the words at her. "You were never my mother. Most parents love a child regardless of their desires. You threw me out as soon as I developed my own opinions."

"You are wrong, of course. Your memories and your mind fail you, greatly."

The people behind began to shift forward, rage bubbling and popping among them. One of the cousins shouted something out, the words mixed with grief and anger, unclear to the human ear. They marched around the desk and grabbed the Director, lifting and pulling him to the office window. Its dirty frame was shifted open, the warm breeze floating into the room, spreading the scents of Artomia. On any other day, the occupants of the room would have closed their eyes and breathed in deeply, enjoying the traces of the sunshine season. But now, it went unnoticed. The Director saw the world he had built turn upside down, and they hung him from the open window by his ankles. He watched the crowd below lift their heads, and begin to laugh and cheer.

Auri watched the display from behind the office crowd and moved toward Wendowleen's hologram. "You must say something, Wendowleen. Speak to the people."

She nodded in response and walked toward the window, gently shifting through the crowd until she stood at the front, beside her struggling son. His face was beginning to go pink from the blood rushing to his head, and he snarled through his shining teeth at her.

"What do you want?" he asked, his voice gruff and strange, a sound she did not recognise at all.

Wendowleen stared at him and then looked at the crowd before her.

"I want justice," she called out. The words she spoke reached the front of the crowd only, and they cheered, causing her voice to be lost to the others. Auri stepped forward silently, guiding the protestors aside until she stood behind the hologram. She reached up, moving her hand behind the hologram's right ear and then letting her arm fall back to her side.

"Repeat it," she whispered. "You have full volume."

"I want justice," Wendowleen called again, her voice now floating down to the people. They fell silent this time, waiting for more.

"Justice. Justice for the people. Justice for myself and for my husband Arthur, whom this man, my son, murdered. Justice for you."

The Director growled by her side, and she glanced at him momentarily before continuing.

"This man has lied to you. He tore my family apart. His staff are mere puppets." She motioned steadily to the Finery officers that remained standing at the gates, who now stood, chins raised, staring at their Director and Wendowleen alike.

"To his officers: He's an academic's son, did you know? An early attendee of university? A murderer? A thief?"

They stared back in silence. Of course, they knew that he was a murderer, though they had never labelled him as such. His work was done for the country's good, and that work sometimes involved the death of the enemy. A few of them stared up at Wendowleen now and wondered whether she was, in fact, the enemy. She was his mother. How could your mother be your enemy? And yet, there she was, next to her son, who was being dangled out of a window by his ankles.

And in this moment of contemplation, something within Wendowleen stuttered. Auri closed her eyes and breathed in. This was a moment that the partisans had warned her about. The crowd in the streets below watched as Wendowleen jolted strangely and then fell from the window, hurtling toward the ground. The upside-down Director let out a single bleat of noise, a laugh that echoed around the air. The people stared, open-mouthed.

Chapter Fifty-Four

There are sayings throughout all lands about what might happen when your back is turned. The one you are familiar with is about a tree falling in a forest and whether or not noise exists if one is not there to witness it. The answer, by the way, is yes. Of course, the noise still exists, and this sound is heard and felt by all of the animals in said forest. If you are still unsure, do go and check with them.

The shot that rang through the air as the barman and his mother joined the protest was just one of a significant number of possible scenarios. It was not the one that the Vice-Chancellor had predicted or intended. As the oak door of The Switched Dragon closed, the two Finery officers stared at each other. The one with the gun, who was now untied, stood before his colleague.

"We should leave via the backdoor, and then we can hide until this is all over," he said quietly, the volume of his voice barely audible over the noise from the street. He quickly loosened the twine around his teammate's wrists.

The jobsworth allowed himself to be untied and then stood, nodding. "Okay. Quick now, hand me your gun."

Unfortunately, though many large and small decisions had led the ambitious aspirant vet to this moment, this decision was the most fatal. He handed over his gun and was promptly shot through the heart. The jobsworth did indeed slip out of the back door, but not before donning one of the barman's jackets, disguising the top half of his Finery uniform. He correctly assumed that no one would notice his shining boots in the incessant din.

The officer had taken some of the dingy back streets of Finer Bay, his feet avoiding and then finding the protest, slipping effortlessly and unnoticed through the crowd. His goal was to reach the Finery Headquarters, of course, and to be beside his brethren in this time of crisis. The man he left dead in The Switched Dragon was not what he considered to be of good Finery stock.

As the crowd pulsed and shifted, he reached the street on which the headquarters were based. He saw the commotion, watched his fellow officers and their complete failure to control the crowd, and witnessed the dangling of the Director and the short speech of his supposed mother. It was clear to him then what he needed to do. The only difficult decision to make was who to shoot. Should he shoot the Director, there was a real possibility that he could then take his place. The people might lift him aloft, celebrate his triumph. However, should he shoot the old woman, the Director may provide him with a worthy reward, and perhaps even promote him to head of staff, allowing him to effortlessly slip into his place when retirement came. The jobsworth chose his moment with some care, and yet even as his finger pulled the trigger, his hand wavered between the two figures at the open window. The one that he shot was Wendowleen.

The reaction of the crowd was instantaneous. The jobsworth stared as the people turned from the scene to face him. He lowered his gun, watching them carefully. His only reward was the single barking laugh of the Director, and he saw suddenly the error that he had made. He should have shot the Director. A man beside him looked him up and down, taking in the knee-high shining black boots with suspicion. He grabbed the jobsworth suddenly, stripping him of his jacket and revealing his uniform beneath. The onlookers howled at him in outrage, angry for his tricks and actions. The portion of the crowd nearest to him fell on him without a care for his bullets and then pulled him aloft, lifting him above their heads as though he weighed nothing at all. They began to march toward the Finery Headquarters with him, and as he went, he stared at the sky for the first time that Artomia, watching the stars fall into each other. A woman beneath him hissed into his ear.

"Take a good look at those stars, son. You won't be seeing anything like them again."

And that, he thought to himself, is probably correct.

Underground Wendowleen was, of course, still safe. The screen had gone fuzzy and strange, flickering before her eyes. She had watched an abnormal assortment of brickwork and ground fall toward the screen, and then, it went blank.

"Damn," she said quietly. "I was getting the hang of that. What do we do?"

An elder sat down beside her on the root and stared at the blank screen. "We do nothing for now. There is nothing that we can do. Auri and Seneca will deal with the body of the hologram and fix it up as soon as they are able, but that won't be for a few days, I shouldn't think."

Wendowleen shook her head in disbelief, fighting back tears for the first time in at least a decade. "But we were so close. I was so close to doing something. I created the fall of Rytter, and I am not there to help."

The elder moved an aged hand over her own and squeezed gently, eyes still facing forward. "We must be grateful for your safety, Wendowleen. After all, that is why you are here. Many deaths are predicted for us all, and it only takes one to be successful. We must be grateful that this is not your ending, and we must have faith in the people of Finer Bay. So far, they do good work. And there is often a catalyst for this sort of historical event, a turning point, a tipping of passions. Your 'death' may well prove to be the making of the city."

Wendowleen nodded sadly and placed a hand on the top of Wolf's head, who sniffed it gently before giving it a mollifying lick. Wolf knew that this was against his training, but something in the air led him to do it. As it was, this led to a chin scratch, and so he understood that he had done the right thing.

Chapter Fifty-Five

Auri leaned out of the window and stared down at the crumpled body of Wendowleen's hologram lying on the ground. The crowd thundered and roared as far as the eye could see, a mass of people lining the streets before her. She saw the jobsworth being carried and thrown atop the crowd, heading toward the Finery Headquarters. And then, the chant began.

"LOCK THEM UP. LOCK THEM UP. LOCK THEM UP."

Those who held the Director by the ankles nodded in fervent agreement, and then one turned to the other.

"We could just drop him. Saves us a bit of time."

Auri glared at them quietly and then cleared her throat. "No. That is not justice. Listen to the people of Rytter. They wish for him to be sent to his own jail. Here, lift him from the window."

The Director was pulled up and into the office once more and flung heavily onto the ground. He lifted his crimson face, blinking through the stars that flashed in his vision, the blood that had rushed to and made a home in his head now trickling back to normality.

"Bob," he said quietly, blinking at his head of staff.

Bob, still sat with his hands tied behind his back, simply stared at him in response, partially in disbelief that he was actually using his real name.

"Bob," the Director said again, with slightly more force.

"Yes," he responded.

The crowd stood quietly and watched with interest.

"You must radio for backup," the Director said.

The silence in the room expanded, and members of the small crowd blinked at each other and then stared at Bob, intrigued at what he might respond to this impossible request. He looked at them uncomfortably and shrugged. Auri stepped forward and knelt next to the Director.

"It's gone beyond such a thing. There is no backup to call; the people have taken over the city, if not the land. And you, Ayin, are on your way to a cell."

The Director glared at her and spat on the floor in between them. "Well, your ringleader is dead."

Auri laughed and shook her head, lowering her tone so that the rest of the room did not hear her words. "She is not dead, Ayin. For it was not her."

Behind her, Seneca placed a firm hand on Bob's shoulder. "Bob, would you be so kind as to lead us all to the cells?"

He nodded solemnly. Auri stared at Seneca and beckoned him to the corner of the room, as the team pulled the two men to their feet.

"Seneca, I must head home. I need to contact my parents."

Seneca glanced at those in the room and then smiled firmly. "We shall lock them up and await your return."

Auri left the Finery Headquarters with great care, leaving not through the front door but the Finery kitchen, located in the east of the building. The chefs, it appeared, were long gone, a pile of dirty plates and dishes left on the side, and actions abandoned. She stepped lightly past the half-peeled carrots and slipped out into the darkness of the back-alley way. From there, she crept through the streets, careful to take longer routes that might avoid the mass of people. As she neared the street of The Malted Mash, she moved steadier still, pausing with care at the end. She saw there, with great surprise, that the street was almost empty. Auri walked down the lane with purpose, stepping past a few signs languishing on the side of the cobbled roads, and the odd wooden spoon flung into a forgotten embrace with the lid of a saucepan.

Once inside The Malted Mash, Auri rushed to the coding machine in her bedroom, bashing out a steady request.

.. ‑ .. ..‑ ..‑ .‑. .. ˙‑˙‑˙‑ .‑ .‑. . ‑.‑‑ ‑‑‑ ..‑ ‑ .... . .‑.
. ˙˙‑‑˙˙ [It is Auri. Are you there?]

She paused, awaiting the answer, imagining her mother underground, sipping on her chestnut broth and musing. The machine came to life suddenly.

.‑ ..‑ .‑. .. ˙‑˙‑˙‑ .. ‑ .. ... ‑.‑‑ ‑‑‑ ..‑ .‑. ‑‑ ‑‑‑ ‑ .... .
.‑. ˙‑˙‑˙‑ .‑‑ . ‑. ‑.. ‑‑‑ .‑‑ .‑.. . . ‑. .. ..‑ ..‑. .‑ ‑. ‑.. .‑‑ .
.‑.. .‑.. ˙‑‑˙‑ [Auri. It is your mother. Wendowleen is safe and well.]

Auri smiled and then tapped out a response.

‑ .... . ‑.. .. .‑. . ‑.‑. ‑ ‑‑‑ .‑. .. .. ‑... . .. ‑. ‑‑. .... .
‑. ‑ ‑ ‑‑‑ .‑. .‑. .. .. ‑‑‑ ‑. ˙‑˙‑˙‑ ... ‑‑‑ ‑‑ . ‑‑‑ ‑. . ‑‑ ..‑ ... ‑ ... ‑ .
.‑‑ ..‑ .‑. ‑ ‑‑‑ .‑ ... ... ‑ ˙‑˙‑˙‑ ‑.‑. .‑ ‑. ... . ‑.‑. ‑‑‑ ‑‑ .
‑ ‑‑‑ ..‑. .. ‑. . .‑. ‑... .‑ ‑.‑‑ ˙˙‑‑˙˙ [The Director is being sent to prison. Someone must step up to assist. Can she come to Finer Bay?]

.. .‑‑ .. .‑.. .‑. ‑‑ .. ..‑ . .‑‑ . ‑. ‑.. ‑‑‑ .‑‑ .‑.. . . ‑. .‑
.... . ‑.. . .‑‑ ... ˙‑˙‑˙‑ ‑‑‑ ‑. .‑.. ‑.‑‑ ... . ‑.‑. .‑ ‑. ‑.. . ‑.‑. .. ‑.. .
. ˙‑‑˙‑ [I will give Wendowleen the news. Only she can decide.]

Auri nodded and tapped out her farewell.

.. ‑‑ .. .. ‑.‑‑ ‑‑‑ ..‑ ˙‑‑˙‑ [I miss you.]

Her mother's response stung Auri's eyes, and she blinked away tears with haste.

.. ‑.. .‑. . .‑ ‑‑ ‑‑‑ ..‑. .‑ ‑ .. ‑‑ . ‑ .... .‑ ‑ .‑‑ . ‑‑ .‑‑.‑‑
... .. .‑ ‑ ‑‑‑ ‑‑. . ‑ .... . .‑. .‑ ‑‑ .‑ .. ‑. ‑‑ ‑‑‑ ‑.‑‑ .‑.. ‑‑‑ ...‑ .
˙‑‑˙‑ [I dream of a time that we may sit together again, my love.]

The Director and his head of staff quickly found themselves being marched through their prison block beneath the Finery Headquarters, a venue that both of them knew only too well. The dull thud of footsteps was quickly swallowed by the dank air, which floated and swam around the small crowd's faces. It smelled like mould, tinged with the scent of something fouler. To the discerning Finery worker, that scent was very recognisable – it was fear. Plastic buzzing electrical lights fuzzed down the stretch of the wall, in between dark oaken doors that hid darker surprises and secrets. The unlucky officer's cousins pushed the Director forward until they came to a cell on the left, in which someone was calling. They stopped the march and strained slightly, unable to hear the voice.

"What is that?" one cousin asked the Director.

He sniffed in response and shrugged.

"It is a young man not from here," Bob said glumly, from behind them. They glanced at each other in mild surprise that it was now so easy to obtain information from these men. Seneca stepped forward and held out a hand to the grimacing head of staff.

"Keys," he said, waggling his fingers.

"In my right-hand blazer pocket," Bob responded.

Seneca reached his hand inside the pocket, despite feeling slightly uncomfortable about the intimacy of the action. He would never usually reach inside the pocket of a stranger. He grasped the key and pulled it forth, raising his eyebrows slightly.

"Just one key?" he said to Bob, suspiciously.

"That's right. It fits all cells."

"It's safer that way," the Director said suddenly, causing the small crowd to flinch. "Just one key is easier to keep from prying hands. Supposedly. If your head of staff doesn't just give it away like a common dog."

Seneca rolled his eyes. "Even at a time like this."

Bob gave a slight smile at the acknowledgement, feeling that he had some sort of recognition for the first time in a very long time.

More shouts came from inside the cell beside them, and Seneca stepped forward, pushing the key into the lock and turning it with effort. He pulled the heavy door open and blinked into the dim light. He could just about make out a figure standing in the middle of the room.

"Hello?" he called inside, squinting. There was no response. Seneca's vision began to adjust slightly, and he saw flashes of the whites of the person's eyes.

"Hello?" he tried again. Still, no response came from the dank room. "This is not the Finery..." he said, "You should feel free to talk."

A murmur floated forward, and Seneca leaned in further to catch the words.

"Careful!" the voice suddenly shot through the room. "It is ice cold."

Seneca looked down and saw that the floor rippled and moved. It was water. "What did you do to be put in here?" he asked carefully.

"I do not know. I worked at a hotel. They asked me to spy on someone, and I did my best to please them."

Seneca turned and glared at the Director, who stood with a bored expression painted onto his face, arms still being held by the cousins.

"Is he speaking the truth?" Seneca asked him.

"He failed at his task," responded the Director, his eyes cold and heavy.

There was a sound of splashing in the cell behind, and Seneca turned to see the figure becoming clearer in the light of the buzzing electric lamps. He leaned forward and held out a hand, which the boy grasped, pulling himself up. He was shivering, soaking wet from his stomach to his feet, his torso barely covered in torn clothing. His skin was pallid and grey, and Seneca stared at him in amazement for a moment, wondering how he stood before him.

"What is your name?"

"Roscoe. I want to go home. I work at The Squid's Inn, but my family lives nearby in Oaksham." The boy stuttered and slurred his words, shaking the entire time.

"Yes. Come, we will get you some dry clothes and food. And you," he turned to the Director and head of staff, shaking his head slowly. "You will have to last as Roscoe has, in a cell not made for human life. I don't doubt that you'll be pulled out if there is to be a trial, so just try and hold on, eh?"

The cousins dragged the silent Director to the door, and flung him in, hearing the splash of the water. Bob was thrown in next, and the crowd paused for a moment and listened with morbid interest, at who would claim the post in the middle of the room for their own, their only hope for survival. Seneca pulled the door behind them and locked it firmly, handing the key to the cousins.

It was the first full night's sleep Wendowleen had been able to enjoy in days, but it seemed to her like months. Her entire body melted into the soft hair-filled mattress, and, along with Wolf, she slept as soundly as she once had in her well-worn bed.

When she awoke, Elagwet had already prepared breakfast for her and Wolf and was sitting with her back to a roaring fire in the kitchen, nursing a broth. Wendowleen wandered in and smiled at the display of food.

"You didn't have to do this, Elagwet. You mustn't wait on me. But thank you very much."

Elagwet waved a hand dismissively and smiled. "It is no bother. I usually wake up well before everyone else anyway. It's the curse of being a farmer's daughter. You never lose the affinity with the early starts."

Wendowleen sat down and pricked a slice of charred cauliflower with her fork, feeling the warmth of the fire spread to her toes. "How do you diffuse the smoke?" she asked curiously.

Elagwet glanced at the burning embers. "It goes through a series of small tunnels, and by the time it reaches the land above, it disperses at foot level only. Besides, those who have crossed the mountains are few and far between. The people of Rytter prefer the cities and towns these days."

Wendowleen popped the cauliflower into her mouth and raised her eyebrows in surprise at the taste of it. It burst with flavour, the charred elements adding to the earthy saltiness.

Elagwet smiled. "Auri contacted me last night. She would like you to go back to Finer Bay. The Director has been put in jail, along with some of his staff...and she would like you to assist with a trial. But you must know, it is entirely up to you, Wendowleen. I know your entry into our little home was not graced with ease."

"This is true," Wendowleen mused. "But my entire life has not been 'graced with ease', I must say. And swimming down beneath a current must be more difficult than allowing oneself to pop up, like a cork?"

Elagwet nodded thoughtfully. "Yes, I suppose so. I have never gone the opposite way myself, though, of course, I did assist with Auri's exit. So you will leave then?"

Wendowleen looked at Wolf, who was ignoring the rest of the world in favour of his breakfast and sighed. "I will, though the thought of the journey does not fill me with joy. Yes. I will leave after breakfast."

"Seneca will not be able to get to the lake so fast, and the trains do not run from Towen to Finer Bay. How will you get there?" Elagwet asked.

"I will hire a coach or a horse. Something or other. If there is no threat, there is nothing to fear."

After breakfast, Wendowleen readied herself with haste. She removed the now dirty bandage from her arm, noticing with pleasure that the wound was healing neatly. As long as Wolf didn't try and save her again, there would be no problem. There was excitement in the air, though her bones ached a little, and Wolf seemed to sense her nervous anticipation, responding by letting out sudden barks and tail wags, interspersed with whines and nudging. On the whole, he found himself ignored for this behaviour. And then, she was ready. She had nothing with her apart from the clothes on her back, and the partisans took care in lending her waterproof clothing. Elagwet had prepared a ziplock bag of treats for Wolf, along with sandwiches, and passed them over with a squeeze of the hand. Wendowleen stood in an earthen corridor midway between two large doors, in front of an iron exit with the words 'Waterway' written on it in red paint, Wolf by her side.

"Best of luck, Professor. We look forward to hearing of your arrival."

Wendowleen watched Elagwet leave the corridor, and the door before her beeped, opening in a jarring motion. A small ramp appeared before her, descending into the dark water. She took a deep breath, doing her best to push aside any fear, and walked forward with purpose. Wolf trotted steadily by her side the entire way, whining with disapproval.

Auri and Seneca sat in the Director's old office alone, staring at the morning sun's light splattered over the wall. The streets outside were now barren, the protestors having done their jobs and all gone to bed. Auri yawned widely and leaned back in what was once the Director's chair. Seneca blinked at a piece of paper in front of him.

"All right. So, the young man from The Squid's Inn, the Vice-Chancellor, Salky Punet…I mean, those are just the first three we have."

Auri nodded sleepily. "Yes, and there's hundreds more. How many people should you allow to testify?"

"Well, once there is upwards of three digits, surely it's a given verdict?"

Auri nodded. "Yes. You would think so. I'm certain the Director himself didn't ask for much stringent evidence when locking people up."

"Hmmm. Let's get some broth. I'm tired."

It was, as Wendowleen had hoped, much easier than the original swim. She had pushed herself toward the light and then allowed herself to pop from lake bed to fresh air, Wolf beside her. Together they swam doggedly (or wolfedly, in the case of Wolf) toward the shore. Once there, they pulled themselves out, shook off the worst of the clinging water, and began to walk toward the nearest town of Towen, grateful all the while for the brightness of the Artomia sunshine.

Of course, there were many people who did not attend the protest in Finer Bay. There were some who were already asleep and did not realise that there was a commotion at all until their waking hour. There were others who had children sleeping, and couldn't leave them for a march. Some were afraid and preferred to sit behind bolted doors, watching through locked windows. And there were those who weren't sure how it would look if they joined, like the (now demoted) mayor. He had waited inside his house, staring out the window with bemused interest. His wife sat beside him, a glass of malt in hand, tutting occasionally. After a series of tuts and a period of around five minutes, the mayor cracked.

"What? Why do you keep tutting at me?" he screeched, his voice coming out at a much higher decibel than expected.

"Because you should be out there, that's why. Obviously," his wife replied staunchly.

"Is that what you think?" he asked, voice wavering.

"I'm not often in the habit of saying things I *don't* mean. And on this occasion, yes. He screwed you out of your *job*. Get out there and do the right bloody thing." She took a sip of malt and breathed in through her nose in such a way that gravitas automatically seemed to be added to her words.

The mayor said nothing and just continued to stare uncomfortably. He wanted to go outside, he really did, but it was...challenging. His mind swam with the many possibilities of it. He imagined himself going out and being immediately arrested and hauled up in front of the Director. He knew what went on beneath the Finery Headquarters. He'd only been down there once, on an initial tour of the building, but once was certainly enough. There was something about the smell of acrid dampness and the sound of muffled shouts that still came to him in the night. He couldn't go back there for anything, and, he thought as he watched the continued march of people from the comfort of his lounge, those people wouldn't be marching at all if they knew what was in store for them.

Eventually, the mayor went to bed, joining his disgruntled wife with a sigh. Despite the tossing and turning that the night brought, the morning came quickly, and the mayor awoke with his wife placing a cup down beside him.

"Well, your boss is in jail. The neighbours are all talking about it."

The mayor squinted at the steam rising from the mug and then at his wife, lifting himself sleepily.

"Did you hear what I said? The man, and his head of staff, are in jail."

The mayor nodded and swung his legs over the side of the bed. "Bob? He'd done some bad things, but I was quite fond of the man, in a way."

"Are you awake? I've hung your best suit up on the wardrobe door," his wife responded to a baffled-looking mayor.

"What? That sentence didn't make —"

"Get your butt into that headquarters now. Someone is sitting in that empty office and taking charge of this entire situation. They have to be. And that someone should be the one person that was voted into power by the people. You."

The mayor stared at his feet for a moment, wondering when it was exactly that his bed socks had developed such large holes in the toes. He nodded slowly to himself. "You're right; I should be leading the land through this change. You're right." He stood up, rolling his shoulders back and breathing deeply. "I'll put my suit on."

Wendowleen found that her feet moved at quite a pace when she was feeling determined. Around three miles or so from Towen, they passed a farm, an elderly farmer working in a garden near the path that Wendowleen and Wolf strode down. He tipped his hat to the pair as they walked past, and Wendowleen noticed that his garden burst with her once-prized homegrown flower.

"My goodness," she said, pausing in her march, "What a wonderful selection of awatoprams you have grown."

"Oh yes," the farmer responded with a wide smile. "And we rarely get folks wandering through here, so it's a pleasure to show them off, it truly is."

Wendowleen breathed in their piquant almond fragrance and nodded. "Beautiful. I've missed that scent."

The farmer stood up awkwardly and dusted down his hands on his shirt, holding one out for Wendowleen to shake. She did so firmly, a trick her mother had taught her, and the farmer responded in grip.

"Good handshake there. On your way to Towen, I suppose?" the farmer asked.

"That's right. Well, Finer Bay in reality, but we need to rent a coach."

"Is that right? I've a cart you may borrow if you like, miss, and my horse Tengwar."

Wendowleen regarded the man with intrigue, and cocked her head to one side. "Now, why would you be offering to lend something like that to a stranger?"

"Oh, Tengwar doesn't get much exercise these days, apart from the monthly trip into Towen for my essentials," the farmer answered, scratching the grey hair that covered his head. "And I don't get many visitors. If it would be too much to send Tengwar and the cart back after your business, then it's all right to refuse. But I could give you the lift to Towen if you'd prefer."

Wendowleen smiled and nodded. "I don't know when my business will be complete in Finer Bay, but I'll accept the lift to Towen, certainly. Wolf here is better than I am at tramping."

The farmer nodded and hastened off in the direction of the barn. Wendowleen watched him disappear with a smile. "What a kind gentleman, Wolf."

Wolf made no noise in response, nose twitching at the scent of the horse who was, by now, being tacked up ready for action.

The mayor marched with determined brown brogues to the Finery Headquarters, and saw a difference to the building as soon as he approached. The usually closed gates were now open wide, the front door no longer guarded, instead hanging off its hinges. He took a deep breath, nervous to find who, or what, lay within. The building, like the streets, seemed far too quiet for a typical day. As he stepped through the entrance, he gave a little cough, and ventured out a question.

"Anybody there?"

The silence was stunning. He stood in the hallway for a moment, noting that the once varied portraits of the Director that hung on the wall were now smashed to the floor in pieces. He stepped over them with care and headed up the stairs towards the Director's office. That door, too, he was now unsurprised to find, remained open. But there was something different. Voices sprang from within the wall, and the mayor rounded his shoulders once again and stepped into the room with the confidence of a man voted into power by his people, his wife's words ringing in his mind. In the Director's chair, there sat a young woman with short hair, reading a piece of paper with one hand and holding a mug with the other. Beside her, a man sat, tapping a pen against the desk, one hand also wrapped around a drink. The pair looked at the mayor with interest. Auri smiled.

"You're the mayor, aren't you?"

"Yes. Well, I was, I mean," the mayor responded awkwardly. He felt like he had intruded and, although his brain kept telling him not to be, was a little nervous that a mob lay waiting for him behind the desk.

"Sit down," said Seneca, firmly, though not unkindly.

The mayor did so, pulling up a chair he was all too familiar with and sitting in front of the Director's desk as though nothing had happened.

"We're a bit surprised to see you, Mr Mayor," said Auri, placing her mug down. "I don't recall seeing you last night at all. We thought you might have left Finer Bay before the unrest had begun."

"Oh, no. I slept through the whole thing if you can believe it," he responded with an element of bashfulness.

"I don't believe it," said Seneca. "It was quite noisy. It was one of the key moments in the history of Finer Bay, I should say."

Auri gave Seneca a firm look and smiled again at the mayor. "We've actually had a little peek at your file, Mr Mayor, one of the smaller of their extensive piles of notes. I must say, you have a fairly clear record. It appears even the Director thought so, which is saying something."

Seneca placed the tapping pen down on the table and nodded. "That's right. We're a little concerned with one thing, though, and that's where your *loyalties* lie. We can see that you and the Director agreed on some things, for example, restrictions at the university library. You signed off a few laws that were, on the whole, against the progress of education and free movement."

"Ah," said the mayor, sensing a turn in the conversation and wondering if his entrance had been a little *too* confident after all. "Now then, I didn't want to sign those papers. Those laws. That wasn't the sort of law I would usually pass. But I was...." he paused, staring at the faces of the pair.

"Go on..." Said Seneca, rotating his hand in encouragement.

"I was..." the mayor tried again, finding the words sticking in his throat.

"You were afraid," said Auri, plainly.

The mayor scratched the skin around the collar of his shirt and nodded. "So, you'll testify then?" said Seneca, breaking the peace.

The mayor breathed in. "Against the Director? I will."

"Mr Mayor," said Auri, leaning forward across the desk, "He is just a man. Like you. There is nothing to fear."

Wendowleen tapped the seat behind her firmly for the third time in a row, staring at Wolf. Again, he whined, sitting squarely in between her feet in the passenger seat of the open cart.

"Wolf, back, now," she said clearly. He gave a sorrowful whimper again and attempted to lie down, despite the lack of space. His tail and one back leg slipped off the back of the cart, and Wendowleen tutted.

"Oh, I am sorry about him; he's a nuisance."

"No, no, he's just worried about you, that's all. Doesn't want to leave you up front with a stranger like me. He'll be okay there, as long as he doesn't fall off," the farmer responded with a kind smile.

"The Gods forbid it," said Wendowleen, rolling her eyes. The pair gave a little chuckle, and the farmer clicked his tongue, causing Tengwar to move forward at a steady trot.

Wendowleen leaned back and felt the sunshine on her skin, closing her eyes and basking in the warmth of the sunlight. Her limbs were more tired than she had realised, and as she breathed in the fresh air, she felt overwhelmingly grateful to the farmer for his help.

"Do you live at the farm by yourself, Mr...?" she ventured after a few muddy lanes were put behind them.

"Call me Frick. I do, ma'am. Used to live there with my wife, but she passed on to the pastures of gold around ten or so years ago now. The farm was passed down to me by my mother and her mother before that. It's a funny thing, mind. I got a letter recently that spells the end of my little slice of paradise. They'll be siphoning off the land soon enough to give away. And it's not that I've even got anyone to pass it to, save my nephew, who's more interested in racing horses than farming land, but it's just that it is my own. My family farm, in a way."

Wendowleen nodded solemnly and watched the trees passing. "A letter from the Finery?"

Frick nodded and clicked his tongue once more in encouragement, which had little impact on Tengwar's steady gait.

"And what do you think you could do about that?" Wendowleen asked, watching the old farmer's brow crease in frustration.

"Well, ma'am, I don't know how much you know about the Finery, but to put it bluntly, I could do bugger all about it. Maybe as a young man, I would have given the Director a good talking to, but at this time in my life...." Frick broke off into silence and then darted a quick look at Wendowleen, shaking his head briefly. "I shouldn't really have said that. After all, I don't know much about you, do I?"

"Wendowleen. As a matter of fact, Frick, the Director is my son."

"Ah. Now then," Frick began, his brow furrowing further, "you must forget what I said there."

"No, no, you don't need to worry about me. In fact, let me tell you exactly why I am on my way to Finer Bay."

The mayor now sat beside Auri and Seneca, contributing to the list of those he was certain would be interested in testifying against the Director. His panic had eased, and he began to talk with confidence, altering plans and ideas with grace. Auri smiled at him.

"So, will you take up your seat as mayor again, once all this is done?"

The mayor smiled in return and stared out of the window for a moment, trying to find the right words. "I would like to say yes, of course. I didn't even get to finish my term, after all. However...the last thing these people need is a leader shoe-horning their way into power. Not after all this. I should have been stronger. I see that now. The job I took was not necessarily the one I signed up for. That's the problem."

Auri nodded, and laid a reassuring hand onto the mayor's shoulder. "We all do things out of fear. Even Seneca and I were only able to stand up when we had an army of like-minded thinkers beside us. And for you, it wouldn't be the worst thing to regain your position. After all, the people need someone to help them. You were voted in fairly. But I think that – no – I *know* that there has to be one overriding difference between you then, and you now. You must be honest. Be honest with us. Be honest with the people of Finer Bay. They will repay you with support."

The mayor nodded. "Have you ever been to the cells beneath this building?" Both Seneca and Auri nodded in silence. The mayor glanced between them and sniffed.

"I've been once. The Director took me on a tour of them when I was first elected. And he made it very clear that were we to work together, I could expect a life of normality. The sort of life I was used to, going home to my wife, eating my favourite foods, nothing hugely out of the ordinary. But he painted a clear picture of the other side of that coin, and I saw first-hand what happened to those who disagreed with the Director's ideals. And sometimes my staff, the public, even my wife, would ask me about a particular action, why I agreed to certain things. I could say nothing about it. After all, they had never seen what lay on the other side."

Seneca stared at the mayor and leaned forward. "Agreement to things...like what?"

"Oh, some you know. And I'm proud of none of them, for none of them were helpful. A short time ago, I signed off to have a professor's house destroyed, forcibly actioning the house law onto her while she was away. I mean, that isn't legal, not at all. But every time I thought about disagreeing, my mind would take me back to those...those pits of despair."

Auri coughed slightly, frowning at Seneca. "You're speaking of Professor Cripcot."

"I am," responded the mayor, glancing at the pair in mild surprise. "So you saw the file."

"No," Auri said, shaking her head. "We know her. And actually, we hope that she is on the way here now to testify against the Director."

The mayor shifted uncomfortably and shook his head. "I am sorry to be the bearer of bad news, but my wife informs me that she died last night in the mayhem. Her body lies at Smith Creek Mortuary, awaiting a funeral."

"It is not so, but your gentleness is appreciated. There were a couple of deaths last night, it is true, and both were officers of the Finery. One reported by the Vice-Chancellor in fact, in The Switched Dragon."

They mused on this for a moment, and eventually, the mayor shifted in his seat and spoke again. "You are right. The people need honesty. I shall give them as much as I have."

Frick wiped his brow as the cart ploughed forward on the dirt track toward Towen.

"And you're going to testify, that's where you're off to?" he said, glancing down at Wolf to make sure he hadn't slipped off the cart.

"That's right."

"Against your son?" Frick spoke again, a little nervously.

"Yes. His actions are not the actions I raised him with." Wendowleen lifted her chin proudly.

"Well then - I'm coming with you," Frick said, clicking his tongue once more. Tengwar broke into a sudden canter, veering off the path and into the woods.

Wendowleen shrieked slightly at the sudden change in speed and direction, reaching for something to hold on to. "You're doing what? Where are we off to now?"

"I didn't tell you this, but my wife was from Finer Bay. I used to take this route many a time in my youth, and though I'll wager it's a little overgrown now, it'll still be a shortcut."

"And what then?!" Wendowleen asked, her hands finally settling on the corners of the wooden seat below her, the wind whisking her hair about her face.

"And then we'll testify. You say you didn't raise him to take people's land and livelihoods, and I, for one, believe you. I'll testify for the farmers because I ain't bloody having it!"

Wendowleen laughed, the noise whipped from her lips and climbing into the sky. As they cantered forward through the trees, Wolf pricked his ears up and pulled in his lolloping back paw.

The mayor gazed at the quiet streets of Finer Bay from the very window the Director had been hung out of less than a day ago. It was lunchtime already, but he felt a busyness within that seemed to fill his stomach completely.

"It's too quiet out there. Why is it so quiet?" he asked the room, which still comprised of Auri and Seneca.

"People are afraid of the fallout. They don't know whether it is safe to leave the house," Auri responded.

The mayor nodded as though that was what he had been thinking this entire time. "Yes. You're correct. We must begin this court case immediately against the Director, for what else can we do? The people need to see a new day. How do we do it? How do we announce it?"

Seneca smiled and raised his head. "It is fairly easy – the Finery have access to the frequencies across Finer Bay."

"Yes," Auri said, sitting up suddenly, "We'll announce it now. Why not? The mayor is right – if we begin the process, the people will know that they truly did make a difference."

"We'll broadcast the entire thing!" said the mayor, a new enthusiasm in his voice. "And then the people can listen."

The three stared at each other triumphantly, and there was a pause. The mayor raised his eyebrows slightly, blinking at the pair before him. "So...how do we broadcast?"

Auri laughed. "How would we know?!"

Seneca sighed, and his eyes fell on an Artomia card that sat on the Director's desk. He leaned forward and picked it up, opening it. "It's from Bob," he said, smiling. "There's our answer. Let's fetch him from the cells. He can help us set it all up."

Bob blinked at the bright light of the office, his eyes adjusting from the darkness of the cell, his skin damp to his waist but with a blanket draped over him. He held a plastic cup of cool chestnut broth, which was the result of a heated discussion about whether or not a mug of hot liquid would be enough to allow him to escape. He took a sip and sighed.

"It's a bit confusing; one minute I'm in a cell, fighting over the only dry space with a man that I've been trained to protect against all else, and the next, I'm up here with a blanket over me. Where's your army gone?"

The mayor laughed. "They're resting. They'll all want to testify soon enough, I should think."

"I shouldn't count on it," Bob said, smiling honestly.

Auri sat back in the Director's chair and stared at the head of staff with interest. A damp and decaying stale scent was floating around him, and it reached her nostrils with a sting. "You're a confusing man yourself, Bob. I could have sworn that your allegiance to the Finery might have been wearing off before you went in that cell, but now I'm not so sure."

Bob laughed a singular, lonely bark. "I'm a polite man, but you seem to think that just because there was a protest last night, the whole of Rytter agrees with you. That is not the case, I'm afraid. Plenty of people benefitted from the Director being in power. The streets were safer, more jobs were being created, fairer positions. And I'll bet that a good number of those who joined the protest last night came out of morbid curiosity." He shrugged. "Such is the nature of the common man."

The mayor clucked his tongue against his teeth, shifting in his chair. "Well, nevertheless, I've got a couple of things I'd like your assistance with."

"Is that so? The mayor again, are you?" Bob questioned, his stare hard.

The mayor pursed his lips. "I'm not giving myself a title as yet, but the people did vote me in, and my term wasn't finished."

Seneca placed a steady hand on the mayor's arm and shook his head. "You don't have to answer to him."

"No, no, I know," he responded.

Bob laughed again, a chortle filled with genuine mirth.

"So," the mayor began, "first things first. Do you want to testify against the Director?"

Bob blinked lazily in response, taking the opportunity to create a little tension and sip at his cool drink with care. After a moment, and cleared his throat. "People are complicated. Some, like the Director, strive for greatness in a way that we mere mortals could never understand. What I'm saying is, they do things for the greater good. You don't have to understand that, but it doesn't make it wrong. And that's all I have to say about it."

Auri nodded. "And you, have you 'done things for the greater good'?"

"Of course," Bob answered simply. "I am the head of staff for the Finery, the Director's second in command."

Seneca frowned. "Can I just say that you seemed far more... helpful last night?"

"You can say what you like," Bob responded, "And I'll admit that I was more willing to be of *jovial* assistance to you last night. But then, you locked me in a cell filled with freezing water, and so I learned what sort of people you truly are. You do not treat people fairly. You elect to treat two men to the same punishment, knowing that one of those men will excel where the other will not. You knew that I would not be able to take the dry podium in that situation. To do so would be to undo my entire career."

The mayor sniffed and shook his head. "But you have no career. No difference could be made to your situation. It would be the same whether you had drowned the Director in the water and took the podium for yourself, as it would if you had spent the evening swimming in it."

Bob shook his head. "I respectfully disagree. What else do you want me for then?"

"We would like you to tell us where the equipment is kept for accessing the frequency..." Auri said.

Bob moved his head from right to left and considered this. "You don't know the building. That's obvious. I can help you. I can even show you how it works. But you'll need to do something for me first."

"We're not letting you go," said Seneca abruptly. The head of staff's head swivelled to look at him, and he rolled his eyes.

"Do I look stupid to you? I'm not going back in that cell. Actually, come to think of it, there's a much better place for me to be kept upstairs. It's where the Director kept his aunt for a short period. There's a bed, and some books in there, and a lock on the door, of course. And you know, I am feeling *awfully* cold. It would be a shame for me to die before I can even show you how to address the people."

The mayor nodded and spread his hands. "All right, I'll put you up there and then-"

"Hang on a moment," Auri said firmly, "what happened to the Director's aunt?"

Bob's look of satisfaction faltered slightly, and he breathed in. "She died."

Auri nodded slowly. "Did she now? You can have that room, with the books and the warm sheets. We'll even throw in your dinner. But you have to be honest with us first. Your voice carries a lot of weight. Did the Director kill his aunt?"

Bob stared at the young woman, imagining a night in the waterlogged cell, and pulled the blanket on his knees up a little higher, shivering. He nodded once, his eyes closing slowly.

Wendowleen sat and stared at the dappled light that played through the leaves of the trees above. The steady and quicker gait of Tengwar moved them with ease across the leaves underfoot, and the gentle sway of the open-air cart took her back to a simpler time in her childhood. She closed her eyes for a moment and dreamed of the journeys she used to make with her mother from the market, their old wooden cart pulled by the family donkey. She felt the warmth of the sunshine on her face and smelled the scent of her mother's flowery perfume mixed with the fruits of their labours, piled behind them in hessian sacks. She smiled as she remembered the crumbles that would always conclude the day, the sweet taste of the sugary topping crisped to perfection in the ever-warm stove. These were such memories that she had tried to recreate for Ayin when he was a boy. They had been somewhat successful, though his taste was for the savoury snack and not the sweet, and he had preferred hanging around with his friends in the town rather than coming with her to market. She opened her eyes, and the smile fell from her lips as she thought of Ayin in a cell. And then, as farmer Frick clucked his tongue and Tengwar ploughed on, she brought to mind the fateful day of the plagiarised test. That was the death of her son, she mused, and another boy, a stranger, had left the house that day. The boy she thought of no longer existed.

The radios and screens across Finer Bay buzzed into action, flicking from shows and diverting music. The people waited cautiously, staring at the machines. This is exactly what they had been waiting for – an update. The mayor's voice sprang into their homes.

Good afternoon, people of Rytter. As you may know, there was an event last night, and it was an event that resulted in the disbanding of the Finery. Please, do not panic. I am requesting that all officers return to Finery Headquarters immediately for instruction. You are not in trouble. We still require officers on our streets, keeping our people safe. Those who are unwilling to work in a new world are asked not to attend. And be assured, to those who listen with allegiance to the Director, that this is a new world. The world that you know is a world based on lies, trickery, and theft. We will continue to broadcast beginning tonight, at sundown. It is suggested that children are not invited to listen, hence the hour of the broadcast. Should you have a testimony to lodge against the Director, you should contact us directly. Until sundown, then.

The broadcast finished sharply, with a screech and a fizz. The people blinked at each other with quiet confidence, soundless in their consideration of the new world.

As the mayor had requested, the previous officers of the Finery began to make their way to the headquarters. The mayor watched them troop into the great hall of the building from his place on the stage. They were a mismatched crew, some in their uniform and others in their own clothing, clutching their previous skins in shaking arms. A couple strode with confidence, unconcerned by the change in the situation. The mayor watched, observing them gather together as though it was the first day of school, veering from excited chatter to nervous glances at the stage. After around two minutes, they fell into silence, staring back at him. He glanced at Auri, who stood at the door. She gave him a swift nod.

"Okay, though more may join us, we may as well begin. If you could all…look to the front. Yes. Thank you. Some of you may be thinking, "Okay, what now? Do I still have a job?"

There were a few nods from individuals in the crowd. The majority just blinked.

"And the answer is," the mayor continued, "yes. Yes, you do. But that is a yes that comes with a caveat. For those of you in uniforms, this will not do. The Finery no longer exists. The sight of those uniforms will scare the public. And if you are wondering why, let me please remind you of something that occurred last night. The Director ordered you to shoot at the people. He ordered you to shoot into the crowd – a crowd of peaceful protestors. And we know that some of you missed on purpose, others chose not to shoot at all, and some of you missed by accident. I don't want to know who did what. What I want *you* to know is that orders to murder are not right. You don't murder members of the public. And, for those of you now thinking of other grey occasions and wondering if your orders, training, or perhaps even intuition were correct – I would not hesitate to tell you that they probably weren't. If you are questioning your actions, then they must have been worth questioning. And this is the spirit with which we move forward.

You do not use the training that you have previously had – you will receive more rigorous training. You do not fall back on old ideas of violence and threat to get a job finished. That is not the way the world should be run. In this new world that you find yourself standing on the threshold of today, we ask you to be patient with us. Be patient with each other. You will learn a lot over the next twenty-four hours, and what you learn will make you question who you are. It will make you wonder about your behaviour and strip away your own belief system. I trust that you know what is right, and I know that you have a moral code. After all, you turned up here today, willing to embrace the new world. In turn, you must let yourself be embraced. So, as to what will happen next! In around an hour, the Director will be brought in here."

Murmurs rose from the crowd of officers before him, and the mayor spread his hands, palms facing downwards, in an effort to quiet the troops.

"The Director will be brought in here, and others will join too. The right honourable Justice Kyon will be presiding. And you, should you want to, may come up and testify. It will be broadcast to the general public. But – I cannot stress this enough – should you choose to leave today and go home, as is your choice, you will have to find another profession. You will not be able to work for this government again. You have around half an hour to decide. Anyone not back in this room by then will be dismissed from their role."

The mayor nodded once at the crowd and turned away, stepping off the stage. He strode toward the door, brogues clicking over wood, each step punctuating the low discussion that began to fill the room. Auri greeted him with a smile, and then they exited together, striding toward the front of the building, where Seneca waited.

"All good?" he asked as they neared the front door, his shape silhouetted in the light of the setting sun.

"Yes, they have the message, I think," the mayor said confidently.

Seneca smiled. "Good. There are a few more people out here to see you, Mr Mayor."

The three stepped out of the door and stared at the street before the Finery Headquarters. It was filled once more, like a déjà vu of the night before, but this time in a far more orderly fashion, and sans pots and pans. The mayor cleared his throat in an effort to hide his surprise and glanced at Seneca.

"There are a lot of people here who want to tell their story."

The mayor looked out at them, a strange sting reaching his eyes. He felt, for the first time in a long time, as though he was standing on the right side of history.

Chapter Fifty-Six

The sun waved at the burgeoning moon as the mayor took his seat on stage. To his left sat the judge, Justice Kyon. When he had arrived, the mayor had made his usual joke, "Funny how you all have the same first name, isn't it?" to which the judge had answered with a grimace. In fact, the mayor had never really had a positive response to that joke, and he had met a fair number of judges in his career. Still, he mused, always best to set off on a jovial note.

The crowd now sat on chairs that had been laid out in the great hall, stretching far and wide. It was made up of officers, the public, and some members of staff who had been located in the street outside and ushered in to take a seat. It was accurate to say that, yes, a few of the Finery officers had left. Auri had halted a couple of these as they strolled past her and asked them why they were leaving. Her curiosity needed to be sated. One had shrugged and kept walking, but another had paused hesitantly.

"I just want a change of career, miss. This has all been a bit of a wake-up call for me. My mother owns a button shop in Towen, and I thought that I might go and learn the family trade."

Auri nodded and watched the officer trundle away, a pang of concern in her heart. To have the officers watching the trial had been the idea of all three of them, herself, the mayor and Seneca, in a bid to de-Finerize them, to open their eyes to the truth. But you couldn't force anyone to stay and to stare at something so hideous. That would be an action the Director would have taken.

Auri and Seneca now sat at the front of the room, watching the stage. Both were feeling anxious; Wendowleen had made no appearance. On the stage, the Director sat facing the judge, a couple of non-uniformed officers at his side. He sat with his eyes at half-mast as though he were asleep, and this was all a minor concern. Auri and Seneca had ensured that he had received a change of warm and dry clothes, as well as a meal. They felt that this would enable him to be present during the hearing. He had taken these things without a word, silently glaring into space. Despite his fall from grace, there was still an air around him of menace and intimidation, and the officers beside him glanced down occasionally, fearing that their cooperation in this coup would lead to their own personal downfall. At the side of the stage, the queue of testifiers began, waiting awkwardly on the sidelines.

After a moment, the mayor stood and nodded at an officer, who was standing nearby with recording equipment ready for action. He flicked it into life and gave a thumbs up.

"Welcome, all across the land of Rytter, both in your homes and in the room. Today we are present at the trial of Ayin Cripcot, the Director of the Finery. We have —"

"I see a judge, I see the mayor, and I see people queuing up to testify against me," blurted the Director. The mayor glanced over at him, now sitting tall in his chair, one leg nonchalantly crossed over the other.

"What I do not see," he continued, "is my defence. And you would have the people of Rytter believe that this is a fair trial? I think not."

The mayor cleared his throat. "Actually we —"

"And so, I have made arrangements for my own defence," the Director continued, "my head of staff, Mr Bob Snid —"

The mayor turned suddenly and strode toward the Director, holding his hand up before his face. "Enough. You know the laws of Rytter. However, you chose to ignore them in your previous life. There are those among these people who may be here to defend you. You understand the way that the system you often flouted works, but just to clarify and to put an end to any confusion, I will state it now. Those who wish to testify in any way are admitted to do so. In the end, the people of Rytter will submit their vote. Though usually, of course, the vote would be permitted only for those who have joined us today in the Great Hall, we are extending the vote to the greater country with Justice Kyon's permission. And so, aside from the people you see before you, you may elect one additional defence, should there be a soul here who does not have a story that derives from your barbarity."

The Director cocked his head to one side and smiled. "I should say that there are plenty, you included. And, happily, Justice Kyon and I have shared many a joyful time. I shall represent myself."

The mayor nodded, "as I assumed you would anyway. Any further interruption will extend this already long process. Let us begin." The mayor strode toward the front of the queue at the side of the stage and nodded to the first person.

A young man nodded at the mayor and climbed the short steps to the stage. The mayor shook him by the hand heartily and gestured that he should move forward. The judge beckoned him over and tapped two fingers on a laminated piece of paper before him on the desk.

"You must swear by the map of Rytter that you will only speak with honesty."

The young man nodded, and placed one hand on the map. "I swear it, by the map of Rytter," he said quietly. The crowd watched in silence.

The trial began. There were many stories, some you know. There were stories that you have heard but try to forget, and some that come back to you sometimes and dwell in your consciousness.

Of the hundreds of stories that were told, the judge, the mayor, and the people listened intently. The Director, however, only heard a handful properly. As he stared at the people standing in front of him, one after another, his mind blurred and unfocussed on the words that they said. At some points, it was as though they were not speaking a language he recognised at all. When they looked at him, he felt only pity for their fake courage. The way they squared their shoulders and lifted their jaws was amusing, if anything, as though they believed that it might have some semblance of impact on him.

The sun had long disappeared as the journey continued. Wolf remained sleeping, curled between Wendowleen's legs, and she and Frick began to see shimmering lights speckle in the distance, drawing them forward. Tengwar was almost spent, his steady canter now an easy walk, and Frick allowed him to set his own pace.

"You're a good horse," he said into the air. "We'll get there soon, and there will be a fine meal for you."

Wendowleen smiled at this and nodded. Her bum cheeks were beginning to protest, and she moved around a little to get some blood back into them. "How long do you think?"

"Oh, we're close now. It'll be around half an hour, I should say."

Wendowleen shifted again on the wooden seat, reminding herself that to walk would not be preferable.

The Director stared at the latest testifier with heavy eyelids, bored by the events. An elderly man stood, holding onto a cane, staring at him with hatred in his eyes.

"And you had me dragged to the cells, and I was kept there for over three years. Without sunlight, with the bare minimum of food and water. When you eventually agreed to my pardon, the officer told me that you had forgotten that I was there at all."

The Director snorted at this comment. "Of course! Do you expect me to remember every single bit of information that passes by my desk? What a laughable thought. This is why we have files and staff."

"The officer told me that even you yourself had said that, upon looking at my file, three years in prison for a petty street crime was far too harsh a punishment," the elderly man responded, shaking with anger.

"Listen to me; I would never have said such a thing to an officer. What nonsense you speak. Your opinion does not come from my mouth. And three years in prison for stealing from the market is not such a long time after all. It is not acceptable to steal. Your mother must have taught you this."

Justice Kyon banged his gavel onto his desk and glanced at the Director sternly. "The testifier is making a valid point that to take a loaf of bread when suffering from poverty does not necessarily warrant a prison sentence. Do not lecture the people here so. This is a democracy. The man must be allowed to speak."

The Director leaned back in his chair and barked a laugh. "Democracy? Democracy has been failing in Rytter for years. These things that you accuse me of may be crimes in a democratic world, but they are not crimes in this one. And further to this, you should be aware that we only hold traitors in the cells beneath this building. There is no other type of person kept there. You should be thankful that you were let go at all."

BANG BANG BANG. The judge held his gavel aloft, threatening to smash it into the wood again. "This *is* a democracy Mr Cripcot. One cannot change the rules without first asking the people."

"Yes, Justice Kyon. And you are aware that the Finery were voted in generations ago," the Director snapped back.

"Mr Cripcot, the Finery was a democratic party. What happened when you took over the Directorship is something altogether different. I believe that you know this and that it is what you strived for."

The Director rose to his feet, the officers beside him suddenly grasping at his arms, fearful that he might walk away. The mayor hesitantly stepped forward, taking the elderly man's arm with care. However, the Director was now focussed on the judge, who raised his eyebrows and remained seated.

"If this is what you believe, then why are we still here? What are these people doing, lining up to list their petty grievances against me? It cannot be borne, such a dull and useless series of accounts. I would rather the entire country vote tonight and hear no more of this nonsense."

The judge breathed in and considered this for a moment. "You understand that by saying this, if I agree, you may be forfeiting your opportunity to be defended. Not all of the people in this line are known to be testifying against you."

The Director nodded. "Is that so? Well, let us hear from someone who is defending me because I have been here for hours, and I have heard nothing yet." He turned to the crowd, who sat in the dim light before the stage, and shook his head in disbelief. "There is no one grateful for the increase in jobs under my watch, the better housing, the rise in safety on the streets? There is nobody who is thankful that I allowed Rytter to bloom and flower beneath my watch? Did you not receive letters stating that you would be given farmland? Could you not see the glorious future that lay before you?"

"I could," a voice said, quietly, at the front. Those on the stage shifted their attention to the space where the noise came from and focused on a sheepish looking Bob. He stood between two officers, and awkwardly stepped forward.

"I could," he said again. "I could see the good in it all." He stared at the queue of people and frowned. "You couldn't see that the streets were safer, that the presence of the Finery kept them free from thieves and beggars? Like this man, on stage. If it was your bread that he stole, wouldn't you want something done about it?"

The people murmured and glanced from one to the other. After a moment, a young woman stepped forward from the queue and shook her head.

"No. We wouldn't want it to happen like that, would we?" She looked around at the people beside her. "We would want a proper hearing – an investigation into the reasons behind it all. And you, Director, and your head of staff, might find this hard to understand: We, too, have Rytter at the front and centre of our hearts. Your staff did not create a feeling of safety on the streets. People were afraid to commit crimes, yes, but people weren't even sure what a crime was! We've heard many instances of that already today. If writing poetry is a crime, if asking for a book that you do not want us to read is a crime, if owning your own land is a crime...how are we to keep from committing them?"

BANG BANG BANG. Justice Kyon held up his hands and gestured for those talking to be quiet. "This is not a round table discussion, and we cannot keep going this way. It is inconceivable. Here is what we shall do. I will take a vote from the room – Mr Cripcot, will you please just sit back down – and if the aye's have it, we shall end the hearing here. You, and the rest of Rytter, who have heard this over the frequency, will be free to send in their votes tonight."

The Director shrugged and stepped back to his chair, pulling his arms from the grip of the officers with a grimace. Justice Kyon nodded at the mayor, beckoning him over. He nodded, shaking the elderly man's hand before directing him off the stage, and then approached the desk.

"Are you in agreement Mr Mayor?" the judge asked him, plainly.

"I am, Justice Kyon."

"And so it is. All right, people in the Great Hall of Finer Bay." The volume of the judge's voice shot up. "If we end the hearing of Ayin Cripcot here, do you feel that you have adequate information to decide on whether the accused is guilty of Domestic Crimes Against Humanity? First, let us have the nays."

There was silence in the room, the crowd all straining to listen. Auri closed her eyes. Suddenly, a bark sounded from somewhere outside. She opened her eyes and looked at Seneca, who grinned in response, nodding. They knew that gravelly bark. It came again, shooting into the room from the corridor.

Auri stood and shouted, "Nay!" as Wolf galloped in, tongue lolloping from his mouth. "Nay, Justice Kyon, for you are about to hear from Mr Cripcot's mother. She has travelled far to give her testimony. I beg of you, allow her this."

Wendowleen and Frick strode into the room.

Chapter Fifty-Seven

Wendowleen stood before her son. He looked different, of course, as different as any man would having spent the night in a waterlogged cell, but his eyes were the most changed. From the snippets of memory that had been returned to her, his gaze shone the brightest in her mind. He stared at her now, unrecognisable. His once hazel gaze was almost black, his pupils darker than the night sky, devoid of light. Wendowleen breathed in quietly, the air around her crackling with tension. It was silent, too quiet, indicative of the eyes that fell upon them, the ears that waited for her words. She began in the only way she knew how, with the truth.

"You were responsible for murdering your father, Ayin. There is no respite for the things that you have done. I do not doubt that you would have murdered me, also, had you been given a chance."

The Director raised his eyebrows and licked his lips, his cheeks sucked in out of frustration. "I thought you *were* dead. Your standing before me now is like a strange mirage. I want nothing to do with you."

The air grew stale before them, causing those on the stage to give a light shiver. Such was the time of night that the already desperate scene before them seemed more so, and Wendowleen gave a small sniff, smelling the strange school hall scent of detergent.

Frick stepped up, and stood beside Wendowleen, squeezing her hand. The stranger was a comfort to her already. He murmured quietly into her ear, "You are right. He is no longer your son. You have spoken your part. What more can we do?"

Wendowleen nodded, squeezing back. She stared into the eyes of the Director one last time and blinked sadly. "Though you have broken my heart many times over, Ayin, I will love you forever." She turned away as her words hung in the air, not waiting to see, or hear, his reaction.

The Director rolled his eyes at her back and shifted in his chair. "She's just trying to manipulate them," he murmured to the officers beside him, who ignored him with some discomfort.

Wendowleen and Frick stepped to one side of the stage, and the mayor nodded at them kindly.

BANG. BANG. The gavel hit the desk again, clouds of dust billowing from each impact.

"Once more," Justice Kyon began, "if we end the hearing of the Ayin Cripcot here, do you feel that you have adequate information to make a decision on whether the accused is guilty of Domestic Crimes Against Humanity? Let us hear the nays."

Silence filled the great hall. The judge nodded. "And the ayes."

Beyond the hall and into the street, 'Aye' was heard far and wide. From farm to kitchen, from school office to home, all that listened to the trial nodded to themselves and said, 'Aye'.

Justice Kyon banged his gavel once more. BANG. "The ayes have it. Mr Cripcot, you will be held in a holding cell while the judgement is collected."

Of course, the people of Finer Bay had the first say due to their proximity to the great hall. The queue of those testifying turned into a voting queue rapidly, with officers doing their best to speed up the process, hopping along the line with boxes of slips of paper. Further afield, queues formed outside council houses across Rytter, homemade voting slips being folded and slotted into the post-boxes.

After voting, Auri, Seneca, Wendowleen and Frick left together, and after a silent walk through the streets of Finer Bay, sat with a malt each, behind the door of The Malted Mash. Wolf lay at their feet, chewing on a very welcome supper, relieved to be resting in a now familiar setting. Wendowleen sighed heavily.

"It is a strange feeling. I shall always be fearful of that which I forgot, for so long."

Auri reached across the table and placed a reassuring hand on her arm. "You mustn't fear that, Wendowleen. Where there is closure, the mind does not hide away."

"That's right," said Frick, taking a little sip of his malt. "And now, we must look to the future."

Wendowleen stood carefully, making her way to the door of the bar, flanked by Wolf, and quietly turned the key and opened it to the night sky. The soft and warm air of Artomia welcomed her, coiling its summer breeze about her skin. She welcomed it.

"Artomia has arrived."

Wolf looked up at his owner and licked her hand, the breeze trickling across his coarse fur.

Acknowledgements

About the Author

Rachel Grosvenor is a writer from Birmingham, UK, with a PhD, MA and BA in Creative Writing. With a passion for telling fantastical tales, Rachel has written poetry and short stories for reviews and anthologies worldwide. When she's not writing, she spends her time editing, coaching, and wondering what's for elevenses.

About Fly on the Wall Press

A publisher with a conscience.
Political, Sustainable, Ethical.
Publishing politically-engaged, international fiction, poetry and cross-genre anthologies on pressing issues. Founded in 2018 by founding editor, Isabelle Kenyon.

Some other publications:

Social Media:

@fly_press (Twitter) @flyonthewallpress (Instagram)

@flyonthewallpress (Facebook)

www.flyonthewallpress.co.uk